Fire in the Hole

a novel by
Greg Scherer

Editing and Proofing: Rebecca Barry

Cover art: Carl Wittaker

Cover and Interior design: Rick Soldin, book-comp.com

ISBN: 978-0-9849654-2-7

Printed in the United States of America

FOREWORD

A number of large strikes occurred on the Mesabi Iron Range in the early 1900s. In 1907 the Western Federation of Miners supported the largely Finnish miners and demanded an eight-hour day and a pay raise. The mining companies recruited thousands of strikebreakers and hired special "deputies" to secure their safety. It lasted two months and thousands of miners were fired and replaced with European immigrants.

In June 1916 the Workers of the World, Wobblies, supported a strike for better pay and shorter hours. It lasted until September of that year with no tangible results although a 10% wage increase was granted soon after.

The Wobblies had a history of violence and promoting the downfall of capitalism through anarchy. Some of their leaders were exiled from Europe because of their organizing practices. On the Iron Range the names Sam Scarlett, Carlo Tresca, Bill Heywood and Helen Gurley Flynn became household words.

Bill Heywood

Helen Gurley Flynn

The miners and the Wobblies stood alone against the mine owners; the Minnesota governor, the general public and the hundreds of armed mine guards. Violence was common even to the point of mine guards beating picketing women and exchanging gunfire with the miners. The Wobblie organizers were arrested and charged with murder and instigating riots.

World War I was setting Europe aflame and the demand for steel was huge. By striking, the miners were seen as aiding the German side of the conflict, an easy assumption since most of them were recently arrived from Eastern Europe and had little command of English.

Finally, with the intervention of the Minnesota National Guard, the exportation of much of the Wobblie leadership and the disarming of the mine police, order was restored and the mines reopened although it left a lasting distrust for big business and a strong unionization zeal.

FIRE IN THE HOLE is a fictionalized story of the strike. Many of the actual characters are included in this book. Others are purely of the writer's imagination. One of the objects in writing this novel is not to pick sides but to show the futility of the actions taken by both sides and the effect they had on individual lives, in this case, the Jenensice family.

I hope you enjoy the reading and if you've never been there, visit and explore the historic Mesabi Iron Range, its museums and, primarily, the immense excavations that the miners wrought.

Chapter 1

Sadie stepped tentatively through the monuments of the long abandoned town. She was looking for something in particular, but it had been so long, fifty years at least. It was so hard to remember how it once was. Had she forgotten after all these years? In the weedy gravel her nine-year-old grandson darted over the crumbling foundations and old stone walkways. The sudden sound of a thunderclap gave her a start and she almost fell over an old curb. It brought on a sharp stab of pain from the old wound in her chest. She straightened and raised her head to the dark cloud scudding across the broad horizon. It was far off. She gave a soft murmur of satisfaction and let her gaze drop to a pair of weathered angels on a nearby hill. That would be the entrance to the old cemetery, she thought. She nodded at the verification their presence gave to her search and made a mental note to visit them. Another day. The boy tripped over something, tumbled and rolled over once before jumping to his feet. He spread his little arms like the angels and grinned at her. Sadie caught her breath and gently scolded him.

"Eric, you be careful now! I don't want you falling in any old cellars. Or worse yet, some old well or sewage pit that I could never pull you out of. What would your mother think of me? And be careful of rusted metal. Old Mammoth is full of it." Then she said to herself. "I'm sure it was here, somewhere." She stopped and looked around as if she were not quite sure. It was then that Eric turned and shouted, "Jeepers, Gramma, come here. You got'ta see this!" She hurried over to him on her tired, worn legs.

Before them lay an immense chasm, the great yawning hole falling away beneath their feet, plummeting to a water-filled pit that stretched out to rusty four-hundred foot tall embankments over half a mile away.

"Look, Gramma," Eric 's voice quivered with excitement. 'That's the biggest hole I ever saw!" I bet that's the biggest hole ever."

She laughed, her own search forgotten for the moment. "That's actually not just a hole, Eric, honey. That's the old Mammoth Iron Mine. But yes, it is the biggest hole ever."

"Wow, Gramma, did mammoths dig it?"

She laughed at the silly thought." No, child. Mammoths did not. But they probably lived here at one time. Your great-uncle dug it and he might have had a little mammoth in him back then."

"Boy! All by himself? With a shovel?"

She shook her head in wonderment. The thought of a lone man doing all this work with just a shovel? What nonsense! She stared with him into the old, abandoned pit. Her eyes followed the gully-washed road that hugged the near edge. Far over on the east side, the rotting vestiges of an old wood trestle angled up and out of the hole. There, the cog railroad tracks topped the level ground and disappeared into a long, ruined warehouse where the ore was once pulverized and loaded onto the Mesaba Railway cars outbound for Duluth, then onto the ore boats that took it to the steel mills back east.

The old memories slowly came back to her. She remembered the road once filled with red-faced, dirty miners trudging out from their shifts, passing clean-faced men trudging in for the next one.

Over there on the face, the old steam shovels threw their giant shovel maws into the broken red ore and dumped it into the waiting tramcars. And there, towards the middle was the hole, still unfilled. That's where the dynamite shack had once stood.

She could still see the hundreds of men; like tiny ants they had looked down there, working with pick and shovel, drills and hammers to break the rock face laden with the rich, red ore.

It all came back to her, the foremen shouting above the banging and whining of the machinery as they prodded the men on in their relentless task of removing the ten billion cubic feet of earth and ore to uncover and reveal the immense hole that had held it. She shook her head. All that back breaking work to end up with just a big hole. She thought it a quiet epitaph for all life in the end.

She still felt the wonderment of it, this big old void in the earth that had once signified greatness and unspeakable human pride. It would remain as long as the world turned as a witness to the exhausted and defeated greatness of the iron range. It was the virgin land that had held the key. The millions of tons of iron that came from it had fueled the nation's blast furnaces, built its bridges, skyscrapers and battleships and had won two major wars. Still, because she had grown up next to it, the mine, itself, drew no particular awe from her. It was the men she saw down in it; rust-red and worn out fathers and sons working in the dangerous pit for wages that bought them just enough nourishment to have the strength to go down again the next day. It was enough to go down and up but never enough to crawl out of it forever.

She thought it strange that all of it should be so much more breathtaking in its emptiness than it had ever been as an undisturbed and vast pocket of richness under the Minnesota forests. It was always so, she thought. Man's disruptions of nature, his unending efforts to make his own indelible scratches on God's creations always drew admiration; at least from other men if not God. She knew people to be like that hole—more glorious when seen in their basic humanity. Most complete when stripped of all but their most basic being, of their simple essence, that being their dignity.

She shook her head at such ideas. So unlike her. She had always lived life with a pragmatic resignation. Like her mother, she had been cut and cultured from simple cloth of a deep European ancestry.

She stood there, seeing the old energy that had once surged about this now dead ground, sensing the ghosts of the men who had worked and died there. And then, all she could see was her brother. Michael. She would always see the Mammoth mine as Michael's scratching.

"No, Eric," she breathed deeply. "He had a lot of help. A lot of good help. Maybe a thousand shovels held in the grip of strong hands."

The boy's interest waned and he resumed his play among the old foundations. She watched him for a while and then, satisfied as to his safety, resumed her own search.

She moved away from the pit, fifty, a hundred feet, counting out the old home sites as she went. She checked herself, turned down a weedy rock path and began moving faster. At the shattered remnants of a picket fence she smiled and walked directly to a big granite rock that lay half buried in the ground at the base of a grotesquely twisted basswood tree.

"Hello, my old friend," she whispered, laying her head against the trunk. "Yes," she added, comforting herself, "this is it. I am home." She settled herself slowly onto the rock and soon became lost in her reveries. Presently, Eric came over to her.

"Gramma," he said, his voice edged with concern. "Are you okay?" It wasn't like his spry old grandmother to quit on him like this. She was touched by his concern but knew she could never make him understand how really okay she was right then. How good it was to be back here after so many years. She wanted him to know the story; why her heart was so full of happiness.

She smiled. "Yes, Eric, darling, Gramma's fine. Old, tired, worn out, exhausted, but very, very fine." She wrapped her arms around him and drew him lovingly onto her lap. "Eric, I lived here. A long time ago."

Eric looked around at the barren town site and then at Sadie. He was confused. "Right here? What happened? I bet a big storm blew your house down into the hole."

"No," she said reflectively. "There used to be a whole town here. It was moved when they wanted to get at the ore under it. The houses, people... everything had to go. They just put everything on wheels and rolled it away. Just about everything, anyway." She spoke the last to the guarding angels. "Oh yes, a real town. And this was my home. I had a swing in this old tree. And right where we're sitting was Mama's garden. She had a beautiful garden. Mama used to grow the biggest cabbages and the reddest currants in the whole town."

"Did you really live here, Gramma, or are you telling me another story?"

She set him back on the ground, held him teasingly at arms length and tousled his hair. "Why, Eric, don't you believe your old grandma now?" She took a red all-day sucker from her coat pocket and gave him a playful tap on the head with it. "You sit here and I'll tell you all about the old Mammoth and Zenith and Aurora locations and my big brother, your great-uncle, the iron miner, Michael. Then you'll believe me. Besides, it's time you get to know something about your kin." She desperately wanted someone to remember to keep it from just fading away.

He sat beside her and unwrapped the candy treat. "Grandma?"
"Hmmm?"

"What does this spell?" He was poking at the rock. She put her hand down and felt the markings.

"Well for goodness sakes. I'd forgotten all about that. Oh my, look here, Eric. You can still see his name carved there. He was your great-uncle, my big brother." And then the tears began to run down her cheeks.

He squinted at the deep moss filled letters scratched into the boulder, and slowly sounded out the name. "Mi… key. Mikey? Gramma, who is Mikie?"

Chapter 2

"Mikey!" Kiril's shrill cry broke through the incessant hammering of the steam-drilling rig. Michelangelo DaVinci Jensen glanced up from his clipboard, his face nearly hidden by the brilliant red kerchief he wore to filter out the red dust that was drifting thick around them. The shift foreman called him Red Mike because of the distinctive kerchief into which his sister, Sadie, had sewn his initials. His friends from childhood on just called him Mikey.

Kiril held his thumb and forefinger three inches apart to indicate the free travel left in the drill bit. Mike shrugged and nodded, then reached over and closed the steam line. The thumping drill lost its momentum and gradually settled into silence.

"Das goot genug. Good enough," Mike shouted over the ringing in his ears. "These bits are shit anyway. They're shot. It'll take all night to get that last inch. You would have more luck with that drill in your pants than this one, Kiril. Tear it down." Michael was known for his blunt direct manner.

The four man crew drew out the blunted shaft uncoupled the steam lines and dragged the heavy rig back from the rock face. They worked with the precision of a well-practiced team, speaking only occasionally and then in a mixture of English, German and Slovenian. Michael and Kiril spoke good English but Constantine and Anton were recently off the boat from Europe and knew only enough to draw their pay and buy groceries. Then too, they were a little lazy in their speech. Most of the miners at Mammoth, at least the ones that lived in Zenith location, were Slovenian and still spoke the heavy native language of northern Yugoslavia. Those raised in America from childhood spoke either equally well.

Mike walked over to a heavy, oak handcart and opened one of the wooden boxes stacked in it. He picked up the lantern and passed it to Kiril who backed off a respectful distance and held it high to let the light flood over the crate. Mike pulled out two of the red cylinders and rubbed his fingers over their surfaces. He swore softly, like a man whose cuss words were only meant to impress him.

"Greasy crap." Then to Anton who had come up to him. "Aw, hell, look at this shit, Anton. See how slick it is? You think that's butter for your biscuits but it isn't. That's nitroglycerine, Anton. It comes out of the sawdust and charcoal in the stick because it gets old and unstable. It's leaking right through the paper."

Anton nodded and kept staring at the dynamite.

"Nitroglycerine," Mike repeated in Slovenian. "Old nitro. Bad shit. Boom!" He threw his arms out dramatically. Anton jumped back and stepped away while Mike dug through the second and third layers in the box.

"Yeah, it's all crap!" he verified. "They give us a mountain of solid rock and tell us to blow it up with this? Why do they give us this crap, you ask? That's a very good question, Anton. Kiril can tell you it's because the United States of American army won't take it. It's too dangerpous to ship to Europe and kill soldiers with so they send it up here where no one will hear it when it takes a man's head off, specially a dime-a-dozen Slovic's head." He looked at Anton again and winked. Anton smiled at Kiril and shrugged. Kiril smiled back and yelled, "Boom!" and Anton dutifully took another step back. Constantine swore at Kiril and they all laughed at the joke.

"Pack it in," Mike finally relented. You'd better ram it in with your peckers or something just as soft. One little bump could set it off; or maybe it won't go off at all. Hell, I don't know."

It had taken ten hours to drill the twenty, ten-foot deep, one and a half inch diameter holes in the solid rock face that they were now filling with the rotting dynamite, pushing the sticks in gingerly with long wooden poles. Eventually they had packed one hundred and eighty sticks into the rock, pushed blasting caps into the last twenty and connected them to the single blasting cap with detonation cord. When the cap was ignited by an electrical charge it would blow the spider work of detonation cord—high explosives in a fuse- and ignite the first stick in each hole and blow the rock face into fist-sized chunks of high-grade iron ore.

Kiril crimped the electrical line onto the metal cap and, threading it through his hands to check for cracks in the wire, ran it back to where Mike squatted over the generator box. The crew gathered around him, pulled their handkerchiefs over their faces and covered their ears. Mike wrapped the wires around the terminals, raised the detonator handle, counted heads one last time, screamed, "Fire in the hole!" and threw his weight on the handle.

The cliff erupted in a thunderous explosion, enveloped for an instant in a flash, then flame, and jets of ore spewed a hundred feet out of the drill holes. The face of the cliff held firm for an instant, reluctant to give up its tenacious lodging of thirty million years. Then it just slid away, slowly at first, picking up speed, and finally cascaded to the ground in an avalanche of red ore that rolled out like a tidal wave over the floor of the pit and covered the drilling crew in its smothering dust.

They huddled against each other, drawing slow, shallow breaths until it began to settle. Eventually Mike stood up and pulled off his kerchief leaving a clean slash of skin across his grimy face.

"God dammit, boys, it's time to get another hundred feet of wire, eh? This one's gotten mighty short."

Kiril got to his feet, blew his nose clear of the dust and wiped his fingers on his pants. "Let's get one long enough we can set it off over beers at the Ore House."

Michael walked back with Kiril to inspect the results. Two hundred tons of fractured ore lay piled up in front of the face. Michael bent over and picked up a dusty red chunk, turned it over in his hand several times. It was the size of a muskmelon.

"Too damn big," he swore. "Look at this shit, Kiril." He thrust the rock into Kiril's gut. "Didn't I tell you the nitro was no damned good?"

"Ah, well, Mikey," offered Kiril good-naturedly. "Tomorrow we can add another stick."

"But we don't have the bits to drill another stick deeper, do we, donkey. Look at this crap. How do we explain this?"

"Nah, it's okay," insisted Kiril. "Let the crushers worry about it."

"I want it perfect. I'm a driller, Kiril. Maybe that's not much, but I'm a damned good one. This is my life and this," he threw down the rock, "is not good work."

Kiril stared at him for a moment trying to get a handle Michael's attitude. "So who cares? We can only do as much as the tools let us. Who gives a shit, anyway? I don't. Yesterday it weighed three hundred ton. Now it weights ten pounds. That's a big change in a rock in just one day. So who gives a shit? Besides the rock, maybe?"

Mike was surprised because Kiril rarely used rough language of any kind. "Where do you learn that crap, Kiril? I think you pick your proverbs from the trash, too." Then the harsh stare dissolved into grudging laughter. "By the Christ, you're right though, brother. If they don't care, then we don't care." He gave Kiril a playful bear hug, the kind a man reserved for his very best friend. Just then the pit whistle blew the end of the shift. Mike gave the ore pile one last woeful look because he really did care. Mining was his life and his heritage from his father and grandfather and generations before that. Michael's father used to say that, before picks and shovels, the Jensenice men would dig out the ore with their teeth. Mining gave him his identity and he was proud to be the top driller at the Mammoth iron mine. He thrived on the danger and enjoyed the sense of mastery he held over the hard red cliffs that rose above him on all sides.

He slapped Kiril on the shoulder. "I am starved. Let's get some breakfast." They cleaned up the rest of the gear, checked in the leftover dynamite at the shack and started up the long ramp to the head of the mine.

chapter 3

John Paul "Billy" Masterton, chairman and principal shareholder of Mammoth Mines was peering out the window of his mine superintendent's office. His feet were planted wide beneath his heavy frame. His hands were clinched tightly behind his back. His head, crested with an overgrown mane of white hair, was bowed forward in silent challenge to the men he was staring at. Outside the office the miners from the night crew were engaging in short conversations with the men on their way down to work. Like all the open pit mines on the range, Mammoth ran twenty-four hours a day; a ten-hour night shift for drilling and blasting, with a ten-hour day shift for loading and hauling out the ore. The other four hours were spent on repair and upkeep of track and hoses, moving pumps about, greasing and oiling the giant steam shovel and performing maintenance on the hundred of other pieces of rolling stock that made the mine function efficiently.

He watched them trudge by, docile and ignorant. Men in tattered, stained overalls passing men in tattered, clean overalls. Faces drawn, exhausted, their feet plodded mechanically down the gravel road. The only difference between the two shifts was the color of their skin and the weight of their lunch pails. The color difference was only a matter of shading; the red dust eventually got into a man's pores and worked its way so deep inside him that it never washed out.

They stirred no affection in his soul because Masterton considered himself to be superior, a pioneer and self-made success, scorning anyone who would trade ambition and independence for the security of an hourly wage. Men who came to him begging for work and so willingly sold themselves into servitude deserved no better than the small paychecks he tendered them. To him, such men were of little difference in demeanor or worth than the mules he used in his mine.

"The bastards are going to try and shut us down, Fleming. I goddamn swear it. These feeble-minded foreigners can't read or write. They don't even know enough English to buy a beer for crissake. I swear they just open their maws and point their fingers down their throats. They wouldn't have a pot to piss in but for me and now, just because we're at war, and with their cousins yet, goddamn it, they think they wear britches so big they can shut me down. Well, balls, boys. If you got 'em then let's see 'em!"

Masterton turned from the window, took out a linen handkerchief and blew his nose loud enough to rattle the window. "Damned cold! Every fall, every spring, ever since I was a whelp I get a damned cold." He thrust the kerchief into an inner breast pocket and adjusted the gold cufflinks of his tailored shirt. "Another damned nuisance is what it is."

At sixty-four he was still an imposing man and still spoke with the bravado that had helped him make his fortune. But his body was losing its vigor. His legs hung beneath him like stovepipes, too thin for the big gut and chest that overhung them. He still had that leonine hair and wore it unkempt and over the collar from the old days when barbers took up more time than they were worth.

John Fleming stood up, came around his desk and took Masterton's place at the window. He had come to Mammoth thirteen months ago, fresh out of the University of Pennsylvania School of Mines, a replacement for Masterton, himself, and already he could name most of his three hundred employees on sight. He made it a point to personally pass out the paychecks every week and that helped him keep in touch with the temperment of the crew. He respected his men for their efforts and, in return, he felt they gave Mammoth as good a production record as any outfit on the range.

"Sir," Fleming offered in a soft, placating voice, "I don't mean to disagree with your assessment but I really don't think…"

Masterton cut him off in mid-sentence. "I wish to correct you John. The truth is, you don't know! You don't know a tinker's nickel about people and less of life. Ain't your fault. Not at all. None of you school boys have spent enough time in the trenches to link up book learning with experience. Well, you're young. I forgive you that. Wish I had a little of it myself. Just don't use it as an excuse to make up crap that won't even place last in a bullshit contest."

The titan of industry looked at the portrait hanging behind the desk. He had commissioned it ten years ago and it captured him in all his masculine glory. His head was held high, his shoulders broad and squared and a vision shone from his eyes. We were men back then, he was thinking now, bastards maybe, but men nevertheless. Even the ones that didn't make it through the hard times were tougher than the toughest today.

Masterton came back to the window and put his arm on Fleming's shoulder. Fleming fought the urge to pull away.

"John, do you realize how far we've come? Not you, of course, but me and people like me?" He shook his head. "No, you weren't here twenty-six years ago when we opened the Mesaba. Hell, you weren't even born yet, were you? But I was here. I was one of them once, and I busted my ass with shovel and pick and I fought my way to the top of the tailings pile. I left them all sitting on their bums in the saloons. I saw opportunity and, by god, I nearly died going after it. Do you think I'm going to let some immigrant toad take that away from me now? Not for a minute, by god."

Fleming nodded condescendingly and, slipping out of his boss' grasp, went back to his desk. "Sir, I've got an order here for quite a lot of replacement equipment, drill bits, hoses and I think our explosives are below safety standards. We are getting a lot of complaints from the crews."

"What? Oh, bullshit. Order what you need but don't go throwing away anything repairable. Work it to the nub first. And don't bother me about this piddling crap again. I gave you the authority. Use it. But be sure you use up all the old inventory first. Understood?" With that he was back on his old scent. "Those men, they didn't put their sweat and blood into ripping out the trees and scratching off the overburden. Thirty-five feet of rocks and roots and dirt! Three years of starvation before we drew our first royalties. But they're here now, reaping the benefits and they want to shut me down. Me! Billy Masterton."

Fleming had heard Masterton's "We were here first," speech a dozen times before and tried to head it off. "They work hard, sir. I just think the company owes them some measure of…"

"We owe them nothing more than a weekly check and they get that, don't they?" His voice rose again. "Fleming, you're a damn fine manager but if you've got one weakness, you're too damn weak. You can't be everyone's friend. Don't be their friend. You're their boss. It don't mix. The boss has to make calls that a friend never would. Hear what I'm saying, now? This week they're on the payroll, next week we might have peace and then a recession and you'll have to can half of them. Hear what I'm saying? It starts with the workweek and ends with the paycheck. Whatever we owe them is paid in full at the end of every week. They get a check every damn Friday, the slate is wiped clean and Saturday they start over. Do not misunderstand me. I don't begrudge them a living. They've got their three bucks a day and they've got their homes. Send them back to Europe and they'd have nothing. They'd starve and that's why they are here and they know it. I know it."

"And that's another matter. I hear you go out there and pay them off in person. I don't like that. You're the boss, the lord, laird and overseer. Keep apart from them and they respect you. Get familiar and they'll see your shit smells just like theirs. You understand what I'm saying? Let the paymaster pay them off from now on. Makes sense, don't it?"

Fleming knew it all, even the parts Billy always left out, the mud streets and poor schools, and the shortage of doctors and lack of sewers. He had walked past the run-down houses Mammoth rented them at profitable rates. He saw the old newspapers stuffed in the cracks in the siding to blunt the fierce north winds. The children wore hand-me-down clothes and the men and women who looked old before they had a chance to enjoy being young. The scores of middle-aged pensioners that sat in the sun and tried to remember exactly how the mine had taken their arm or leg or manhood. He kept his eyes on the paperwork before him. "Yes sir, J.P. I will do that."

"Fifteen years ago," Masterton droned on, "those Finlanders thought they could railroad us too. They walked out on us. We said, fine, just keep walking, boys. Today they're scratching out a living in the woods and getting drunk on spruce beer. I drank it. Tastes like pine piss. Today I can drink twenty-year-old scotch. The smart ones stayed. There were damn few of them. But if these damned Pollocks…"

"They're Slovenians, sir, most of them." Fleming had wandered back to the window and only dared interrupt his boss because he was distracted by something going on outside. His secretary, Mary Savich, was coming across the street to the office. She had stopped to talk to a group of men and was just now coming up the office boardwalk. She was being carried in the arms of a young miner. She had a face and figure enough to make most men lose their train of thought.

"What? What did you say?"

"Excuse me, sir. I just said they were Slovenians. Austrian and Slav."

"I know what the hell they are!" J.P. bellowed. "I hired them. What the hell difference does it make? Pollocks, Slovenes, it's all the same."

"It does make a difference to them." This time Fleming barely let the words escape him.

"What? Speak up, man. My hearing is shot and you talk like a man with a fishbone in his throat."

There was a quick rap on the door and Mary burst into the room. She came halfway across the office before stopping.

"Oh! I'm sorry, John. I didn't know you were busy."

Masterton grinned at Fleming. Mary thrust out her hand to J.P. "Good morning, sir," she offered boldly. "I'm Mary Savich, John's personal secretary. How do you do?"

"I do well," he returned. "And how do you do?"

Fleming interrupted. "Mary, I'd like you to meet J.P., Billy, Masterton, Chairman of Mammoth Mines and principal stockholder. J.P., this is Mary Savich," adding lamely, "But you already know that."

"Call me Billy." Masterton reluctantly gave her hand back. "That's what my friends, few though they be, call me. It's been Billy since I was in diapers."

"Good morning then, Billy," she said pumping harder and holding her smile until it became obvious Billy would find nothing further to say. Fleming cleared his throat.

"Mary, are those yesterday's production numbers?"

"Oh!" She held out the paper in her hand. "I forgot. Yes they are. I'll just put them on your desk." She put down the document and excused herself, lingering a moment in the doorway.

J.P. stared at the door for some time. Finally he clasped his hands behind his back and rocked back and forth on his heels, chuckling. "You hired quite a pistol, Fleming. Quite a looker, too."

John looked up from his figures. "I'm sorry about that. They don't stand much on formality up here."

"She called you John."

"She isn't bashful. You saw that… how friendly she is." Then he caught himself. "She's an excellent secretary though. I will say that. Excellent."

Masterton frowned. Fleming was either naïve or holding back, probably naïve, and either was enough to cause him to be suspicious. Still, he took the fatherly approach. "Listen, son. You said it yourself. She's one of them. Slovenian, right? Only this one seems to have the ambition to get ahead and the right attributes to get her there."

"Sir?"

"Are you two shacking up?"

"Mr. Masterton!"

"Don't get me wrong, son. Wouldn't blame you if you were. I'd enjoy a helping of Miss Savich myself. I'm just saying be discrete about it. Never compromise. Let her know up front what the limitations are, that it's just for jollies. I'll tell you a secret. That's what I do and I've kept a happy marriage for thirty years."

Fleming, blushing heavily, hurried to change the subject. "Would you like to go over these numbers now, sir?"

"Let me tell you something about women. See, it was man that created virginity, not women. Men prize it in a woman until she becomes *their* woman and then it's a door to be unlocked, a trophy to be taken. We ignore it in ourselves because it's an embarrassment that separates us from true manhood. Women? They're born with it by accident. If they die with it, it's their own fault. Men don't understand the concept because we are never really virgins anyway. The ones that are, aren't very good at it. So go get your trophy if you want. Just be discrete."

"The numbers, sir?"

"In a minute." J.P. had returned to the window. The street was nearly empty now except for some early commercial traffic farther down at the business end. He started his rocking motion again. "I'm sending a man over to you. His name is Karsch. He'll work for you but answer to me."

"For… ?"

"He was a police sergeant in Chicago. Tough. Hard as nails. You can strop a razor on his ass. He's a real throwback to the old days. I want him to oversee the mine security if it comes to trouble."

"Security? J.P., I don't think we need that here." He had a familiarity with mine-run police forces, goon squads, moving into the Vermillion range northeast of them. The Mammoth had never had so much as a gate guard in the past. "I know most of these men. They're…"

Masterton cut him off and drained the last of his patience. "Don't ever take that tone with me, son. Don't go thinking again about what you don't know. You read the papers. Out east they're marching with signs. Down the main streets of half the towns on The Range. Hibbing Chisholm, Virginia. Next week they may just march the hell away and where'll we be then?" Masterton sat down, exhausted by his own tirade. "I admire your work here. You know mining, I'll give you that, but with people you're green as hell. I've got a three million dollar investment here with war contracts to choke a hippo. I'll be damned if I'll let some drunken, immigrant miners destroy it over a penny-ante strike. You understand that?" He didn't wait for an answer. "Doesn't matter. I told him to hire as many deputies as he needs and he answers directly to me. Understood?"

Fleming blanched but said, "Yes sir. Understood."

"Fine. I knew you'd see it my way. You go out and buy all the drill bits, dynamite and other equipment you want and leave the worrying to me." He turned his attention to the papers on the desk and his voice lost its bite. "Now let's take a look at those numbers you are so proud of."

Fleming turned back to the reports with relief and he felt the anger slowly drain from him. He was an engineer by profession. Production was his real love, not people. Maybe this Karsh would be all right to handle that side of the operation and let him concentrate on the important things.

Chapter 4

It was Michael who had stopped Mary on the street. He did it the same way he stopped all the pretty girls in town, planting himself in front of her as she carefully picked her way around the muddy puddles.

Carefully putting her feet where the mud would do the least damage, she abruptly found herself looking down at a pair of dirty, size eleven boots. Her gaze lifted past the patched canvas trousers and jacket but stopped when she reached the boyishly handsome face before her. Clearing her throat, Mary forced out the words, "I beg your pardon. I would like to get by."

Michael put his hands on his hips and grinned. "Not until you tell me your name. Maybe, then I'll let you pass. But when I tell you mine, maybe you won't want to."

She gave his a withering look that cost him much of his swagger. "Michael," he volunteered abruptly. "Mike. Special friends call me Mikey." He shrugged then, gesturing feebly. "Yours, please. Name?"

Mary had recovered her sense of composure. "I know who you are Michael Jensen," she answered. "You work the night shift on the bottom, run a drill crew, by all accounts the most productive, and I am not quite as impressed with you as you apparently are with yourself." She started to elbow her way past him but Michael quickly reached down and swept her into his arms.

"Okay, you win. I'm your slave."

"Put me down this instant!"

"Not until I save your shoes from our streets." He said carrying her over to the boardwalk.

"Are you impressed now?" he asked matter-of-factly. "I could come and help you like this every day if you desire." She was kicking pretty well. "Will you go out with me?"

"Are you serious?"

"Yes, I am. But it will be better if I know your name before we see each other again. I think there should be less gossip that way. And it will certainly be better for the sake of our children. We will have six, don't you think?

She stopped kicking. "I do not believe your audacity."

"My what? Oddacy?"

"I said audacity. It's... Oh, you wouldn't understand if I read it out of the dictionary. But if you don't put me down at once I will scream. I can scream quite loud."

That did it. The other men were watching with some relish and as much as Mike savored attention, he knew that things were not going his way. He set her down on the boardwalk. She indignantly straightened her dress and hurried to the office door.

He called after her. "Why did you find out my name if you don't care?"

She stopped and looked at him. He had beautiful dark eyes and the kind of face that any mother would want her children to bear. His hair was black and curly and his body, young and muscular, had not the squat stature of most of the others of eastern Europe extraction. He was dressed in proper fitting, though worn, trousers and a light-blue flannel shirt under the jacket. All in all, she thought, a very attractive catch under different circumstances. But he was, after all, just a miner, eking out a living. But her ego had been stroked enough to warrant him something.

"Mary," she said with just a shadow of a smile and then she was gone.

"What was that all about, Mikey?" Kiril asked when Michael caught up with his friend again.

"Nothing," he shrugged. "She just wanted to know my name. Very insistent about it."

"She's pretty," Kiril said. "She would make a handsome girl-friend, for a handsome man." Michael threw a hammerlock around Kiril and began choking him. Kiril playfully danced like a puppet on a string and then broke free. Michael took one last look at the mine office then shrugged.

"Ah well, Kiril, who needs girlfriends? I have more women than I need already. But you!" He punched Kiril in the arm by way of emphasis. "You need a woman desperately, not me. I have women knocking down my door. Peeking through the windows. They throw notes tied to rocks for me."

"They throw rocks disguised as paper at you."

"They make impossible demands on me."

"Yes, can you possibly stop bothering us?"

Kiril and Michael had been friends and siblings since Michael's childhood. Kiril was five years older but Michael was, in many ways, the older brother. Kiril was the bigger though shorter and quieter except when they were together. Where Michael would rush into flirtations oblivious to the consequences, Kiril would stay on the periphery of romance until he found his own comfort level. In truth, he was actually scared of most women, loyal as a dog to his friends, and loved the Jensen family fiercely. His ears poked out of his swarthy bearded face in a way that made a bit of a buffoon that he was not but often acted like. Like Michael, he wore trousers but kept his up with a single red suspender that crossed over his chest. He didn't need any advice from "Mikey" on women.

"I do have a girl, Mikey," he replied. "Your sister."

Michael laughed. "She's too young for you by twice your age."

"I will wait."

"Hah! I believe you will. But make sure you wait long enough," he cautioned. "I have a shotgun, you know."

"I won't need a shotgun to go to the altar with my beautiful Sadie."

"I wasn't going to use it that way."

"Aw, Mikie. Love fears not those that try to come between the loved ones."

They had come to the small commercial district of Meridian, Mammoth's main street, and stopped in front of Wong's Laundry. No one knew Mr. Wong's first name but most of Mammoth assumed that a Chinaman's first and last names were interchangeable anyway. Wong was sweeping the sidewalk clear of the red dust that constantly drifted out of the pit. At the adjoining shop, Abe Izerman, the laconic owner of Abe's Clothing Emporium, was also sweeping his sidewalk because that was something they invariably did together.

"Good morning, Mr. Wong," Michael called. "What is the news of the day?" Wong and Abe both subscribed to the Duluth Herald.

Abe would read his and then use it to wrap merchandise but Wong always pinned his to his front door and, over time, the entrance to his laundry had become the ersatz town bulletin board. Rather than poring over copy, Michael preferred to listen to Wong's synoptic summary. Wong enjoyed and took the social obligation seriously because it gave him a small measure of social prominence. Beyond that he was an enigmatic and private person. No one ever visited his home nor were they invited. To the town, Wong was a functional washer of clothes and, in an area where even the best water turned red in ten minutes from its iron content, Wong managed to turn out a good clean shirt. People felt that Mr. Wong and Abe had a necessary place in Mammoth and both of them seemed to be aware of what it was.

In an ethnically diverse town they were the absolute minority. The nearest Jewish community large enough to warrant a synagogue was twenty mile away in Hibbing. Abe made the trip every Friday noon so he would be there before the Sabbath. Only Mr. Wong knew how his own spiritual needs were met. They were part of the Mammoth community and yet not so. Jews and Chinese were an oddity on the iron range and, maybe because of this they were accepted as a tangential facet of the local society. This made them unusually objective observers of the social activities of the town.

Wong finished his sweeping, tucked the broom inside the door and sat down in a chair set beside a small table. Izerman did likewise and began setting up the pieces of an ivory chess set. They were quite the pair, well past middle age, white-haired and mildly paunchy but otherwise possessing the energy of men who still worked for a living out of choice rather than necessity.

"Good morning, young Michael," Mr. Wong replied with great civility and then launched immediately into his recitation. "The first of May, 1916. In Virginia, Minnesota, five hundred Finns, Italians, Slavs and Scandinavian socialists marched in the May Day parade demanding new work conditions: Eight hours labor, three dollars a day minimum, half holiday Saturday, the right to adjust wages and an end to the speeding system." The speeding system was set up so that the machine set the pace of the work. It normally set a faster pace than the average man working at a comfortable pace could keep up with.

"And a damn poor system it is," shouted a man behind Mike Kiril. They looked around at the man with a raised fist. "We should do like them and refuse to also work."

"Yes!" agreed another. "Strike if that's what it takes. A strike they will understand."

"A strike is very likely," Mr. Wong concurred. "Many were waving signs that read 'Workers of the World Unite.'"

"They'd be damn fools to walk out," said Mike to no one in particular but he glanced at the two behind him. Strangers, but he didn't bother to ask who they were. Anyway, the mine news didn't interest him as much as other things. "What about the boxing card?"

"Ah, yes. The boxing card is very interesting. On Saturday night in Mammoth Slovenian Hall Jack Ruffcorn from Milwaukee will box ten rounds against all challengers for cash wagers."

Kiril jabbed Michael in the ribs and grinned knowingly but Mike had another question.

"And who is Mary, that woman who came down the street to the mine office just now?" Mike asked quickly before anyone else could interrupt but also so no one might place any particular importance on the question.

"Mary?" Mr. Wong repeated the name tentatively and scratched his wispy beard. "Michael Jensen now wants to know about a certain woman named Mary."

"Stop teasing, Mr. Wong. Just give it to me. She works in Fleming's office, right?"

Wong's face brightened. "Ah, yes. Mary Savich by name. Recently hired personal secretary to Mr. Fleming, himself. From the Duluth Secretarial School. Nineteen years old. A proper lady by conventional standards and currently unattached although that would be of small importance to you."

"You do her laundry?" Kiril blurted.

Mr. Wong winked.

A voice from the back brought laughter. "Does she have ribbons and bows on her bloomers?"

"Now you watch your manners." Mike protested protectively.

"I agree with him," said Kiril. "You said I need a woman and I do like women with fancy underwear."

"That's enough B.S., Kiril. Stay away from any woman I got my eye on. And she will be mine, if I want her to be," he finished emphatically.

Kiril knew that a worm could more easily escape from a robin's beak than he could take a woman from Michael. That was why he enjoyed the game… as long as no real prize was in sight.

"What of it, Mr. Wong? Her bloomers? What color are the ribbons?" Kiril asked one last time.

"No, no," Mr. Wong shook his head. "Professional ethics bar such a wonton disclosure. I protect the privacy of my esteemed clientele."

Michael pressed on. "Where does she live?" There were only three real choices: Zenith, the company location where most of the workers lived was one. He knew she wasn't from there because he was. Then there was Aurora, on the other side of town, where the company managers and town merchants had most of their homes. The last choice would be somewhere on Meridian Street in downtown Mammoth.

"That is curious," Mr. Wong agreed, wagging his head. "She had, for a short while, taken a room with the widow Pryzmus, but when Mr. Pryzmus' brother came here to take a job in the sorting mill, she was required by common decency to move."

"Where?"

Mr. Wong's face swelled in a Cheshire cat smile and he pointed to the second floor of his store. He had three apartments up there, one for himself and two that he rented.

"You devil!" Michael snorted. "You knew all the time."

"She moved in three days past, Michael. I am surprised that a man of your acute senses did not know this."

"The suckers are running in the creeks. I'm been smelling of fish, not women," Michael said in his own defense. That brought some laughter. I've heard enough nonsense, Kiril. Let's go home. Thank you, Mr. Wong."

Wong touched Kiril on the shoulder and whispered, "Blue."

"Home" was Mike's house where he lived with his mother, Katla, his sister Sadie, Kiril and three male boarders who slept and took meals for fifty cents a day. Katla had been taking in boarders ever since her husband was killed eight years earlier. Michael was twelve at the time and Sadie still unborn. Mike had insisted on helping out, something, which would have been necessary even if he hadn't wanted to. He went to work for Mr. Wong at the laundry for two years. He hated it at first. Stirring the big tubs of boiling laundry and then squeezing out the blistering-hot clothing on the hand-cranked wringer left his arms numb by the end of the day to the point where the young man thought they might fall off. Instead, they grew larger and stronger. Later, he spent more time delivering and picking up the orders and got to meet most of the young girls on both sides of town. He came to prefer the lusty spirits of the Zenith women to the wealthier and often snobbish ladies of Aurora who only favored him with a penny tip if at all. But he also came to learn that soft lips and curving hips knew no geographic boundaries. A warm, yielding body on a summer evening was as close to heaven as he thought he'd ever get, something his pastor, Father Basil, would have been quick to second.

As handsome as he grew, Michael still had to credit the Chinaman with assisting in most of his conquests. From Wong, he picked up the ability to be comfortable around anyone and he learned enough philosophy to impress most of Mammoth's poorly educated population. He received enough formal education to know how little he really knew, but he felt he knew enough to get ahead of most people and let further book-learning go. He loved the Chinaman as the father he had lost. For Wong's part, Michael was as close to having a son as he would ever get.

When he was finally old enough to get what was considered a man's job, he went to work in the mine. By the time he was fifteen he was loading out ore and at seventeen he was a drill-blaster. Mike inherited his father's attitude that mining rocks was as good a way as any to make one's daily bread and a hella'va lot better than trying to farm a field full of them. The work was hard enough to challenge a young man's body and had more than enough danger to appeal to his hubris sense of immortality.

He thought the wages enormous at the time and still thought them comfortable now. He had no family of his own to support and still gave most of his wages to Katla. His needs were simple. He drank less than most men and his horizons extended no further than the tailing piles surrounding the pit. His loyalty to the mine was total.

Kiril had been with them since he was a young boy in Yugo-slavia, before Michael had even been born. He lived forty miles from Kranj in a village back in the mountains. One winter a fever swept through the province and took almost everyone that couldn't get away. Those that could escape did. Kiril survived but his parents didn't. There were so few adults left they couldn't bury the dead. Instead they piled the bodies inside a house and set fire to it to deter the wolves from eating them. To stay there was to die so Kiril left. He put a loaf of dark bread in a sack and started walking out of the mountains. Somehow he remembered the cousins he had met two years prior at a wedding and, like a homing pigeon, the little boy, not yet ten, came to the house of Ernst and Katla Jesenice. He opened his sack and presented Katla a gift of the bread and was taken in and he was one of them ever since.

Katla and Sadie had breakfast waiting. The other boarders had already gone off for the day shift and Sadie always waited for "her boys" before she ate.

"And how is my big-eyed girl," sang Kiril, picking her up and swinging her around the room.

"Kiril, stop that," said Katla. "You will muss her hair that I just spent so much time getting the snarls out of it." Kiril put down the squealing girl and kissed her on the forehead.

Sadie was an eight year-old reflection of her father. She had dark, expressive eyes, glossy, thick black hair that reached halfway down her back, and honey-toned skin that made her beautiful face glow. Katla had braided a long ponytail down the middle of her back and tied a big blue ribbon in it. Sadie liked it until Michael asked the name of the boy she was trying to impress. After that it became a circus with Sadie tearing out the bow and Katla patiently retying it.

"You children eat now before it gets cold," scolded Katla with mock anger. "The next time I will just put out some raw potatoes for you to gnaw on."

They ate up the hot cakes and fried side pork with the relish of men who had just spent ten hours at hard labor. All the while Michael grilled Sadie about her schoolwork with only an occasional tease about boys.

Finally Katla came in from the kitchen to chase her off to school and Mike and Kiril trooped upstairs to sleep.

Chapter 5

At one that afternoon, Michael came downstairs and filled a bowl with boiled potatoes and cold sausage from the pantry. He sat at the kitchen table where he could watch his mother through the window and ate. The temperature had climbed during the day into the fifties and the sun was working hard to dry off the remaining wetness of the spring thaw.

Katla was in the garden, laboriously turning over the lumpy brown loam with a potato fork. At every turn she raised the fork and brought it down like a sledgehammer to break up the clods. From time to time she bent over to pick out a rock, which she'd throw over into the Kracov's garden. She always insisted that was where they came from anyway. Mike finished his meal and went out to her.

She saw him come down the back steps and straightened up from the work. With a weary gesture she put her hand on the small of her back and rubbed.

"Ma, you're gonna kill yourself. Why do you do this?"

"Because my lazy son will not is why. Just like he will not paint the house until I start up our broken ladder." The south side of the two-story framed house was weather checked to the point of being bare of paint in many places.

Katla was only forty-five years old and had the dark features and sturdy frame of her Slavic race but she was not so heavy as some like Mrs. Krakov as she liked to remind others. Her hair was already slivered with grey but the skin of her cheeks was alive and olive smooth. Her eyes were the large, beautifully dark eyes of the Slavs. She liked to claim a little Hungarian blood in her ancestry.

Michael moved behind her and began to massage her back. "Mama, Mama. You think we are still back in Kranj and have only wrinkled potatoes and turnips to eat. So tell me this. How can you even dig out here without hitting all the jars of money you have buried and forgotten about?" He was saying this only partly in jest but what he would never fully appreciate was the experience etched deeply in her soul that, once poor, you would live forever with the fear that it could come upon you again.

She answered him in Slovenian. "Oh, go on with you, lazy youth. We haven't so much money that we can waste it buying the same food we can grow ourselves. The day will come when we may have need of it. Remember the grasshopper, Michael. He played his violin and then he starved."

"I always thought the ant took him in and cared for him."

"Not so. The ant took him in and ate him. People who don't care for themselves must rely on the kindness of God. And God has already been kind enough to give me a garden." She thrust the fork into the ground and grunted with the effort of turning it over.

"Okay, Ma. You've made your point and now you're breaking my heart." He took the fork and began rhythmically turning over clods while she watched.

"Your father, Michael, always had a garden, a beautiful garden. The neighbors would beg for his seeds, they grew such wondrous vegetables."

Mike understood the meaning of her statement. Her garden was really a memorial for Ernst. He had died in the Mammoth mine in a fall from the trestle he was helping to build.

The trestle was a long timbered ramp that stretched from the bottom of the pit up to the crushing mill beyond the rim. Ore trams were pulled up the tracks by a big steam winch. It was the only way to get the ore from the deepest level and, once designed, the foreman pushed hard for its completion.

It was in the winter, cold and snowy. Ice was glazed over the timbers and Ernst was working near the top when a thousand pound steel rail broke loose and came at him. It hit him in the chest, crushing ribs and a lung. He had fallen forty feet from the top of the railway trestle and, even then, might have survived that but he landed on a piece of ironwork. A steel rod had pierced his back and came out his chest between the ribs. The men still talked about how pieces of his heart had filled the threading of the rod. Kiril was one of the first at the scene, his screams of "Papa, "Papa," tearing the air. He had never called Ernst Papa but this once. Michael was too young to view the corpse and it wasn't until years later when they were both working in the mine that Kiril had told him how it had happened.

Today there was a fine stone monument in the cemetery west of Zenith. Still, she slept with her own memory of him alive behind the house. A small statue of Our Lady of the Assumption, protectress of Slovenia, stood on the large granite stone in the corner of the garden; the one Kiril had used a broken drill bit to carve "Mikey" on years ago.

Pausing for a break, Michael drove the tines into the ground and turned to his mother. "Mama," he said patiently, "I will turn over the garden for you. I don't want you to do this."

"When, Michael?" She appreciated that he was a young man with many interests, none of which involved gardening.

"It's early May, Mama. We'll have frost for three weeks yet. Last night I would have froze my nose off were it not for Sadie's kerchief."

"When, Michael? Your father would have it done by now."

"Father would have done it last fall," he conceded, knowing the ground would have been broken and the clods raked down before the snow. Potato sets would have been in on Good Friday. Father was like that; busy all the time with no hobbies but for watching the boxing matches, drinking the beer at the Slovenian Hall and smoking the matches that he was constantly striking and waving over his balky pipe. On any given day, no more windy than normal, Ernst might strike two hundred matches to burn less than an ounce of Sir Walter Raleigh. Suddenly remembering the boxing gave Michael his excuse.

"Sunday, Mama, I promise. I will finish the garden. Next week I might go in the ring with that big palooka, Ruffcorn, and win five dollars to put in one of your jars. If I dig today, I could hurt my arm and then how would I knock out that big palooka?"

"Oh you. Just like your father with his boxing and now working on Sunday yet. I have raised an atheist, may God forgive me." But there was a tease in her voice as she saw her Ernst in Michael and, anyway, her back hurt too much to dig anymore today. She would do a little each day before he came home and maybe on Sunday Michael would finish it.

"Ma, I have to go." Mike said, giving her a quick hug and peck on the forehead. "Kiril and I want to spear in the creek this afternoon."

He hurried off. "Come back to walk Sadie home from school," she called after him. But she knew he wouldn't forget. If there was one responsibility Michael took seriously, it was taking care of his little sister.

There were more once; a brother who died on the winter crossing from Yugoslavia and another sister who perished from pneumonia the second winter on the range when they lived in a thin, drafty tent. Ernst fell from the icy trestle in December, a week before Christmas when Katla was still carrying Sadie. Winters were never very kind to the Jensonice family and she often dreamed of romantic places like California or Kansas where the fruit trees would flower in early April.

She sat on the rock, ran her fingers over Kiril's etching of 'Mikie', and let the sun warm the stiffness from her back.

"Katla, tell me the truth. This place, it isn't so bad is it now?"

"Ernst, it is a terrible place when you get old. You died a young man before the arthritis." She closed her eyes. "I do miss you, though. Very much."

"My beloved girl, I am always here with you. I loved you then and I love you now. In the children I love you."

"Yes, I know," she smiled. "In the children we will always be together."

Michael and Kiril came back from spearing with four egg-laden suckers and two pike and met Sadie at the little one-room school-house. On the way home, Kiril swung her up on his shoulders so she could touch the sun and, when Michael asked if she'd ever marry Kiril, and she said no, his face was too scratchy, she relented when he began to cry.

"Kiril, I will marry you if you grow a real long beard so you'll be like a fuzzy bear." Kiril promised to start immediately.

chapter 6

That afternoon Michael was downtown earlier than normal. He waited at Wong's for Mary to come from work, stopped her on the street and came straight out and asked her for a date.

"No, thank you. I'm quite sure I would rather not," she answered straight out. The coolness in her tone set spring back another week.

Michael went straight to the heart of her snobbishness. "So are miners beneath your social status so far that it would embarrass you to be seen with one at a dance?"

She wasn't. "Certainly not. No more than being seen with you anywhere else. You have a reputation you must be aware of."

"I don't think I do."

"Well, it's generally known that you are self-centered, egotistical, shallow and a bit of a conquistador with any woman that strike your fancy. Shall I go on?"

His healthy ego made it possible to ignore her assessment. "How about in the dark, by Lake Park? Only the owls will see us and they don't care who goes there unless you're a rabbit?"

"You really are a case, aren't you?"

"So what about in the daylight? A picnic?"

"Even worse. But what if we arrange to go on different days together."

He had rarely been rebuffed so emphatically or effectively. "Is there another man?"

"One would certainly hope so." But the way she fluttered her eyes took the sting out of it. While her cool reparte was hard for him to stomach, playing the coquette only made Michael preserver the harder.

"Who? Tell me and I'll tear his heart out."

"You don't know him."

"Is it Mr. Wong?"

"My secret is out! Yes, Mr. Wong is my beau and my lover."

"Of course. It has to be. He washes your petticoats."

She blushed. "I don't wear petticoats."

He shot his last arrow. "Then it has to be John Fleming."

"No!" But she added quickly, "He doesn't wear them either."

"It is Fleming. Oh my, Mary! We have our sights set a bit high, don't we? I think you might be aiming your shot a little over the buck. Mr. Fleming is at least second-generation east coast high society."

He had angered her now. She turned and opened the door to go upstairs but he was blocking her way just enough. It forced her to respond.

"I don't see that's any of your concern." But he had struck a nerve. She did have her sights set on something better than just a miner and she was playing the aspiring Philadelphia debutante as she imagined it. She had no interest in explaining to Michael the hardship of growing up on a failing dairy farm near Hinckley, milking cows twice a day and helping in the fields. She studied at night and as soon as she was accepted to the Duluth Secretarial School, she packed a bag and left home. There had been a boy, one that she felt was a good fit. He was a member of the local society and gave her all the affection she craved, right up to the point of her going to bed with him. She discovered she was just a casual conquest for him and he didn't think her worth further attention, she being just a farm girl after all. Yes, she did set her sights high and would continue to do so until she was successful.

"Have you gone out together? Yes, of course. You see him in his office, don't you? Has he proposed yet? Did he tell you of his wife? His mistress? His wooden leg? His glass eye? He has so many defects or have you already seen them all? Doesn't it just drive you insane? Mike was talking fast and foolishly but he had her laughing at his inanity.

"I'm going in now and don't you dare come any farther," she said.

"I might dare anything I set my mind to. One last time," he pressed, "Can I see you?"

"One last time," she answered. "No, you can't." She was not about to settle for what she saw as having no future."

"Then I won't ask you again until tomorrow," he said gallantly. He took her hand, kissed it, and then turned away.

Every day for what seemed like weeks he repeated that scene, with the same results. It wasn't until the following week that Fleming remarked to Mary that he had seen them in front of the Chinaman's and asked who Michael was other than a miner.

"Is he a relative of yours?" It was an inadvertent reference to an obviously lower class than himself and it stung her.

"Of course not! He's just a man. I barely know him. He works for you, as you are aware. His name is Michael Jensen." Then she guessed where she might take this conversation and changed her approach. "He's a rather friendly gentleman at that, actually, and quite handsome I'm told."

And that's all it took to start the flow of John Fleming's competitive juices. Hadn't he, after all, been first alternate on his schools' eight-man rowing team? Wasn't his the name on so many dance cards of some of Scranton's most notable debutantes? John Fleming always considered himself the master of his own destiny. Masterton's caution about fraternizing and conquering put the brakes to his line of reasoning for only a minute before he boldly moved forward. The paper on his desk was open to the local news and glancing at it he asked the question of the moment.

"Mary, may I ask? Are you engaged Saturday?"

She reminded herself not to be too eager. "I have been asked to a picnic, if the weather is mild."

"Oh! Well, I certainly don't mean to spoil that," hastening to add, "There's a boxing match at the Slovenian Hall Saturday night. I don't normally attend but I thought you might like to accompany me there."

How utterly unromantic, she thought. "How utterly thrilling," She said. "I'd love to, John. Are you a boxer?"

"Heavens no. I mean I certainly could have been. But without training properly I'd have my nose bloodied in a second. Well, it might take several minutes actually. But I do enjoy watching it," he lied.

"So do I," she lied back.

On Friday when Michael again asked her for a date, she accepted, not because she especially cared for him, but because she had begun to think of him as the draft that would fan the flames of John Fleming's desire.

chapter 7

"**What's** the news today, Mr. Wong, if you please?"

"Ah, the news, Michael." Wong sat back in his chair and stroked his wispy beard. "It is being whispered that Michael Jensen has a personal and private picnic date today with one Mary Savich at Lake Park and other unrests of the labor kind continue to mount."

Michael blushed. "How did you know that? Did she tell you? Kiril?"

"Uh, Uh. Professional ethics. Of course, she might have possible requested a personal reference from me."

"And what did you tell her?"

"Only the truth. I told her that you were the model of gentlemanly behavior and like a son to me. I told her that to put trust in you was to put it in a temple of honor."

"In other words, you lied. Thank you. So, tell me about the labor unrest? Where?"

Biwabik. Hudson, Mohawk, Miller and Fowler mines all shut down. Four hundred and sixty men have walked off their work. Labor leaders have come up to the range to agitate to shut down every mine."

Mike and Kiril were stunned. "Holy Jesus, they really did it," stammered Mike. "The fools really did it. Well, it can't happen here. Mammoth isn't like other mines and we aren't like other miners. We're proud of our work and we work because we want to."

"Oh? You had better be more observant, Michael," said Mr. Wong. "There are many things happening all about you that your eyes do not hear, your ears do not see."

Kiril laughed. "See, Mikey, I told you. You only have ears for skirts and eyes for dancing music. The rest of the world has passed you by."

Michael scoffed. "Well, my nose still works fine and I think the union stuff stinks." He gestured at Wong. "That would be a lot of laundry passing you by, Mr. Wong, if there are no paychecks. And a lot of trousers that won't leave your shelves, Mr. Izerman, if there aren't miners to wear them out."

"How sad, but you are correct," agreed the stoical Jew.

"And you know what? If I can't work it wouldn't bother me in the least. I'll just go fishing. I'll even have time to get Ma's garden in properly."

"Garden?" Mr. Wong perked up. "Please plant Bok Choi for Mr. Wong. Chinese cabbage. Like celery. Very good for you."

"Okay, Mr. Wong," Mike said as they left. "Bok Choi for you and currants for ma. You believe that, Kiril? The woods are full of them and she wants me to plant currants in the garden. Next she'll be wanting blueberries, too."

"She's wanted currants for years, Mikey. It's a Slovenian tradition. If you have currents your memory will live on whenever someone picks one. They last forever."

"Bullshit, Kiril. Nothing lasts forever, not you, not the town, not me. Every thing changes. Everything gets forgotten."

Chapter 8

"**The** situation is changing constantly out there," he said through a coffee belch. "Here's the big picture." The heavily muscled man with the large florid face and short-cropped salty hair was addressing Fleming in his office. Like Masterton had done earlier in the week, Karsch was looking out the window at the passing foot traffic. Fleming's eyes were focused curiously on the hand Karsch had clasped behind his back. The fingers on it only extended to the second knuckle. In fact, the man' entire body seemed to be made up of damaged goods. His left ear lobe and the tip of his nose were missing and a sickly scar connected the two misshapen parts. When he turned and moved about the room there was a noticeable limp in his bow-legged step. Still, he had an air of raw power, like a high-pressure steam line charged to the point of bursting. He appeared to Fleming like a junkyard dog that had been in, and won, more than his share of fights over the corner hydrant. He was scarred and crippled but he could still stare down or beat down any man he wanted to.

"They've walked out in Biwabik. Hibbing and Virginia are next. They're taking out the big towns first and then they will go after you, Greenway, Coleraine, all the rest." He spoke with the steady beat of a man describing a military campaign. "It'll start with a march and some crackpot demands. Mammoth miners will be stomping in support of Hibbing strikers. They'll be asking for crap they don't need, want or deserve. Anything to raise a little hell over. Next thing we know, Buhl will be marching down the streets of Mammoth."

Karsch locked onto Fleming's eyes. "Masterton said you ain't a believer. He said you trusted your people. Bullshit!"

Karsch waited for Fleming's response but John looked silently away. "Doesn't matter. They'll do it anyway, regardless of what you think. I've seen it before; meat-cutters, stevedores, coal miners. They're all alike. What one does they all got to do. Like lemmings they are. You know what lemmings are, Mr. Fleming?"

"I assure you I am familiar with lemmings, Mr. Karsh."

Karsch and Masterton were confidants, Fleming knew. They would share everything with each other. He wondered if the boss had told Karsch about Mary Savich, too.

Karsch wasn't through. "It ain't the miners so much as the agitators. Those damn Wobblies ain't good for nothing. Like having an extra hole in your butt. They got two of their big wheels on the range right now. One's this Tresca guy and a man by the name of W.D. Scarlett. My old buddy Scarlett. I've had a run-in or two with his like. A guy named Heywood is on his way, too. They'll demand twice as much as they ever hope to get and convince your miners it's doable. By the time their promises come back down to earth, there'll be hell to pay."

Fleming was familiar with Bill Heywood. Although he had never met him he knew Heywood to be from Colorado and was the treasurer and an original organizer of the Industrial Workers of the World. He had helped organize the Western Federation of Mine that boasted of seventeen thousand members. He was a staunch socialist, probably a communist, and was active across the country.

Karsh broke into his thoughts again. "You following this, Mr. Fleming?" It was a loyalty check to be dully reported back to Masterton. Fleming recognized it as such. "Certainly, Mr. Karsh. Go on."

"You got your job and I got mine. When they walk out my job is to make sure the scabs can get to work and the strikers don't bust up the equipment. Security, that's what I do. Me and the Mammoth police will see to that. Your job is to keep Masterton's ore moving out of this hole."

Bill Heywood

Helen Gurley Flynn

"Mammoth police?" The very name sounded strange to Fleming. Mammoth had no civil police force. Ithasca County Sheriff's deputies always handled the law enforcement duties.

"Mammoth Mine police, Mr. Fleming. I'm going to hire twenty-five deputies for starters, maybe more later. Legally deputized by the County Sheriff and ordered about by me." He pointed a crooked finger at Fleming. "They will work directly and only for me and they will do what I tell them"

Fleming started out of his chair but Karsch stuck out a hand. "Right now there's probably four or five agitators in your work force you don't even know about. Not your fault. There's a war in Europe. I don't have to tell you that. Steel demand has never been greater. Immigration is shut off. You hire who you can. The owners don't fault you for that. My job is to check out everyone and get rid of the crud. Your job is to take the rest and ship iron ore. Agreed?" Karsch smiled for the first time since he had walked into the office half an hour ago. The number of missing teeth amazed Fleming. An instinctive rush of pity welled up in him, then revulsion swept it away and John Fleming's judgment of people was reinstated.

"Mr. Karsh, just so we are in agreement in principle at least, I want you to know something. I work for Mammoth Mines and I am one hundred percent loyal to their policies. My employees, until they demonstrate differently, are the same. I know that if some divisiveness comes between the company and its people, it won't be me that causes it and I certainly hope it won't be you."

Karsch held his smile longer than called for. He filed Fleming's comment for future use and picked up his valise. "We'll be moving into the watch house then." The watch house was an empty dormitory that once housed the mine's fire fighting crew. Ever since the formation of the city volunteer fire company it had been used solely for storage.

"Yes, Fleming muttered. "Well, goodbye then." He returned to his work with such a vengeance that he snapped off his pencil lead. The young superintendent flinched.

chapter 9

They had their picnic on Saturday rather than Sunday because Michael worked Sunday nights and was hoping to make this more than just an afternoon outing. He picked Mary up at eleven that morning. The weather was as mild as expected for late May in northern Minnesota. There were no mosquitoes as yet and if there had been, the warming sun would have soon driven them under cover. It was too early for the swarming gnats, black flies, deer and horse flies. All in all, it was a delightful Iron Range day.

They walked down to Lake Park on the southeast corner of Aurora, Michael chattering like a squirrel the whole way, not out of nervousness so much as by design. He always had his best luck with a woman when he was in control of the conversation. For her part, Mary worked hard to keep a proper physical separation from the constantly encroaching Michael.

On the shore of Buck Lake, he skipped rocks for her amusement. It was a skill he felt he was especially adept at.

Across the water to the northeast was the huge tailings pile where they had piled the overburden when the mine was developed. It rose eighty feet above the lake. The gravel that spilled down its eroded sides washed into the lake and tinted the water red. In the winter, children tobogganed down the pile and out onto the ice. When the wind blew hard enough and swept the snow from the ice, they could cover most of the quarter-mile over to Lake Park on a single run.

North of the tailings and out of sight of the park stood the trestle and sorting and crushing mills where the ore was trammed up, washed free of gravel and loaded onto the train cars for shipment to Duluth. The low hum of the machinery was punctuated periodically by the sounds of ore cars banging together. There, also, were the sidings of the Mesaba Railroad tracks and most of the mine's machine ships.

To the east, beyond the lake, was cut-over forest, mostly second-growth birch and aspen, creeks, bogs, lakes and then more mines that ran all the way to Ely a hundred miles away.

Mary spread a blanket under an oak tree that was still clothed in last summer's leaves. She laid out a dinner of cheese and finger sandwiches and a loaf of walnut potica. Michael plunked his last stone and, opening a bottle of Caliari wine, he took a long drink. Mary giggled.

"What's the matter," he said, a dribble of red running down his chin.

"Nothing," she laughed. "I just hope you thought to bring a glass for me."

He wiped his chin. "I did," he smiled, holding out the bottle, "but it has a pretty small hole in the top."

She took the bottle and generously drank as he had, the cheap astringent liquid sliding warm and satisfying down her throat. Up to this point she had found him to be an amusing though not an especially fascinating person. He reminded her of most of the young men she had dated: unfettered by responsibility, confident in their youth and immortality, and always living for the moment. Hopefully, she thought, he would go deeper than that before the day was concluded. It would be a shame to waste such a beautiful day on a raw youth of such low social standing.

They ate and looked out over the lake. A small flock of blue-billed ducks rafted out in the middle, taking a rest from their trip back north.

"I bet I killed nearly a hundred ducks last fall," Michael said nonchalantly. "Probably that many grouse, too. Not to mention three deer and God knows how many squirrels."

Mary's eyes wandered over to a heron fishing down the shore. "Why?" she asked.

"Why what?"

"Why did you kill them?"

"Well, to eat, of course."

"Are they good? To eat?"

"Sweet as honey," Mike said. "Sweet like you," he added flirtatiously.

"Oh, God!" she exclaimed, reaching for the wine. "That's bad. To be compared to a duck carcass. We'll need a lot more of this if that's your idea of romantic talk."

He finished rolling a cigarette and stuck it in his mouth. "How about this," he continued, nonplused. "I think you're about the prettiest girl in Mammoth. No, I take that back. I know you're the prettiest girl in Mammoth because I know all of them. No one else comes close to your looks. And that goes for the whole range. You have smoky eyes, raven hair and a smile that could melt a glacier. And I'm not even close to getting to your shapely figure."

Nor will you any time soon, she thought. "Well, sure," she giggled. "Tell me something I don't know."

Michael lit his cigarette and, taking a long drag on it, blew an expansive smoke ring. "What about me? Do you think I'm handsome?"

"Handsome?"

"You know. Good looking? Manly, attractive, fetching to a young lady?"

God yes, she was thinking. "Well, maybe, in a rough chiseled way. It's not dissimilar to a sculptor taking a jackhammer to a block of fine granite after a night of heavy intoxication."

He laughed and began to move closer to her but she held him off with one hand and took the cigarette from his mouth. Mike was ready for the kiss but, instead, Mary drew deeply, arched her head back and exhaled. A series of perfect, round smoke rings came out.

"Damn! Where'd you learn to do that?"

She stubbed out the cigarette. "From my brothers, out behind the woodshed."

"I didn't think nice girls smoked tobacco."

"They don't." She winked at him and reached into the picnic hamper. "Here," she said pulling out a book and handing it to him. "I have a gift for you."

"What's this?" He took it and turned it over in his hand.

"I'm sorry. I thought you'd recognize it. It's a book." She gave him a beguiling smile."

"I guessed that. What do you want me to do with it? Hey! Let's see how far I can skip it." He started to get up but she grabbed his arm.

"Don't be a tease," she said. "I want you to read to me."

"What for?" He looked at her incredulously. "Oh my god, can't you read, Mary?"

"Of course I can. Can't you?" she countered.

Mike stared at her. It came to mind that her 'gift' was really more of a test.

"Have you had any schooling, Michael?"

He puffed out his chest, a little more than warranted. "I certainly have. Eight years, front row. And I still have most of my knuckles in working order."

"Good. Show me." She opened the book to a marked page. Start here."

Michael looked at the passage for a minute. "It's been a nice day so far, Mary. Let's don't ruin it."

"It's from The Taming of the Shrew, a play by Shakespeare."

"A shrew is a garden rat," he stated indignantly. "Who'd ever want a tame one?"

"It's also a strong-willed woman," snapped Mary, equally indignantly. "Go on, please me."

He looked it over. It had words like their King James Bible but otherwise didn't look too difficult. He grimaced and plowed into it.

"But Kate," he read hesitantly, "the prettiest Kate in Christendom, Kate of Kate Hall, my super-dinty Kate." He stopped, a wounded look on his face. "Super-dinty?"

"That's probably how all your ducks felt," Mary grinned. "It's lovely. Please go on."

He reluctantly read on.

"For dainties are all Cates and therefore Kate.
Take this of me, Kate of my consolation,
Hearing thy mildness prais'd in every town,
Thy virtues spoke of, and thy beauty sounded,
Yet not so deeply as to thee belongs,
Myself am mov'd to woo thee for my wife.

"There," he snarled, slamming the book shut. "Is my lady now pleased?"

"You really should go on."

"Never," he shuddered.

"No. I mean in school. To better yourself."

"I'm as good as I want to be right now," adding, "and better than most of the other men in Mammoth."

"For shame, Michael. That's hubris. "He stared at her. "See? That's my point. It means unwarranted bragging. That's a word you could learn in secondary school instead of remaining so placid by comparing yourself with far less educated people.. You could do much better than to spend your life turning red in a mine. You are intelligent. You could probably manage one if you set your mind to it."

"Like your boyfriend, Fleming? No thank you, Mary. My father never set foot in a schoolhouse in his life and he kept a job, a house and a family and did pretty damned good until,…" He stopped and rolled another cigarette and lit it. His hands were shaking noticeably. He blew a smoke ring, then another and another until he began laughing and choked on the smoke.

"What happened to your father?"

Michael shrugged, trying to act nonchalant. "He was killed in the mine." She waited for him to continue. "I only smoke," he added, "when I'm excited about something… or someone."

She nodded, ignoring and thus deflecting his advance. "I always thought people smoked because they were bored. You were telling me about your father."

"I told you, he was killed in the mine."

"How? How was he killed? Unless you would rather not talk about it."

Michael breathed deeply, and related it as he knew it. "The big trestle. He was working with the construction crew. It was December, cold and icy. There had been a sleet storm but the foreman made them go up anyway to work on it. It was too slippery for a cat to crawl on much less a man. He fell." His shoulders heaved. "I was just a little kid then," he added by way of indicating that was all he knew or cared to say.

She reacted, as she reflected later, without thinking. "See? See? The iron mines offer no future at all." She began to laugh a little and caught herself. "Oh, god, Michael, I'm sorry. That was so insensitive of me. I'm not laughing at your father or any miners. But doesn't it prove my point or at least support it?"

Even with her apology it still hurt. She was stirring up emotions in him that had been deeply buried. He had anticipated an easy conquest, but now he was starting to wonder who was conquering whom. She was smarter than he and had a sharper and wittier tongue about her. Taken together with her sultry looks, she was fast becoming more than a casual conquest to him and he wasn't sure how to handle it. This woman was definitely more woman than he had ever encountered before.

"You were laughing at me just now, weren't you?"

"No! No, honestly I wasn't, Michael. Well, maybe just a little but I'm so sorry I did." She had no intention of giving into his vanity. She had her own to cope with. Still, she reached up and gave him a comforting touch.

Michael took her arms and, pulling her to her feet, and tried to reassert some measure of control as best he could. He kissed her hard on the mouth.

"No!" She pushed him away and almost made to slap him. "You had no right to do that."

He shrugged. "Why not? I'm a man and you're a woman and we're obviously attracted to each other."

"And it's the rutting season? Is that all you men think of? Bed a woman and have another trophy to brag about?" She was shouting at him. "And to think I almost started to like you." She began to run off. He started after, then returned and, swearing at his stupidity, threw everything into the basket and ran after her. He caught her by the little bridge that crossed Buck Creek, slipped around her and planted himself in her path.

"Don't try to stop me," she demanded. Her face was flushed and angry but Michael held his ground.

Michael was confused now and desperately wanted to fix things. "I will but first I want to show you a trick." He put down the basket and, grabbing the handrails of the narrow bridge, did a handstand.

"What do you think?" he asked while hanging upside down. "Can Fleming do this?"

She was still angry because she wanted to dislike him. "Frankly, I wouldn't be impressed if you could twirl your nose around your head and whistle Flow Gently Sweet Afton through your rear."

"No, but I can do Coming Through the Rye." Then he started laughing so she pushed him and he went over into the creek. He went under in a cascade of water and stayed submerged for the longest time. When he finally surfaced he squirted a fountain of water from his mouth and said, "I love the way you talk, Mary."

"Oh, God. You scared me half to death! I thought you drowned." He waded to shore and climbed up on the bank where she threw the blanket over his shoulders.

"Did you push me? Mary, I think you did."

"Me? No! Well, I… a little. I wanted you to get down. I thought the blood rushing to your head might wake up your little brain if you weren't careful."

"Here, I'll do it again. I can do a somersault off this bridge," he said putting his hands back on the rail. "I won't do it if you kiss me again."

Mary grabbed the basket and ducked past him striding purposefully off the bridge. "Honestly. I didn't even kiss you the first time. You are such a child."

He ran after her and caught up again. "I am not. I'm a man, Mary. A silly man, maybe, but still a man. That may not seem like much to you but in Mammoth it's something."

"I certainly haven't seen any indication of that." But she had slowed her pace so he kept talking.

"Do you like boxing?" he asked quickly changing the subject.

Are all men in this town so crude, she wondered? "I should say not."

"Come to the hall tonight."

She stopped. "Why?"

"There's a boxing exhibition. Let's go together."

"Mr. Jensen." Her voice was firm and final. "That's the last place I'd be seen with you this evening. Besides, I already have an engagement."

He kept trying to smooth over her irritation with him all the way back to Mammoth but at the door of Mr. Wong's she mouthed a quick goodbye and disappeared inside.

But he found himself standing on the sidewalk with the complete works of Shakespeare in his hand and had no idea how it had gotten there.

chapter 10

The Mammoth Slovenian Hall was a wood-framed building three times the size of the one-room schoolhouse and stood on the south end of Meridian Street. Fifteen years earlier it had been called the Finnish Socialist hall but then the Finlanders walked out on the mine owners and the mines imported eastern Europeans to work the pits. The Finlanders moved out to the logging camps, selling the hall to the new migrants for forty-five dollars. There were dozens of such fraternal organizations on the iron range, national touchstones for the newly franchised that had left their homelands in search of the American dream.

They were the towns' living rooms for wedding receptions, anniversaries, funeral wakes, family reunions, dances and, on this occasion, a boxing match.

There were over two hundred people packed into the hall on wooden folding chairs and benches. The outer rows were standing on stepladders. A few men squatted up in the rafters. Most of the women were sitting up on the stage, demurely waiting for the night's entertainment while they worked over stacks of knitting neatly piled in front of them.

Jack Ruffcorn was sitting on a stool in the corner of the make-shift ring set up in the middle of the smoke-filled room. He was chewing on an unlit cigar and trading banter with a small circle of admirers.

In his best years Ruffcorn was, at most, a journeyman who never made more than fifty dollars a night as a legitimate professional. Long past his prime, he finally struck pay dirt fighting 'All Comers' exhibition matches in Northern Minnesota. He took eighty percent of the gate and paid out five dollars to anyone who could last one three-minute round against him. He was a natural showman, playing the part of a brawling and bawling villain in the ring and, afterwards, would sit around in the saloons and regale his admirers with stories about his big championship shot against Jack Johnson six years earlier.

"I went twenty-four rounds with old Jack," he'd brag. "Toe to toe and spit in the other man's eye, we slugged it out in the middle of the Cody, Wyoming stockyard. Then he broke three of my slats"—here he'd point to his ribcage—"and I started spitting blood. Blood, by god, boys! I had him covered in my blood so bad he couldn't hardly see. Finally my tank ran dry and we threw in the towel. By then, that was covered with my blood, too. We threw in a red towel. Afterwards, Jack came to my tent and said it was the hardest fight he had ever fought."

Ruffcorn threw his cigar in the spit bucket and nodded to the referee who grabbed a megaphone and hailed the crowd.

"Ladies and gentlemen," he intoned in the time-honored tradition. "Ladies and gentlemen, may I have your attention please. Tonight's bare-knuckle fight card is about to begin. In this corner, weighing two-hundred and ten pounds, former heavy-weight challenger of the world, Joltin' Jack Ruffcorn." A rich mixture of cheers and boos swept through the hall. Jack, resplendent in black silk tights and naked from the waist up, strode out of his corner and, grabbing the megaphone, began to harangue the crowd.

"And over there, in the other corner," Ruffcorn shouted, gesturing to a burly, bearded miner, "sits three-hundred pounds of scared, quivering lard! Let's get the pig slaughter started." He threw down the megaphone and began shadow boxing around the man.

The bell sounded and the miner came out, his hands held high in a pose he imagined a fighter would affect. The fight was shorter than the introduction. Ruffcorn raided his fists high. The miner matched his stance. Ruffcorn reached higher and the miner did the same. An instant later, Ruffcorn's left feinted a jab in the face and his right hand swept down and into the man's huge gut, doubling him over. A hard left to the side of his unprotected face followed and the miner fell back against the ropes and collapsed to the floor.

Attendants pulled him out of the ring, boots first, while Ruffcorn went back to his corner and popped another cigar in his mouth. Five other fakers and fools followed, only one of them lasted more than half the time limit and then only because he ran around the ring until Ruffcorn finally backed him into a corner. The man ducked under the ropes and lost himself in the hooting crowd.

Jack stayed in the center of the ring, exchanging taunts and daring another man to come forward. He was, if nothing else, a great showman and knew that the evening was still well short of completion.

Suddenly, Michael climbed over the front ranks and slipped through the ropes. Behind him came a laughing Kiril, a beer mug in each hand. Ruffcorn took one of the proffered beers, saluted the two inebriates and downed it in four gulps.

"Thank you, my good man," Ruffcorn nodded. "I will treat your friend civilly. Then he retired to his stool. Michael took off his shirt and laid it over the top rope. Kiril poured the other beer over a towel and rubbed Michael down with it. Friends and advisors leaned into the corner, massaging his shoulders, whispering tactics in his ear. An amused Ruffcorn patiently chewed his cigar.

The bell clanged and they came to the center and touched hands. Ruffcorn's were half again larger than Michael's, but whereas Ruffcorn's gut was large and expansive, Michael's stomach was flat and etched with muscular definition. He may have been playing the fool but he certainly didn't have the body of a faker.

Ruffcorn backed off and raised his hands as before, trying to get Jensen to expose his belly. Mike feinted up but, beating the brawler at his own game, drove his fist into Ruffcorn's stomach. Ruffcorn let out a gasp and looked up in surprise, just in time to absorb another blow to his face.

"Damn!" he swore, staggering back and covering up. He took two more quick shots on his forearms and then fired back, glancing a blow off Mike's forehead and then landing a better one on Michael's chest. The shot drove Mike harmlessly into the center of the ring and he danced away grinning.

"Damn, you are a feisty little shit,"spat Ruffcorn, "I'll give you that."

Joltin' Jack gathered his senses and came at him, swinging from the floor joists but hitting nothing but air. Mike bounced in, landed another blow in the face, and then skipped away. Blood began oozing from Ruffcorn's often broken nose. He blew it out and wiped his face with the back of his hand.

Mike drove in with another right but this time Ruffcorn blocked it and came back with one that caught Mike alongside the jaw. Stung hard, he reeled back, his legs struggling to keep up with the rest of him, until he was finally backed up against the ropes. Ruffcorn was on him like a tiger, battering his body with short vicious uppercuts. Mike swung back, landing a few harmless punches. Then, he grabbed Ruffcorn around the waist and hung on until the bell rung. Mike dropped his hands and smiled up at the old veteran.

"You little punk," Sneered Ruffcorn. "You hit like an old lady. But I said you are a feisty little shit and I'll say it again. I give you that.

He gave Mike a playful tap on the chin before roughly pushing him away. He went back to his corner and dumped a bucket of water over his head before demanding his cigar. Then he sat there, five dollars poorer, a scowl covering his wet and blood stained face.

Kiril jumped over the ropes, threw another bucket of water over Michael and began hugging him.

"Mikey, Mikey! You killed him. You beat the former, once was, world champion contender." They danced around the ring, Kiril dragging the still stunned and groggy Jensen until the referee came over and paid him off.

"Here," he said. "Now get the hell out of here and you better get drunk tonight because you won't be able to open your mouth tomorrow."

Mike held up the money and waved it to the cheering crowd. His eyes swept past the stage, came back, and rested on Mary seated in the front row. She was smiling at him, a big, open-mouthed, disbelieving grin. Her arm was slipped casually through John Fleming's.

"Come on, Kiril," he said, stepping out of the ring. "I see someone I want to talk to."

Pushing through the backslapping crowd, he jumped onto the stage, stumbled and stood up. His face was six inches from hers.

"You told me you hated boxing. Or was it just boxers? Or was it just some boxers? I don't remember."

"I shouldn't wonder the way you were beating on his fists with your head. You look awful," she sympathized, refusing to be embarrassed. She touched the welt on his cheek. "Your eye is going to go black. A badge of honor among men, no?."

"Michael flinched away. "I was killing him, Mary. I had him beat. One more round and he was done. Just one more." Mike began shuffling, doing a little shadowboxing until Mary poked the red mark under his ribcage.

"Really? How does this feel?"

"Ow! Be careful there. It's a little tender."

"It might be a little cracked," said Mary.

Fleming laughed. "Just one more round and he would have had you on your knees, I should say, young man."

"Who are you calling a young man?" Mike challenged.

"Oh, John," Mary interjected. "This is Mike Jensen. He runs one of your drilling crews. Mike, John Fleming."

"Oh, yes," he nodded on cue. "Jensen. What's your crew number again?" He knew who Michael was but by virtue of the young man's apparent relationship to Mary, he was determined to keep a distance.

Mike's face registered mild disgust. "Three," he said proudly.

Fleming sifted through the data in his brain. "Three? That is a good crew. A very good crew."

"Best damn crew you got, Mr. Fleming," Mike corrected. "And with some new equipment, we'd be better yet. You don't need a number to tell our work from the other crew's either."

Fleming smiled wanly. The young miner was as good a boaster as he was a pugilist and it made him uncomfortable. And it didn't help to see Mary running her fingers over Michael's unclothed body either. Masterton was right. Mixing with the help in their element wasn't a good thing. He felt very out of place at that moment.

Michael pressed his advantage. "Maybe you'd like to try your luck, boss."

Fleming shook his head and laughed haughtily. "No thank you. Not my sport. I'll leave that to you muscular types."

Michael looked down at his bruised body and, having made his point, began to put on his shirt. "You should do that. Yeah, us muscular types."

"Mikey, who is that guy?" Kiril broke in, pointing down to the ring. A big, rough-cut man with close-cropped hair was stripping to his trousers. Where Ruffcorn was large and blocky and Michael was lean and sinewy, the new man was a combination of both. He had a massive body that actually could have been chiseled from Mary's facetious granite block.

Fleming narrowed his eyes at the man. "His name's Karsch," he said humorlessly. "He started at the mine today."

"Where?" Mary asked. She had seen him in the office but had no word of him going on the payroll.

"He's a special consultant for Masterton," Fleming fumbled. "He came down to oversee some of our ... special needs."

Mary looked at John quizzically but he ignored her. Ruffcorn warily stood up and came out to meet Karsch. He was three inches taller than Karsch but they were of equal arm reach and appeared to weigh much the same. They stood in the center of the ring and touched hands.

"What in the hell are you doing up here?" whispered Ruffcorn.

Karsch spoke through his toothless smile. "Working. I'm a cop again, Jack. How do you like that? Me on the right side of the law?"

"They've got you on the wrong side of the bars."

"I pick my teeth with crowbars."

"It shows."

"Do me a favor, Ruffcorn. Don't fall down until I put you down. Let me get in a few good licks for these wonderful folks."

Ruffcorn scowled and spat on the canvas but his spittle was sparse and dry.

The bell rang and Ruffcorn began circling warily to his left

Uncharacteristically, he wasn't smiling any longer. His face was clouded with concern and his eyes never left Karsch for a second.

Karsch followed suit and mirrored Ruffcorns movements moving with the stealth of a hunter. Neither man was in a hurry. The three-minute time limit had become meaningless. The crowd had ceased to exist. The hall became hushed, the tension within the ring spilling out and washing over the tension frozen on every face.

"They know each other," Mary barely whispered. "Who is he, John?"

Suddenly they crashed together. Like two mad dogs going for each other's throats, they rained blows on each other. The crowd came to life with wild screaming; the women held the knitting in front of their faces and the needles flew like a gale at sea. The brawlers were cutting each other now and blood sprayed from their faces at each hammer blow and sprinkled the spectators three rows back from the ring. For a minute that became an eternity they stood toe-to-toe taking the other's most powerful blows and returning the same. Then Ruffcorn's arms dropped and he fell back, was driven back, reeling against the ropes and everyone could tell that most of the blood was coming from him. Michael had bloodied his nose but Karsch had obliterated it. A deep cut had been opened over his left eye and another beneath an ear. A steady, thick, red drool was running from his mouth. His eyes were wild with fear now, like a deer cornered by ravenous wolves.

The thin, toothless smile spread over Karsch's face, a face already so scarred that no further damage could be done to it. Ruffcorn slid along the ropes and Karsch relentlessly advanced. He took another stalking step and Ruffcorn swung hard. He hit Karsch squarely in the face with everything he had left. Karsch's head snapped back and recoiled. He staggered, shook his head and bore in. He drove his fist into Ruffcorn's ribs–once, twice, and again. Ruffcorn grunted and doubled over. Karsch hit him twice more in the ribs, breaking them, and then drove his right hand onto the back of Ruffcorn's neck. He staggered and pitched forward to the floor. Karsch looked around malevolently, then bent over and grabbed a handful of Ruffcorn's hair and pulled his bleeding head off the floor. He raised his fist to hit him again.

Jack's manager dove through the ropes and, kneeling beside his champion, grabbed Karsch's arm and begged for clemency.

"I want to hear him cry for mercy."

"He can't, for God's sake! He's out cold!"

Karsch rolled Ruffcorn's head around. The eye sockets had gone white. The ugly brawler lifted his eyes to the stage and found Fleming. He smiled his thin-lipped smile and let Ruffcorn's head drop to the floor. Then he straightened up and surveyed the crowd with contempt.

The referee rushed over and held the five dollars in his face. Karsch took the money, held it over his head and tore the bills into bits before letting them flutter down on Ruffcorn's prostrate body. He took a corner stool and stepped onto it.

"Listen to me! Everyone! My name is Karsch," he bellowed. "Karsch! I can drive a spike into an oak timber with my bare fist. I can bend steel bars like green wood. There ain't a man alive I can't beat in a fight fair or foul. Are there any here who say otherwise?" Then he stared the murmuring assemblage into silence and left the ring. The crowd melted before him as he shouldered his way out of the stunned room. No one had ever seen a man like him before. They had all witnessed the truth of his brag.

Kiril tried to be practical. "Well, if he can run a special operation as well as he can fight, you have quite a man there."

Michael laughed. "Hell, Kiril, he's just another rooster scratching in the dust and showing his spurs.'

"Yes, but what a rooster and what spurs, eh?"

Mary's white-knuckled fingers were wrapped around the pale Fleming's arm. Michael's eyes never left Karsch until the grotesque man was out the door.

Ruffcorn didn't make it to the bars that night. He was lying in a coma in the Mammoth hospital with severe clots on the brain. Michael and Kiril took his place and Karsch was the hot topic. By Monday morning everyone knew who he was. Then they began seeing him down in the mine, patrolling with his deputies whose number increased every day. By the end of the week there were twenty living in the watch house and everyone had a good idea what Karsch's special duties were.

Chapter 11

Masterton exchanged curt greetings with the five sober-faced men gathered in the boardroom of the Duluth Commercial Bank. Tom Booker, chairman of the giant Tolliver Mining Group, controlling eighteen mines in six range cities, sat in the big chair at the head of the table. To his left were two independents: Dick Chambers of the shut down Biwabik undergrounds and one-armed Harry Madlock, owner of the Webb and Meadow's open pits. Across from them, Robert Saperstein, executive secretary of the Carnegie Steel Group, was reflectively turning a pen over and over in his hands. Next to him was Matthew Deering. Like Masterton, he saw himself as a pioneer and independent minded mine owner. In the 1905 strike it was Deering's idea to send flyers to Ellis Island soliciting replacements for the disgruntled Finlanders. The owners had offered a job, free schooling for six grades and a mortgage on a company owned house. The response had been overwhelming. Deering was chomping on a two-dollar cigar and sipping bourbon from a water glass. He looked up at the sound of Masterton's voice.

"Get your ass in here, Billy," he snarled good-naturedly. "I gotta catch a train to Chicago at eleven."

Masterton gave it right back, "Why don't you just buy the damned thing, Deering. Then it won't leave until you want it to." He went around the table shaking hands, finally sat down opposite Booker and poured himself a cup of coffee, taking it black.

"Sorry about Hibbing, Tom," he offered across the table.

"Hibbing *and* Virginia."

"Virginia? When?"

"Now! Today! While we sit here on our dead asses, the whole Iron Range is shutting down. Look," he said fixing each of them with a look of exasperation, "Let's get right to it. The Vermillion mines are gone. Dick and Harry here might as well go fishing for the rest of the summer. Mesaba's on the way and it looks like Toliver's taking the first licking."

Deering thrust his fist in Booker's direction. "I say now what I said before. Screw them all, Tom! If they won't listen to reason and come to work on our terms, our jobs for crissake, then we'll go get some who will. It worked back then and it'll work now."

"No it won't, Matt. There wasn't a war on then," Harry reminded him. "You couldn't get a man out of Europe with a corkscrew today."

"The hell with Europeans. We'll get chinks." Deering shouted, slamming his fist on the table. "You know how many Chinese there are in the world? Hell, if they all spit at the same time, we'd drown in a tidal wave."

"You're never at a loss for bad ideas, are you?" Harry answered, jabbing the stump of his bad arm at Deering. "For one thing, immigrations don't encourage slant-eyes coming to America now that the railroads are mostly built. For another, I don't want them coming up here eating their noodles and talking their blasted gibberish. What the hell do we do with them after the strike, open up two thousand damned laundries and chopstick factories? You think you could grow enough rice in Minnesota to feed them all? I don't."

"We grow wild rice, don't we? We could grow white rice, too."

"Harry's right, Deering," Saperstein agreed condescendingly. "And no, you can't grow white rice in a cold climate. We wouldn't have a productive mine up here for a year if we did that. Chinese don't know mining. Sure they'd learn, but how long would it take? Maybe two years, or five and by then all this current trouble will be a bad memory."

You cross-bred Jew, Deering thought. You're one to talk. You still don't know crap about iron mining. Then he queried innocently, "Well just how long did it take them to build a railroad, eh?"

"I don't go for it either," Booker said. "We can't keep throwing out the crews every time they come forward with a demand for more money and new conditions. It takes experience and time to be productive."

"Just what the hell are they after, anyway," asked Dick Chambers. He was only along for the ride and knew the heavyweights among them would determine the course of action. "What's wrong with what they're getting now?"

Harry snarled. "A whole pile of crap. They heard about that Nolan bill in Congress and want to shirttail on the coal miners. Three dollars minimum, Saturday half-holiday. The right to negotiate wages and hours. An end to speeding. Imagine letting them set their own work pace. The same old bullshit. You'd think they had a blasted union, that's what. Maybe they will in time. What I hear is it's all talk right now. They don't have an organization, just a lot of noise."

"What if we sit down with them?" Booker said. "Listen to what they got to say? A lot of mines are already averaging three-fifty a day after five years as it is. I think we can settle peaceably. Settle now rather than lose six months or a year's production and we still come out ahead, don't we?"

His outrageous comments were met with a chorus of rejections summed up by Deering. "Yeah, that'll never work. Not in a hundred years. In twenty-five years on this rock pile I've never mistreated my men. I pay them well and I house them well. I don't make them throw away their wages in the barroom. I don't tell them to dump their garbage in the streets and I don't make them let their cows walk all over town so the kids got to play in the shit. Dammit, if they want to live like animals, that's their business. I can't help it. There comes a time when they have to take responsibility for their towns and their lives."

"Isn't that what they seem to be doing?" suggested Booker.

Tom caught Masterton's eye. "What about you, Masterton? You've been pretty quiet."

Masterton drew on his cigar, drowned it in a water glass and stood up. He ran his eyes over the assembled men. "Gentlemen, I thought we were getting together to tell each other what we planned to do, not cackle like chickens over what we should have done or might do. I did not come here to listen to Deering's 'How I Created the Universe' speech." He gave Deering the faintest of smiles. "So I'll tell you what I did do. I went out and bought the toughest son-of-a-bitch law officer west of Chicago and told him to go out and hire twenty-five more like himself. I told him to walk the pits and walk the town and, if he runs into any agitators or stiff necks, or anyone else in my town that doesn't work for me, to straighten them out and run them out. Mammoth isn't on strike today and it won't be on strike tomorrow, either. I'm sorry your boys went out. I truly am, but at the same time, I say hang tough and they'll come back like little boys when the groceries run out. You want to get a man's attention, you put a hunger in his children's bellies." He sat down and took a long pull from Deering's whiskey. "Let them walk out and in thirty days they'll be put in the army digging trenches in France."

Booker nodded at him. "I admire your guts, Masteron. I always have, but it's not just a bunch of young Turks talking through their whiskey. They have some real agitators up here all right. The legitimate unions won't touch it. The Wobblies will. They got three guys up there now stirring it up and they can get more. I assure you they won't just march around with cardboard signs. You got yourself a mean son-of-a-bitch? They got 'em too. And they got matches and gasoline and a lot of good hands that know their way around explosives. They can burn down buildings and tear up tracks, and I suspect the hungrier the kid's get, the higher the flames will reach."

Billy snorted, "Sounds like these Wobblie characters already got you by the balls, Booker."

Booker stood up and put his hands on the table. "The Workers of the World movment aren't just a bunch of characters, Billy. They are organized, financed, experienced and well led. I've been doing a little research on them. They preach reforms with a strong socialist approach. A lot of people think they're communists. Bolsheviks. Look at the Homestead coal mine strike out east. It was a full-scale riot. Twenty-one killed in fifteen minutes. They made the Molly Maguires look like Sunday school boys."

"And the soldiers and police won the day. They broke it up," countered Billy.

"And the mill was shut down for six months," Booker said, sitting back down.

Saperstein picked up a pencil. "Who are they? Those three guys?"

"I talked to them. Nice guys in a restaurant but hell on business and born to a picket line. W.D. Heywood's the boss. Then there's a fat little wop, Tresca. Carlo Tresca. He's the bookkeeper; keeps it organized. The speechmaker is another W.D. He loves to agitate."

"Who's that?"

"Scarlett. W.D. Scarlett."

Chapter 12

Scarlett was standing on the running board of a Model A. Three hundred men and women had gathered at the gates of the Hibbing Hill mine to hear him. He didn't intend to disappoint them. Standing proud and tall at six feet, W.D. was a bronzed Roman in a dark blue suit. His long silver locks were parted down the middle and flowed back to his shoulders like a lion's mane. He was born to be an orator and, in all his fifty years, he never once ducked an opportunity to take a podium. His powerful voice carried easily to the back edges of the crowd.

"At Biwabik a strike has been in progress now for eleven days," he began. "Not a single strikebreaker has been brought in. They can't find any. It will be the same here and in Virginia, in Colleraine, Greenway and Mammoth. Your cause is just, your will is strong. You will triumph!" He paused for the applause, which came on cue.

"Your jobs will be yours when you want them. We will picket and we will march. We will be peaceful. You don't need to do anything but keep your hands in your pockets. If any gunmen or thugs try to stop our parades, identify them and turn them over to the authorities. We have been told to leave the city. I assure you, we will stand on our rights as citizens. We have been threatened with deportation. I say, if we are deported, others will return in our place. This strike then becomes a violent strike."

Cheers rose from the miners but Scarlett sensed an undercurrent of concern. He hurried to reassure them.

"If any miner is harmed by a gunman, I say to those who are advocating the kidnapping of the leaders of this movement and thus openly advocating violence that, if any committee of vigilantes or others start violence, then the I.W.W. will finish it." Scarlett shook a clenched fist to the gods of righteous causes. "I swear it!"

This time the crowd erupted in a fusillade of cheers.

Heywood spoke next, succinctly and to the point. "The capitalist," he said, "has no heart, but harpoon him in the pocketbook and you will draw blood. Tonight I am returning to Pensylvania to speak on the last struggle and I am going to make it so plain that even a lawyer can understand it."

A smiling Scarlett climbed up and joined Heywood on the roof of the car and Tresca drove slowly away from the mine. Their procession wound down Hibbing's main street followed by the jubilant strikers. Past the stores, the bank, the creamery; all the establishments that held the credit accounts for all the Hill Mine employees. When they came to U.S. highway 169, Scarlett spoke again. He told them to keep the faith and the flame alive and stand firm. He promised to return in three days then he and Heywood climbed in the car and Tresca turned right and drove off towards Mammoth.

Chapter 13

On Sunday the Wobblies held a sympathy march in Mammoth for the Hibbing miners. The crowd was small, not helped by a cold drizzle that blew out of Canada. Only thirty-five showed up but they were the vocal ones. Many carried signs reading 'Living Conditions Keep Rising, Pay Must To' and 'We Want Safer Mines'. When they reached the gates of the Mammoth pit they were stopped by Fleming, Karsch and his deputies. Karsch was resplendent in a brown trooper uniform complete with Jodhpur riding trousers and a Sam Browne leather belt across his chest. As soon as Scarlett began to speak Karsch cut him off.

"Don't give us any of your garbage shit talk. We don't negotiate. We don't settle matters with concessions. I've got one job here and one job only and that's to protect this property from agitators like you. I'll tell you right now so there's no mistaking. We got clubs. We got guns and we got muscle and we're legally authorized to use them. If any man tries to break up anything in this mine or stop anyone from going to work, I will do them harm."

Counter threats were hurled from the crowd and one child picked up a rock and threw a squibbler that bounced twice and rolled off a deputy's boot. The tiny spark was quickly extinguished when the child's mother ran forward, cuffed him on the head and dragged him off the street by his ear. A ripple of laughter ran over the miners and the deputies relaxed their threatening posture a little.

Karsch turned to Fleming. "You got anything to say?"

Fleming had plenty to say but most of it would have been to castigate Karsch and his harsh talk. He tried to take the only path he could, a conciliatory middle road.

"Good people of Mammoth. Please. We all live here. We all work here. Let's not let emotions control our actions. We have to be patient and keep the faith. Even now the owners of the iron range mines are meeting to, I am sure, arrive at an solution agreeable to all."

"Sure, agreeable to all of them," someone shouted and the catcalls began raining down on Fleming. Flustered, he turned to Karsch for support. Karsch nodded to his deputies and they began rhythmically beating their pick handles against their booted legs. At another nod they took a step forward. The crowd quieted, tense with the anticipation of what might happen next.

Scarlett turned to the miners. "We have finished what we came here to accomplish today. We have served notice that the situation is not going to go away. Let us now leave in peace." With that he walked through the crowd and led them to the other end of town away from the mine.

Karsch's deputies pelted their retreating backsides with insults and Fleming went to his office hoping the matter would end there, but Karsch knew it was only the opening skirmish. It was the way they all started, a holiday at first. Mothers and children come along and picnic with the demonstrators. Then the talking escalates. First the pleading and begging followed by the screamed demands. Finally the anger erupts and the picnics are bathed in blood.

John Fleming had shut the door to his office and locked it. He drew the blinds at the window and peered cautiously through them as if he expected rocks to come flying through at any moment. He was afraid, more of Karsch than his employees. Damn, he thought, the damn stubborn owners. His damn boss! Fifty cents a day and slow the production rate just a little to a safe level. How little to ask for after years of abuse and no improvements in conditions. But Karsch! Karsch was still on the street hurling invectives. Karsch wanted a strike. He wanted the violence. Remembering Jack Ruff-corn, Fleming's skin crawled. Karsch wanted to kill someone.

Over two hundred men and women crowded into the Slovenian Hall that night. They came out of curiosity and they came out of desperation because they were tired of seeing the ambulance rushing into the pit to save another man who had just lost his hands in a gear. They were tired of earning less each day than they paid the mine for food, rent and firewood. They were tired of seeing their children grow up, if they didn't die in infancy, with no chance of a better future than their parents. They were young and old, men and women and for whatever reason they came, they all shared a common wish for hope in a tomorrow that would be better than yesterday.

Scarlett knew his audience because he had seen their like before. He was intimate with the faces and the slow eyes. He had shaken their calloused hands with the fingers permanently bent to fit a shovel handle. The women never ceased to amaze him. There were always more of them than expected; many more than polite society would find acceptable at such a gathering. They were poor people but not at all like the sub-humans they were often depicted as in the newspapers.

Political cartoons liked to depict the women as uncultured animals. Males were often drawn mating with large-breasted females possessing no sense of social etiquette or manners. The men were grotesque, muscular brutes, sexually unattractive and fit only for the coarsest manual labor. But W.D. Scarlett knew them for what they really were: The hearts and souls of the labor movement. They knew the price of a loaf of bread and the cost of winter mittens. They were the backbone of his movement. Scarlett knew his audience well and fed them the hope and respect they hungered for. He had to prepare them for the struggle ahead.

Once on stage he poured on the oratory. "You have not," he shouted, pounding on the podium, "been invited into the American dream! You have not stood in the warm glow of Liberty's golden torch! Your streets are mud, your homes are drafty shacks and your jobs are dangerous and onerous. Your backs are weary and you are given only pennies from the riches that pour out of this region. Stand up today and take your destiny into your own hands!" He paused to let the interpreters catch up with him.

Michael and Kiril were standing in the back, more spectators than participants.

"How do you like that guy?" Mike said. "He says we live like pigs."

"Oink, Oink," returned Kiril, flattening his nose with his finger. "I think I might be turning into one, Mikie."

"Yeah, well, I think he's a troublemaker. Big troublemaker. He sounds like a man heading for a basket full of pain and lonely for company along the way."

They listened for another fifteen minutes then went over to the Ore House for beer. The place was empty, which didn't help Michael's mood, so after three beers they called it a night. On the way home he saw Mary and John Fleming coming out of the Mammoth Cafe. They were walking arm in arm and she was laughing at something he must have said. Mike's mood went from sour to black and he backed Kiril into the shadows to let them pass unnoticed. There, by the light of a quarter moon, he was already ready to dismiss her and move on. Still, when he went to work the next day and saw her sitting at the office window, his heart began to race and when she saw him and broke into a bright smile he waved and grinned. Madness, he thought. It's all madness and possibly beyond a simple miner's comprehension. Maybe Scarlett was right. Miners were pigs and that made him a pig by extension whereas Mary was educated, prettier than any girl in town and spoke like a lady. And there was more.

There was something about her; a spark of life he had never seen in another woman. When he saw Mary, he wasn't stooping to another level, he was reaching up to a higher one. Maybe, he thought, the madness was love. Whatever, it was chewing up his insides.

chapter 14

The Mammoth strike finally arrived, not as quickly as Scarlett had hoped, and when it did come, it wasn't so much his doing as God's, but a strike it became. The feast of Corpus Christi was a major religious event for the Slovenians and even more so for the several dozen Italians in town. Decorations were pulled out of the St. Marin's basement and hung from all the buildings on main street. The church altar was dressed in gold crepe and a gold bow hung from the end of every pew.

In past years the men had willingly worked on the feast day and then hurried off to church for the solemn high mass and then straight home for the extensive dinners that always marked a special day.

But this year some of the men decided to test the 'working partnership' that Fleming was promoting and it wasn't long before everyone decided it would make a nice work holiday. When they proposed the idea to Fleming he retreated into the argument that America's war effort needed their ore and, rather than face the wrath of Masterton, which he knew Karsch would surely bring down on him, he simply said no. It was an impossibility he couldn't discuss. Thus what began as a simple, half-serious request developed into a full-blown test of wills and, in the ensuing dispute in Fleming's office, Karsch stormed in and threw the three spokesmen out.

The next morning three quarters of Mammoth's workforce refused to walk down to the pit until an apology was issued and Karsch and his bullies were made to leave Mammoth forever. Fleming would have given in to this in an instant if Karsch had worked for him but it was Masterton's call and all Billy said was "Screw 'em! Here's where balls are going to beat bellyaching and I still got 'em."

Michael Jensen and Kiril weren't among the no-shows and reported as usual. They weren't Italians after all they said. The others tried to talk them out of crossing the improvised picket line but Michael thought them fools and told them so.

"Come out with us, Michael. Kiril, you too. The two of you carry a lot of weight. If you walk out others will follow you."

"I'll tell you where they can follow me," Michael said. "They can follow me down the pit road or they can follow the rest of you up to the poorhouse and stand in a breadline. I'm going to work just like yesterday and as I will tomorrow and that's all I have to say."

Not even Scarlett could change his mind although he sorely wanted to because he had become aware of Mike's popularity and influence over many of the younger men. He couldn't help but admire a man like Michael who could work through and hold a position on his own. He had done the same thing years ago when he threw in with the labor movement. He certainly had no admiration for Michael's abrupt and brutish manner of speech nor his philosophies as rudimentary as they were, but he still wanted him on his side. He wanted everyone on the side of his Wobblies.

"It's much like theatre," he told Tresca one night in the café. "There's always a protagonist and an antagonist. Through them the whole drama of civilization is played out in its starkest detail. The strongest wills shall invariably prevail and cause all change. It always happens that way. It's the chaos that often precedes it that makes humanity so ugly so often. Michael Jensen could be our protagonist, our poster child, if you will, if we can only bring him to our point of view."

Tresca, a career accountant, didn't often think in terms of physical attributes. "But is he strong enough? I mean both mentally and physically?"

"He's probably stubborn enough and that goes a long way in any drawn out conflict. It's all good as long as he's stubborn for the right reasons, those being our reasons. At the present time, he's stubbornly opposed to our movement but now that will be an asset once he becomes committed to us."

Scarlett played with the prospect. "Oh yes. Once committed, he would be a real hellion for the righteous cause. Whoever is calling the dance for the other side, perhaps this Karsch person, would have his hands full of Michael Jensen. I think it's just a matter of time until his youthful principles become our greater ideals."

Chapter 15

Pickets were place at the Mammoth mine entrance while Karsch covered the pit gates like a lion protecting his lair. His presence alone was sufficient to get the strikebreakers through the pickets. While Kiril and Michael came and went relatively unscathed, the same measure of respect wasn't always afforded to the other men who stayed on.

Passing through the picket line meant traversing through hell. At first, the strikers joked and cajoled their friends to join them but, as days passed, they turned to pleading and finally began issuing thinly veiled threats just as Karsch had predicted.

Soon they began grabbing at coat sleeves and hands, stepped in front of people and spat on their shoes. Eventually it got to be in the face. Whenever it looked like it might get out of hand, Karsch and his goons would walk through the ranks of the strikers and part the waters. They carried their pick handles, slapping them rhythmically in their palms and they'd lock eyes on the offending striker and wouldn't let go until the cowed man turned away. Tempers were running high but had not yet flared into violence.

Karsch's men, as ordered, never spoke. For all the verbal abuse that was put on them they never answered, never gave the miners something solid to chew on. They just kept patting the pick handle, staring and biding their time. The staring infuriated the miners most, even more than the clubs and even more than the pistols that many of the deputies carried in their belts. If a man was any kind of a man, they felt, he would be man enough to call another fellow out after an insult. Only the mentally deranged and those in love spoke solely with their eyes.

Karsch had other ways of angering the strikers. He gave orders to have his men fed at the gates in full view of everyone. He fed them well; big rounds of beef, whole chickens and racks of smoked ribs. The Slovenian strikers never ate so well on the most sacred holidays much less on a picnic. Most of them were already subsisting on bread and soup; soup so thin that many a bone tossed away by the guards was quietly pocketed, washed clean of dirt and slipped into the cooking pot.

Down in the pit, Karsch didn't spare the strikebreakers from his rancor either. The third night of the strike he watched Michael's crew drill for two grueling hours. When they finally shut down, he went up to them.

"I've kept my eye on you," he told Michael, "for three nights now and I can't figure you out."

Michael was loading the borings with explosives. "I don't know what you're talking about," he said over his shoulder.

"Sure you do. I can't decide what mischief you're up to. I know people and I know you got too much in your craw to keep it in forever."

"Is that a fact now? Then I must be pretty good at it, whatever it is."

Karsch stuck his finger in Michael's face. "Your friends quit and you still work. They think you're a traitor. I think you're a traitor."

Michael straightened up. "They all know where I stand and why. What they think of it doesn't bother me." He grinned at Karsh. "I'm just very lucky to have a job, like you."

Karsch growled back, "If you're happy, why do you bitch so much. I read your file. It's full of complaints. You whine about everything. These explosives. You don't like them much. This drill of yours. You're never happy with the tools or they way they service them."

"No I am not. I've said they're shit because they are. You can find that in my file too. If I was given better, I would work better. Like these greasy sticks of butter we're supposed to break up solid rock with."

"They look fine to me. They look…"

"Like dynamite? You must be a hellava blaster if you think that. Take a closer look." He took a stick and nonchalantly tossed it to Karsch. Startled, he grabbed for the dynamite, fumbled it, and finally let it fall at his feet.

"See," observed Mike. "Now if that was good dynamite it might have blown us both into hamburger and maybe a couple of chops to boot."

Karsch picked up the stick, walked it back to the dynamite cart and carefully placed it in the box. Then he came over to Jensen and put his ugly face within an inch of Michael's.

He spoke so softly, so carefully that the others didn't hear him. "If you want to die young, you're going down the right track, boy, because I will kill you before I let you make a fool out of me. Do you understand me?"

Michael had gone white beneath his kerchief and his facial expressions were dead. All he could see was Karsch beating Ruffcorn into a bloody pulp. Karsch must have been thinking the same thing.

He wasn't done. "I saw you in the ring with Ruffcorn. It made you cocky, didn't it? Well any time, young man. Any time you want to try me." Then he planted a huge fingerless fist in front of Michaels face and growled.

Finally it was Kiril who spoke up. He had come around behind Karsch and alongside him were Constance and Anton. They were holding drill bits in their hands with the ease of young boys about to partake in a hot dog roast. Kiril addressed Mike but all three of them were looking at Karsch.

"Hey, Mikey. These bits are finished. What do you want us to do with them?"

Mike looked over Karsch's shoulder and finally found his voice. "Ask Mr. Karsch. He's an authority on blasting. Maybe he knows bits too."

Karsch turned around and, always the survivor, stepped out of the circle. He looked at each of them in turn. "If you step out of line I'll deal with you, one at a time.

Not as a group. I'm not so stupid as that. I will give each of you my personal and private attention." The next night he came back with three deputies but no one did anything to antagonize the other.

chapter 16

Mary was standing in Fleming's office when the skimpy crews came out of the mine that morning; ten of them left from an original shift of forty-eight. There were an abundance of pickets in the morning. Less than thirty percent of the original number were working now even with the few scabs Fleming had been able to hire.

The strikers didn't bother to talk to Michael's crew anymore. In fact, neither group even looked at the other. While Mike still held fiercely to his beliefs and Kiril remained loyal to Mike, Constance and Anton were beginning to waver. Their friends had been working on them, first with words, then by ostracizing them from the neighborhood pinochle games. For Constance and Anton, America was threatening enough, even with friends and the social hall. Being cut off from both, life was slowly becoming unbearable for them.

"Why do they still do it?" Mary asked as she watched them through the window.

"Do what? Strike? We've been over that." Fleming was at his desk, poring over the disappointing tonnage figures.

"No. I mean Jensen and his crew. I understand the strikers walking out but why are they still working?"

"They want to keep their jobs, I guess. Money trumps principle sometimes. Besides, he has no family or kids of his own to support and as a driller, he gets the top salary for a non foreman."

"But all their friends have quit now. I know a job is very important but wouldn't you think that to risk your standing in the community would be terrible?"

"Oh lord!" Fleming shot a look outside. "Don't go out there and tell them to walk out, too. That's the last drilling crew I have. Thank God it's my best one."

"I won't. You know that. I just don't know what makes them keep on. Imagine the pressure they get from the others. Are they that loyal to Mr. Masterton?"

"I would strongly question that loyalty to Masterton has any bearing on it at all. Why don't you ask him? He's a friend of yours, isn't he?"

Mary gave him a stern look. Fleming backpedalled immediately.

"I just meant you would know more about his attitudes than I. Personally, he always seemed more loyal to himself than anyone."

Mary appeared satisfied. "He does. I think he's basically a selfish, immature man who only pursues what pleases him. I would guess he probably only works for the money and spends it solely on himself."

"So don't we all in the final analysis?"

"Some of us might have higher goals in life, John, maybe because we have a longer way to go to get there," she said partially to herself. "But you may not know that."

She had stood closer to the window than normal, hoping that Michael would see her. He never looked her way. His head was down inside his collar. He and Kiril walked side-by-side, quiet and sullen. He hadn't spoken with her since the strike began, but he had seen her coming to work twice from the direction of Fleming's house. He didn't ask her. He didn't have to.

"He's a boy," Mary said in summary, emphasizing the word and, in her own mind finalizing her relationship with him at the same time.

Fleming felt a tightening in his gut. He came up behind her and traced his index finger down the nape of her neck. She stiffened, then relaxed and a soft murmur of contentment came from her.

"And?" he asked.

"And, I've grown tired of boys," she said in a throaty whisper and turning to him embraced him with a smoldering kiss.

"Mr. Wong. What's the news if you please?"

Mr. Wong was sitting in his chair, studying the chessboard Izerman had set up. He looked at Michael and shook his head sadly. "Very bad, Michael, very bad. Nobody works now so nobody soils his clothing. It is just as you predicted. Or perhaps it was I. Nevertheless, business is dead. Is that not so, Mr. Izerman?"

Izerman nodded but didn't look up from the board. "I think I might close up and go down to see my sister in Milwaukee. She complains that she never sees me anymore so maybe I will let her see me. There are her storm windows, too. At eighty her arthritis gets so bad she can't climb the ladder. At seventy-five I don't want to either. But I should go and hold the ladder for her. Better to change storm windows than stand in my empty store and gather dust like my fine merchandise."

"Is it like this everywhere?" asked Kiril.

"That is the only good news," echoed Mr. Wong. "We all suffer together. The papers say that miners are leaving the range to look for work elsewhere. They are even joining the army. The ones that are still working are being treated most unkindly by the ones that are not. It appears that all sense of our fine community has disappeared."

"Amen," Kiril agreed. "Most unkindly to be treated like an unwelcome stranger. It might be better to join them than to let them spit on our shadows."

"It hasn't come to that," Michael countered. "And it won't."

"I think it already has but you haven't noticed," insisted Kiril. "Mikey, I see no good in what's going on. No good at all." He looked to Mr. Wong for support. "Am I right, Mr. Wong? I am, ain't I?"

"I think you see clearly, Mr. Kiril, like the hawk searching for the meadow mouse. You see the truth and do not chase the dream. Perhaps dreams are only for men with full bellies after all. The hungry, unfortunately, must dine on reality. Dreams make poor fare at the dinner table."

Chapter 17

Scarlett was still busy chasing his own dream of a peaceful strike settlement, but it was reality that came rushing home to him and the striking miners the next day. He had come down from Hibbing and was with them on the picket line when the crew, swelled by the arrival of twenty new replacement workers, mostly displaced farmers from North Dakota, came down to the pit. They were gathering in front of the office to go through the gate together.

Michael and Kiril were coming up from their shift as they came in. There were fewer than thirty original employees now, plus the scabs, confronted by nearly a hundred pickets who had arrayed themselves in double ranks, leaving a defile so narrow that one couldn't help but bump against them in passing. The pickets began taunting and cursing them. They clutched at clothing and stole caps. One man made a grab for a blonde man's lunch pail.

"Hey, Swede," he said, "you got a dumpling for me?"

The Swede jerked away in fright and the handle broke. Food spilled out on the ground and pickets began to stomp on the sandwiches.

"Goddamn you! Damn you for my food!" he screamed in rage. He swung the broken pail and hit the striker in the face, knocking him down. Two guys held his arms and a third pulled a club from his coat and brought it down on the Swede's forehead, splitting it open. The man fell and disappeared beneath a wild melee of brawling men.

Karsch's deputies let the combatants get well involved with each other and then moved forward, methodically swinging their mattock handles as though they were scything wheat. They were taking defenseless men from behind, laying on the blows with dull thuds on the back of their necks only vaguely aware of which side they belonged to. Men were swearing, screaming, begging, caught in the mass of wild milling bodies. Men fell over each other and, desperate to escape to the crush were stampeded by the swinging fists, clubs and metal bars.

Michael pushed his way in and began pulling men apart. He had just separated two and was trying to reason with them when a blow crashed down on the shoulders of one. The man groaned and fell to the ground. Behind him, brandishing the red-stained handle stood Karsch, a look of uncontrolled rage on his face.

"Why did you do that?" Michael screamed at him.

Karsch showed his thin-lipped, toothless smile. "Gettin' my exercise on a agitator. And you're not much better, you bastard scab." He raised his club against Michael but his eyes caught Fleming watching from his office. The piece of hickory slowly came down. "But my job is to protect bastard scabs like you. So get your ass out of here."

Mike lunged at Karsch but the larger man just pushed him off with one arm and Mike was grabbed from behind by Kiril and roughly pulled out of the fight.

"Mikey," Kiril begged. "Let's go home. This is not our fight at all. Look at them. It is sheep against wolves."

Mike looked back at the butchery. Karsch's men had driven back the strikers and were backing the scabs protectively through the gates. A dozen men were on the ground, some not moving, others crawling about incoherently.

Scarlett was trying to drag an unconscious striker away. Blood was running from the corner of his mouth. He was beseeching his people to stop fighting and move back. His eyes caught Mike's for a moment. On his face was the look of someone hopelessly trying to stave off defeat. He was someone in need of a friend and, for that, he was looking to Mike.

Mike turned from him. Friends? All of them were friends once. Now he didn't recognize any of them anymore. None except that monster, Karsch. That man loathsome man deserved to be at the bottom of the bloody pile.

Kiril pulled on his arm again. Trying to drive it from his mind, Michael walked away. What he had just seen left him too empty for anger.

Alarmed by the fighting and wary of farther reaching reper-
cussions, he walked Sadie to school that morning. Her braid was
replaced by a ponytail that Kiril loudly approved of. He was going
to walk with them but Sadie was adamant that only Mike came. She
had something to ask him and it was embarrassing.

"Mikey. I want to know something but I don't know if I should
ask you."

"What is it, Sadie? You know you can ask me anything." They
were walking along the edge of a dirt street that ran the whole
length of Zenith.

"What's a scab?"

"Scab? Where did you hear that word?"

"At school. That's where we learn all the words that you won't
say around me. What is it?"

He tried to make a joke of it. "That's a crust that covers a cut,
isn't it? You know that."

"Well, that's what I said but some kids at school said you were
a scab."

Mike picked her up. "Let me carry you," he said swinging her
up on his shoulders. "I don't want you to get your shoes muddy."
He walked half a block in silence before he answered her. "Sadie,
they said that because I want to keep working instead of leaving the
mine like the others."

"Is it bad to be a scab?"

Next to Katla, his endearing mother, this was the only woman
he had ever loved. It tore at his heart to know that she might think
less of him because of this. "It's just a word, Sadie, but not a very
nice one. Let's not use it anymore. I don't like it. And you know, I
grew up to believe that it's bad to say bad things about anyone and
it's also bad not to do what you believe to be the right thing."

"You are doing the right thing, aren't you?"

"I hope so. At first I was sure it was, but..." He set her down.
"What did you tell those kids, Sadie?"

"I told them that if they didn't stop saying it, I'd punch them."

"Oh you! I'm the only boxer in this family." Michael broke up
in laughter and, sweeping his little sister back up onto his shoulders, they went on to school.

That afternoon he spent two sweaty hours in the garden, helping his mother plant potatoes, beets and rutabagas. She still worried because the weather had been so cool and wet which made the planting late.

"Your father would have set the cabbage out already, Michael," she reminded him. "Cabbage and Brussels sprouts can take the cold air. It hardens them."

"Sure, Ma." Mike was only half listening. His mind was on the battle at the pit. Katla had heard of it even before he got home and she eventually got around to mentioning it.

"You and Kiril weren't in that ruckus this morning, were you?"

He smiled at her watered down reference to the bloody brawl. It was like her to reduce a tragedy to manageable proportions.

"No, Mama. Kiril and I were leaving when it started. We just saw the shouting part of it."

"I am glad of that. Mrs. Kracov was talking to Dr. Ingram's wife. She said he told her that one of the men might die."

"Die? Who?" Mike hadn't heard of it.

"She didn't know his name. It was one of the new men the mine hired, I think. But it could have been anyone. If you were there it might have been you. I cannot think of that happening."

Mike remembered the blonde scab, heard again the hickory club cracking down and saw the eyes roll lifeless up into his skull. It had to be him.

"A strikebreaker, maybe," he said, unable to use the word 'scab'. "There were so many down there it would be hard to pick one out."

"She said someone hit him on the head with something. Some hooligan was swinging at people with something and probably broke his head apart. I hope he is arrested and brought before a magistrate."

"Yes, Mama. He should be."

"Violence is such a sinful thing. Michael, I don't want you to go down there again until the trouble is over. Do you listen to me?"

"Ma?"

She was throwing potato sets into the holes he was digging and doing so with such force that they were bouncing back out. He took her arm.

"Mama, slow down. I think the real violence is what you are doing to your baby potatoes." Katla straightened up and pushed her aching spine back into alignment.

"What, Michael?"

"I said, slow down. I can't stay ahead of you. That's all." He wiped his brow, feigning exhaustion. With her shoe she chased an errant potato eye back into its bed.

"Ma, do you remember the last strike? When the Finns walked out?"

She eyed him curiously. He had been only eight years old at the time. Still, he had walked his father to the mine every morning from the time he was six and she thought he wouldn't remember anything of what had happened. She dropped another potato and covered it over.

"Yes, I remember."

"He went to work, didn't he, Ma? He got his job because of the strike, didn't he?"

"He did," she allowed. "A lot of good men did the same thing."

"Why did he walk through the pickets, Mama? Did he ever say?"

"Why?" To her it was a silly question. "We had to eat. He had to find work and there was a job waiting. He knew nothing of what the strike was about. You know his English was never very good and we had no papers to read about it."

"But a lot of those men were his neighbors, weren't they?"

"No!" she answered fiercely. "They were not our kind. They were Finlanders. Black Finns at that. They were not civilized. They were Protestants that would not even tip their caps to a woman on the sidewalk."

"Still, he did work with some of them."

"Few at best, and not for long. They always acted better than us, Michael. When they walked out, they threw down honest work. That was their choice to do that. Your father went to work so we could buy bread and clothing. Firewood, too. He worked hard to keep us from starving. That was his choice. You do not know anything about that because we tried to protect you from it. All Ernst ever said was that a man had to work to be whole."

"Ma, do you know why I'm still working? Now, when everyone else is not?"

She turned back to her potatoes. "I do not ask or think about such things. You have to make up your own mind." But her mind was filled with her last goodbye to Ernst, his bloody body and her great fear that she joined the caste of widows. "You are not a child anymore," she said trying to end the talk. "But if people are going to try to kill each other with big clubs, you must stay away." She sighed deeply. "You are like your father, Michael. That is why you work."

"Ma?" He waited patiently until she straightened up and gave him her full attention. "Ma, I don't know anymore why I am still going down. I thought I did but it doesn't seem right any more." He paused to consider the question. A sparrow, carrying a tuft of grass, flew past him and disappeared into a birdhouse next to the garden. He thought how simple life was for that bird. "

"If I knew," he went on, "it would be so much easier, but I just don't know why I keep going back. It is a habit, now. If I quit, I wouldn't know why I did that, either." He chopped another half-dozen holes. "I just keep going back because I always have."

Katla came over to him and took his chin in her dirty hand. Her eyes were brimming with tears of love.

"Like your father, Michael, you are. You are a good man." She put a heavy accent on the word good. "When I look at you all I see is your father."

He put his arms around her shoulders and drew her to him. "I love you, too, Ma."

"Good. Now stay home and I will dig up a jar of money for us to get by on."

After he had finished the planting and went to pick up Sadie, Katla went in the house, washed up, made herself a cup of tea and went out on the back steps to survey their garden work.

"It is a nice garden, Ernst. But Michael is so difficult to get to help with it. Not like you. You loved your garden."

"Oh, Katla, my dearest. You would be surprised how much he is like me. Don't you remember? How you had to scold and scold to get me into the garden? I think your memories are making good of some things that were really not so good."

"Perhaps a little. Most of our time together was very good, Ernst."

"Katla. Do you know why I went to work in the mines when the times were so difficult?"

••• 75 •••

"Why, Ernst? Tell me so I understand. I fear for our children and our neighbors. I try to keep it from Sadie but Michael brings it home with him. I think about those other times. They have returned and I'm so afraid that so many will be hurt."

"Katla, I worked with fear too, not for something I believed. Not because I did not respect the Finns. Certainly not to get out of the gardening. I did it for love, Katla. For your love."

"Ernst."

"At that time, my entire world was just you and me. And I wonder who Michael will ever find to love so much as I have loved you."

Chapter 18

Sadie had come down with a bad chest cold and was sent to bed, which was just as well, for the mood at the dinner table was black. One of the boarders had left two days earlier for a job in the Michigan mines. The other two, Karlos and Johann, were marching with the strikers and now their money had run out. Embarrassed and broke, they were trying to explain their situation to Katla.

"Do not think you have to leave," she replied. "When you go back to work, you can make up what you owe."

Michael listened to their clumsy apologies for as long as he could. Unlike his mother, he knew that they took their turns on the picket line and had shouted vulgar words like the others. He still might have kept quiet if not for his mother's softheartedness, which he felt, they were taking advantage of. Two more minutes and she'd be paying *them* to live there. Abruptly, he slammed his fist down on the table and stood up. His hands were trembling as he drove them into the tabletop.

"That's a bunch of crap! They could go back tomorrow if they cared about us, ma. No one is stopping them but themselves." He turned to Johann. "No one is stopping you. So you are ready to pick up clubs and beat on the heads of good men who only want to draw a paycheck? Is that more satisfying than working? Why don't you use the same words on Ma that you use on me and the others? Then she'd know where you really stand."

Johann held up his hands, trying to settle Michael. "No! No! We were not there today. And not to you, Michael. We have no disrespect to you. We with Mr. Heywood in the hall. All day."

Michael shot back. "What does he pay you to sit and listen to pretty speeches, dammit? What's more, when you swear at the people I work with, you swear at me, you lazy bastards."

"Michael!" Katla flew at him. She wasn't one to interfere but she wouldn't have this talk in her home. "You will not use that talk with my boarders. You will not curse in my home. Ever! Apologize now."

"I will not," Michael spat defiantly. "Ma, These men are abusing your kindness. They won't abuse me." He ripped his coat from the back of the chair. "Let's go, Kiril, it's time for working men to report."

"But it's still early," Kiril protested. He was still finishing his bread pudding.

Mike grunted and stomped out of the room. They heard the front door slam and the room was suddenly quiet. Katla busily gathered up some dishes and disappeared into the kitchen. She returned just as Kiril was getting ready to leave.

"Kiril? Before you go, say goodnight to Sadie. Will you do that, please? For that Michael, too?"

"Sure, Katla." Kiril obediently went upstairs. He knocked softly on Sadie's door and peeked in. She was propped against the head-board, picking threads from the edge of her blanket. She looked up when he opened the door.

"Oh, Kiril. I thought you were Mama with another stinky plaster."

"No. Just me. I just came with a big spoonful of Kerosene and pine tar to coat your throat."

"Yeech! I won't take it." She pulled the blanket over her head.

Kiril laughed and sat down next to her. "Come out, Sadie. I'm only teasing." The blanket slowly retreated. She looked at him. "Mikey was angry, wasn't he? I heard him yelling at the others."

"I am thinking all of Zenith could hear him tonight he was so loud. But don't mind your brother. He's sometimes like a young colt and kicks up his heels just to see how high they can go."

She giggled and that brought on another coughing spell. He put his hand behind her head and after a moment she was better.

"It's just awful, Kiril. I can't swallow and I keep spitting up yellow stuff. It makes me want to throw up. Make it stop, won't you."

"Stop cough!" Kiril commanded. "Stop or I will drown you in pine tar."

She grimaced. "Now you sound like Mama again. Read me a story instead."

Kiril frowned. "Sadie, you know I read like a donkey who got booted out of first grade. What if I tell you one, instead? I know a lot of stories and some you haven't heard."

"All right," she brightened, wriggling up against him. "Is it a made up one? What about?"

Kiril nodded. "This story is about Flitter. Did I ever tell you about him? No? Well, he was a very pretty, furry squirrel with a bushy tail and very fat cheeks like yours. He was very little, too, like you, and likely to do things an older squirrel would never think of, like pulling a girl squirrel's tail and dropping acorns on Mr. Hunter's head to make him angry. But he wasn't bad; he was just restless like young people are."

"Like Mikey?"

"So much like Mikie that Mikey was his middle name. Flitter Mikey Squirrel. Now one day, Flitter came running up the tree where his family lived. He flew through the door and scampered into the kitchen where his mother was baking acorn bread. Didn't you know squirrels baked bread? They do. "

'Dit, dit, dit! Mother! Mother!' he cried. He was very excited. 'Heavens, child,' said Flitter's mother." Kiril affected a high-pitched voice. *"Sit down and take a deep breath. Tell me why you are so excited.'*

Flitter sat on a toadstool and his mother said, 'Now, Flitter, tell me what has got you so worked up.'

'Dit, dit,dit. Well, mother, I was playing down by the meadow with Sonny Bunny and when he went home for lunch, I started to come home, too. But just as I was going by the old scraggly oak, I thought I saw a shadow move. I was so scared I froze. Only my teeth were moving and, dit, dit, dit, I couldn't stop them.'

Flitter's mother got worried and Flitter thought he was in big trouble. She finally had to hug him and tell him to go on.

'What happened then?' she asked.

'Mother, I heard a loud click and I ducked real low and, whoosh, something went past me so fast I couldn't see it. I jumped in the trees and ran home as fast as I could.

'Oh, my,' his mother said. 'Did anything happen?'

'Well, yes, mother. That's what happened... but then it didn't happen after all. I mean...' Flitter was confused and rubbed his paws over his whiskers. Mother squirrel gave him another warm, furry hug.

'Well, darling, nothing ever happens when it doesn't happen, you know.'

'I know. I know,' Flitter said. 'I meant, I thought it was going to happen and it didn't. I'm just a lucky squirrel. Nothing will ever happen to me now, will it?'

That made Flitter's mother very concerned. 'Flitter, be very careful, always. Watch and be careful because sometimes bad things do happen even when we don't see or expect them.'

That's the end, Sadie."

"That's a silly story," Sadie said. "You just made that up."

"I didn't, I swear," Kiril insisted. "I heard it from Flitter, himself. We were talking one day when nothing else was happening."

"I don't understand it."

"Well" replied Kiril, let me explain. I think what it means is that we sometimes worry a lot that something, maybe something bad for us, is happening or is going to happen but it doesn't because it almost never does. So we shouldn't worry about those things that don't happen that we think might. Now do you understand, Sadie?'

She nodded. "I think so," but there was a confused look on her face.

Ten minutes later, Kiril joined Michael at the mine entrance.

"What kept you?"

"Flitter the flying squirrel."

"Who?"

"Flitter, a friend of mine. I just told Sadie a little story. Oh, she says goodnight."

Michael grunted. He was finishing a cigarette. He only smoked when he was agitated about something and Kiril joined him in a second one because he only smoked when he could bum a free one.

"You really chewed on Karlos and Johann."

"They deserved it the way they were playing the 'poor little us' line made me sick."

"Sure. Sure they did," Kiril agreed. "But maybe not at the dinner table. You know, with Mama there and Sadie sick and all. It just upsets everyone and makes things worse."

Michael flicked his butt onto the street and grunted again.

"Aw, shit." He said it softly, almost like an apology.

Chapter 19

Since the first day of violence, there had been no pickets down at the mine. Heywood had returned from his trip east and pulled them off.

"Two days of peace, men. We will show them we really want to work this out. But, if we can't, we'll be back with double the number after that. In the meantime we will be the bringers of peace. We will wear the olive laurel." So for two days, the loyalists came and went without harassment.

A steady drizzle was falling and the deputies watched them approach from the shelter of the watch house, the small wood-framed bunkhouse at the bottom of the pit road.

Fleming and Karsch were looking out from Fleming's office at the same scene.

"Look at them dumb bastards," Karsch said, "turning out on a night like this. Don't have the brains to get out of the rain."

Fleming was counting the disappointingly few heads. "One should admire their loyalty, I think," he observed sullenly.

"Loyalty? Horse turds. If they had an ounce of loyalty, they'd put it with the men they drink with, not a cold master like this mine. A dog knows more about loyalty than they do."

Fleming looked at him with disgust. Karsch, the man who put his own loyalty in the hand that held the money and despised all men equally, strikers and scabs alike, had no right to be talking about loyalty. He trusted no one. Maybe, thought Fleming, that was how he survived for so long. Then his mind went off in other directions, first to Mary and the previous night they had spent together. His groin began aching anew at the memory of their tumultuous lovemaking and the anticipation of the next time. Finally he shook her out of his thoughts and got back to the business at hand. How was he going to get any meaningful production out of such a pitiful crew?

The light drizzle began to increase in intensity. By ten that night it was a cold, miserable downpour. The wind whipped the rain about so savagely that the security patrol only came by twice, their heads buried deep in their slicker hoods. An hour later it began to sleet, driving down the work pace even further and, along with it, the crew's spirits. Small cataracts of water spilled over the lip of the pit and doused the unlucky man who had to work too close to the face, hitting him not only with the water, but also the dirt and gravel it carried with it.

Karsch knew one benefit of the storm; there would be no infiltrators tonight. They had begun coming into the pit at night, slipping down the sheer sides on ropes. A favorite game was to cut the steam lines and pull spikes out of the rails. Their favorite game for Karsch was to catch them and beat them senseless. The day before, he had caught two young men and turned them over to the Itasca Sheriff, Clete Meining, who immediately sent them on to the Hibbing General Hospital. Mammoth had its own small, four bed hospital but Sheriff Meining wanted those men put where the others wouldn't see how torn up they were.

They had caught a young Italian immigrant and his arrest and subsequent deportation orders were processed with no right of appeal within six hours of his apprehension.

"Stitch 'em up and send 'em back to Italy," Karsch smirked. "Let them do their fighting from behind a rifle if they're so brave."

By dawn, Jensen and his men had drilled six arduously slow holes. Mike was still angry from dinner and this made things even worse. He cursed the shoddy work the replacement machinists were doing on his drill bits. He cursed the leaking hoses and the low steam pressure and, for the first time ever he cursed his crew.

"Dammit, Anton, move your ass! You want to be here all fucking night? Get another goddamn bit over here."

And near the end of the shift, "Kiril, who the hell taught you to pack dynamite? Get it in there, man. You work like a man with a pole stuck up his ass."

"Easy, Mikey. Take it easy. It is not pleasant night for us either." Even with abuse being showered on him, Kiril was still the bigger man.

"Yeah, yeah," answered Michael, just a little mollified. "Well, sorry. Just do the damn job right."

They finished setting the charges, joined the detonation cords to the blasting caps and ran the cable out to the generator box. With cold, numb fingers, Michael screwed the wires to the posts on the box. He raised the handle, counted heads to make sure they were all accounted for, ducked his own and threw his weight onto the plunger. The crew flattened themselves against the sodden ground and flinched at the anticipated blast. The blast didn't come. Nothing happened at all. The rock face was intact and silent.

Slowly Michael straightened up and wiped his face. He looked around for Kiril. "Shit! Goddamn shit! Now it's the damned blasting caps."

Kiril sat back on his haunches. "No. It ain't the caps, Mikie. I think it's the rocks washing off the face. They just knocked a wire loose."

Michael looked at the generator. "Hold it. I'll try again." he rammed home the plunger once more with the same results. Kiril scrambled to his feet.

"Don't give it a thought, Mikey. I'll check the connections." Kiril scrambled to his feet and ran off toward the mine face.

"No!" Michael shouted. "We have to wait five minutes."

"Don't worry," Kiril called back. "I'm Flitter the flying squirrel and nothing ever happens to me." He comically threw his arms out and began flapping, his laughter echoing back at them.

Mike pulled the wires off the terminals. Kiril was twenty feet from the charges when another small shower of rocks came cascading down. One of them must have struck a blasting cap, set of the entire charge and the ore face erupted. The force of the detonation snapped Michael's bead back and rolled him out like a carpet. Anton and Constance threw themselves down as pieces of ore hammered them like shotgun pellets. The dust came back and settled out quickly, smothered by the rain. Michael lifted his head. Kiril was gone.

"Kirril! Kirrrill!" He ran through the still falling ore, stumbled and fell, got up and ran on. "Kirrilll!" He prayed for a miracle, any kind of miracle.

Michael threw himself down on the pile of rock and began clawing at it. In seconds, Anton and Constance were with him.

"Kiril. Do you see him?"

"No! Look for crissake. Dig!" They tore their fingers on the wet jagged chunks of iron.

"Oh, God!" Michael cried. "Oh, God, no. Not Kiril!" Not Kiril!"

A bolt of lightening tore through the sky.

"Over here!" Constance screamed.

He had found a hand, the fingers sticking out of the pile. Michael clutched at them. They tightened on his.

"Get him out! Get him out! He's alright! He's alright!"

Frantically they cleared away the rock.

"Hurry, dammit! Hurry!" He was screaming in their faces and holding onto Kiril. His arm came clear, and his head and chest. The arm was mangled horribly, the elbow crushed and as useless as a broken branch. Michael cradled Kiril's head in his hands and groaned. He had no face. Then the rain washed over it and the dirt began running off. He was all right. His eyes were open, clear and dark like lustrous onyx and just as distant. Slowly they turned and found Michael. He lifted his hand, brought it to rest on Michael's cheek and held it there for a moment. A smile crossed his lips. They parted and the flow of blood came out. His eyes lost their luster and Kiril's hand fell away.

chapter 20

It was a big funeral, all the antagonism of the strike temporarily set aside. The little church was so full that people were standing in the aisles and waiting outside on the wooden steps. In the front pews sat Katla's family, many of Kiril's closest friends and all the old widows and women of Mammoth who went to every funeral regardless of the politics of the day. Father Basil had decided to hold the service concurrently with his morning mass and that may have helped bolster attendance somewhat but it wasn't necessary because Kiril was liked by everyone. Even so, Father Basil apologized to Michael earlier.

"I'm sorry we couldn't wait a day or two, Michael, for the paper to print the obituary and then have the funeral on Saturday, but you saw the condition of his body. If the weather had warmed up at all..."

Kiril lay in a simple pine coffin. His body from the chest down was covered with a heavy serge drapery. Katla had personally dressed him in the black suit that Kiril always wore to the funerals of others. His face had, remarkably, escaped untouched. He looked in death exactly as Kiril had in life.

There had not been the luxury of a wake, which would have given the family time to let the shock ease. There had been no time to insulate themselves from the community to do their private grieving before the public condolences had to be attended to. They had just an hour before the service when the priest had sensitively locked the church doors so they might spend some time alone.

Sadie had reacted at first like the child she was. She refused to believe that her best friend was dead and, instead, imagined that he was just playing another of his little jokes on her. Even when she saw him in the casket, she talked to him as if he were alive and told him to sit up and climb out of it. Finally, when Father Basil said it was time to begin the mass and he had to let the people in, she burst into tears and tried to climb in with him. She still didn't know what Kiril was doing or where he was going but, in her heart, she was ready to go with him.

Father Basil said the requiem high mass and, after he had blessed the body and closed the casket, Sadie took Michael's hand and they walked up so she could place a flower on it. Of all the mourners, Katla's behavior was the most subdued. She had accepted the news with a quiet resignation and refused to discuss it any further than to acknowledge that she understood and was in quiet acceptance. In the end, she knelt with Sadie and said a short, silent prayer. She had tears in her eyes but they didn't fall and she uttered no cries of anguish. She had been through this before, with Michael, at Ernst's funeral and so many of their friends and knew she would be there again. She was saving her tears to share with Ernst in the garden.

In the short procession to the cemetery behind the church, Father Basil limped slowly behind the casket. Two altar boys who were carrying drowned candles on the end of heavy brass holders flanked him. Another altar boy walked in front of them with a tall crucifix. A fourth held an umbrella over his head. He apologized for it but wanted it to ward off a case of lumbago which he knew was sure to follow any exposure to the elements. Michael, Sadie, Katla and a meager dozen mourners followed him. Everyone else had stayed back because of the cold drizzle and remained in the church hall waiting for the potluck lunch served by the St. Basil's Women's Guild.

At the wrought-iron gates of St. Marin's Catholic Cemetery, Basil pulled a hankie out of his sleeve and quickly wiped at something at the bottom of the casket. It came away red. He looked back at Michael and quizzically gestured to the blood. Michael hissed in his ear. "His legs, father. It tore off his damned legs."

Basil nodded and hurried on. The procession ground slowly up the little rise, coming to a stop beside the open gravesite. The pallbearers lowered Kiril onto the three wooden slats spanning the hole and respectfully stepped back. Father Basil opened his prayer book and methodically droned through the graveside liturgy. He prayed it as if he knew it by heart, which he did. Wherever Kiril's soul was bound, Basil was sure it had already arrived and had done so regardless of what might transpire among the small knot of mourners. Besides, it was cold and he could already feel the chills setting in.

Just before the final sprinkling with holy water, a black Ford pulled up to the gate and Fleming and Masterton got out with Mary and Karsch. They came up the hill to within thirty feet of the grave and stopped. Fleming and Masterton removed their hats despite the rain. Mary was shivering noticeably, her arm tightly entwined with Fleming's. Her eyes were locked firmly on the ground. Karsch's eyes swept over the gathering, memorizing faces and missing nothing. He had developed the habit of always searching crowds, reading faces for feelings and motives, for the betrayal of any suspicious emotions.

In a minute the drone of Basil's voice ceased. He led those present in praying the Lord's Prayer, formally shook Katla and Michael's hands offering his most sincere condolences and quickly led the wet and shivering clutch of altar boys back to the church. The pallbearers were close on their heels, but for the two that lingered for a cigarette before closing the grave.

Michael had noticed Masterton's group arrive. He put his arm around his mother. "Mama, I'm going to stay for a while. Take Sadie back to the church. We'll eat together."

Katla put her hand on his arm and, rising on tiptoes, kissed his cheek. "We have food at home, Michael. Come home after. I'll fix a meal for the family." He nodded and gave her a quick embrace.

It was quiet now except for the drizzle. He could hear it in the leaves of the elm trees in the graveyard and now and then when a larger drop hit one of the larger tombstones, it splattered. Little rivulets of water were wearing tiny gullies in the side of the mound of dirt and carrying the mud into the sodden hole that bore Kiril's body. Staring at it, Mike wondered if the rain kept up long enough, would it eventually fill it up? Nature was like that, always filling up the holes that people dug and reconstituting the earth. Their own handiwork was always relegated to such a short and finite duration. It was a silly thought and he drove it away so he could concentrate on thoughts of Kiril. But those thoughts were strangely empty.

A benign numbness still protected him from the full realization of his loss. That would come later when he would turn to tease Kiril about a little matter and his friend wouldn't be there. Later, when he wanted to share a laugh and he found himself laughing alone. For now, he only knew that he had a big part of him torn away and nothing had been left to replace it.

He heard the footsteps behind him. Masterton walked up and Karsch handed him a wreath that he dropped on the dirt mound. Draped across the front was a silk ribbon that read: 'Our Beloved Friend. Rest in Peace, Kerel.'

Michael stared dumbfounded at the wreath. The hypocrisy of the words screamed out to him. How dare he! Beloved friend? He couldn't believe the man's gall. His mine had killed Kiril and now they came to cry out their brotherhood.

"No!" Michael snapped. "No! You can't do that to him!" He ran forward, slipped on the mud and nearly fell into the grave. Clutching at the oozing dirt, he righted himself and began tearing the wreath to pieces. His eyes were wild and deranged and they locked onto Masterton's

"You damned son-of-a-bitch! You asshole! Damn you, Masterton, you killed him!" Pieces of the wreath flew at Masterton. "Who the fuck… You don't belong here! Love? You don't even know… And you can't even spell his name right." The old mine boss simply stared. He had a crooked smile on his face, half amusement and half disbelief.

"I told you time after time," Michael screamed and pointed an accusing finger. "Someone was going to die. Someone always has to die. I only wish to God it had been you."

Mary recoiled in shock, her face hidden behind her gloved hands. Michael's condemnation turned on her too. She had come here only with the intention of consoling him but he only wanted to make her part of his rage. He screamed curses at her, too, and she ran out of the cemetery.

"Mary, wait!" Fleming ran after her.

Karsch's reaction was different. He moved like an old guard dog in front of Masterton and kicked aside a chunk of the wreath.

"All right, boy," he said. "Think twice about what you're doing here."

Michael grabbed a long-handled shovel and brandished it over his head. "Come on, Karsch. You want to join him? I'll cut your ugly head off, you bastard. Come on!"

Karsch looked back at Masterton. The old mine boss made a show of pulling cigar out of his coat and lit it. The curling smoke created its own pallid wreath around his head. "Do what you got'ta do, Karsch" he nodded.

Karsch turned back to Michael and smiled his thin smile. He took a step forward. Michael stepped back, sliding in the mud, still holding the shovel like a two-handed scimitar. Back at the cemetery gate, Mary stopped and watched in horror. Fleming caught up and tried to pull her away.

Then the dead began to come back to life. Like ghoulish phantoms, ghosts in the misty rain. In ones and twos men began to appear. From behind the trees and tombstones, they came forward. Like the carved angels on the headstones, they spread their wings and descended around Michael. In the space of seconds, over fifty men formed a sheltering cordon around him. He was, above all and after all, still one of their own.

Karsch backed off until he was next to Masterton. Masterton looked at his miners, the hate in his eyes mirroring that in his heart. He curled his lips and flipped the smoldering cigar into Kiril's grave and started to walk off.

Karsch pointed a gnarled finger at Michael. "There'll come a time you won't have so many friends to help you, Jensen. Maybe the next time we can fnish what you started here."

Michael pointed the shovel blade directly at Masterton and yelled, "As for you, you bastard, I quit. I quit your damn mine, I quit being your slave and I quit… I quit. Oh, fuck you all. I quit!"

"You were fired when you tore up my wreath," the mine boss answered.

Chapter 21

The young scab Swede who had fought over the broken lunch pail, died the same day as Ruffcorn. It wasn't clear by whose hand, but the strikers had started it by trampling his lunch so, on the testimony of Karsch and his thirty-five deputies, the Sheriff arrested Heywood and Scarlett as the organizers of the strike and instigators of the riot. They were charged as accessories to manslaughter and sent to the county seat in Grand Rapids to appear before a grand jury. Karsch's deputies were commended for preventing the violence from growing out of control. Except for the timid Tresca, that left the strike functionally leaderless. There were still some minor Wobblie organizers at each mine but no one person the people could rally around. The Wobblie national committee in Pennsylvania knew the movement on the Range was in trouble and immediately sent another leader, in many ways their best, in every way their most attractive.

Elizabeth Gurley Flynn was a sturdy Irish thoroughbred with flaming red hair. A becoming lilt softened her otherwise flint-edge voice and her sculpted lips and country-blushed cheeks accented her clear white skin that she often kept shielded from the sun beneath her wide-brimmed hats. She was twenty-six years old, having been borne in Concord, New Hampshire, the Live Free or Die state, of socialist parents. At seventeen she became a full-time organizer for the I.W.W. working with garment workers, weavers, textile workers and, now, miners. Theodore Dreiser called her an 'East Side Joan of Arc' because, although she had grown-up somewhat affluent, her heart rested with the poor. Already she had been arrested nine times without a conviction and once chained herself to a lamppost in Spokane to delay one of those apprehensions.

This was the woman that stepped down from the Greyhound bus in front of the Chinaman's laundry the afternoon of

June eighteenth and, with the vigor of a twenty-three year old missionary, mounted the sidewalk and climbed onto Wong's chair. It didn't take long for an audience to gather to stare at the woman whose skirt stopped a scandalously six inches above her ankles. Some were already there to greet the bus. Pickets saw her standing on the chair and came up from the mine. Tresca spread the news about this ravishing woman who was about to speak and soon the crowd was large enough to be significant.

Flynn wore black leather boots under a blue serge dress cinched around the waist with a purple sash. Her shoulders were demurely covered with a rose silk scarf. Her hat was crowned with a burst of blue egret feathers. She passed the waiting in animated discussion with Wong. Eventually he picked up her bag and carried it to the second floor apartment above his laundry. Flynn took out a pocket novel and began to read, occasionally lifting her eyes to survey the curious crowd. Most folks thought she was a woman drummer but they still kept their distance because they couldn't tell what she was selling.

Eventually she pocketed her novel, opened her arms, broke into a hugely warm smile and began to speak.

"Greetings to all you handsome men of Mammoth. I am Elizabeth Gurley Flynn. If you like me, call me Libby; if not, call me Flynn. I'm not here to make speech. I'm not here to beguile you with my acclaimed charms. I was ordered here from Scranton, Pennsylvania, by the I.W.W. officers to report on the general state of the strike on the Mesaba Range and learn of what service our order can be to the strikers. On the way here I learned of the arrest of your local organizers, Misters Heywood and Scarlett for the murder of a replacement miner. I am told he didn't even have a name, for God's sake, just the 'scab Swede'. I also heard of the death of another man, a good friend of yours by the name of Kiril, brutally killed by the unsafe explosives you have been forced to work with. I want to say this; I intend to stay here to do more than report. I am going to stand by your cause and march with you in Heywood's place. I don't care what crap the owners pull. They don't matter to me. We'll out-maneuver them. We'll outwit them. We'll outlast them. I am familiar with all their dirty tricks and shenanigans."

She waited for the impact of her mild profanity to sink in. Libby had done enough organizing to know that she must first establish her personal credentials, her toughness, before she could get on with the business at hand. The tone of the response was gratifying. In due course she held up her hand to quiet them and went on.

"St. Louis and Itasca County people have an entirely wrong impression of our order. We are neither murderers nor anarchists. Nor are we communists. We are god-fearing American patriots in every respect. We have more respect for the laws of this country than the big interests have ever shown. They accuse us of starting the trouble on the Mesaba when, as a matter of fact, we had nothing to do with it. The miners at Aurora struck for more wages. Earned wages. Then they held a meeting and asked us to help them. We did not start the strike. We went there after it had begun and at the urgent request of the embattled miners. We seek only a fair settlement to just issues.

"I know how you feel. You feel abandoned, betrayed. You grieve for a lost friend. I tell you this. Do not mourn for Kiril. If he were here today he would not have you mourn. Let the death of this humble laborer be your inspiration, to fight determined until the end of this dark night for your birthright, a fair share in America's riches. In the tears of his loved ones, in the sobbing of his friends, read anew the message of emancipation from the chains of industrial slavery. Kiril died in the greatest of all human causes: man's right to work free from the shackles of serfdom. Let us garland his grave Mith flowers and, in memories' sacred archives, let us cherish the names of all our brothers and sisters who have died in the world-old struggle between the oppressor and the oppressed."

Her voice rose on its flinty sharpness and crested before finally carrying them back to earth with her seductive Irish lilt. She lifted her arms high and in the ensuing applause she congratulated herself for having so quickly turned the gentle scab, Kiril, into a symbol of the cause. Yes, she was good. She was better than Scarlett and Heywood and any of the other organizers the movement sent out. She was sure of that.

"I'm staying here!" she shouted over the rising roar. "Upstairs." Libby pointed to the second floor of the Chinaman's "Men, for the sake of propriety, we'd better not meet in my parlor. It seems our movement has enough scandal to live down already." There was good-natured laughter. "Instead, we'll make that our head-quarters." She pointed to the Ore House across the street. "And the first round is on the I.W.W. Come on, boys. Let's tip a pint in Kiril's memory."

She stepped off the chair and strode confidently across the street followed by the entire cheering, laughing crowd. In the space of five minutes she had breathed fresh, new life into a corpse, using Kiril's name as the bellows.

A large oak table, the 'Director's Table' called such by the regular clientele of retired and crippled who used it, dominated one end of the room. Sensing its significance, Libby walked directly to it. When she sat down she found herself seated next to a very curious Michael Jensen.

Fleming had watched the pickets walk away from the gate and when he saw the attractive woman begin to speak he walked outside to listen. Mary was already on the sidewalk. She turned when she heard the office door open.

"Look, John, it's a woman. And such a woman at that." She turned back to stare at the gaudy, vibrant speaker.

"Mary," he asked with a touch of concern, "are you alright? You seem a bit stunned."

"The movement sent a woman. I can't believe they sent a woman up here. Listen to her. She has those men right in her palm."

Fleming grunted. "Any pretty woman with a feathered hat and exposed ankles could have those men in the palm of her hand. Still, I am curious about her. Well, no matter. With a woman leading them, at least there'll be no more violence."

"Why would you think that, John?" She looked at him as if she had just unearthed a dyed in the wool chauvinist beneath his veneer of gentility.

"Well, I mean... just look at her," he said with a sense of the obvious. "Can you picture a frail thing like that charging our gates, club in hand, manicured nails covered with blood?"

"And if she did, I suppose your gentleman, Mr. Karsch, would strike her down with a bouquet of flowers with the same glee he displays on your employees with a mattock handle?"

But he had gotten her hackles up and she wanted to carry it further. "No, John, you just meant a woman hasn't the right nor the ability to do what she's doing. You don't think she's qualified to lead and, more specifically, to lead men."

"Lead? I hardly think so. Perhaps you can tell me exactly what she is intending to do up on that chair besides getting those men pointlessly worked up?"

"It seems she's intending to fight for a cause she believes in."

"Maybe," he admitted grudgingly, "and maybe she should be doing something she's more physically suited for. Besides, if the cause has no inherent value, then how much good can come of it?"

Mary sniffed. "I believe 'value' is a subjective term and apparently they find much more value in their movement than you ever can. As for this lady that you feel should be home birthing and raising children, I think she's doing quite an adequate job despite the distraction of her physical endowments. And, judging by the obvious interest you are taking in her, I don't think you're nearly as critical of her physical attributes as you pretend to be."

Even from a distance she was a striking woman. Pretty, like Mary, but with a stronger air of maturity as well as experience. John caught himself wondering how far that experience went.

Fleming took her arm and stepped in front of her, his concern shifting from the female labor organizer. He tried to kiss her but she turned her face away. "Mary, what is happening here? This isn't right."

"What do you mean, right?" she said, keeping her attention riveted on Elizabeth.

"The tension I'm feeling between us. What is it, Mary?"

"Nothing."

"Ever since that Kiril fellow's funeral," he persisted, "you've been different, distant, as if... well, you just seem to be sympathizing more and more with these men."

She took his hand off her arm to draw her sweater tighter about her shoulders even though the cool weather of the past week had cleared into bright, warm summer. She spoke very deliberately.

"I am beginning to think they have some noble purposes about them. I don't see that in the mine owners."

"Don't ever think that about these miners," Fleming insisted. "They have no nobility whatsoever. They only walked out because the other mines have. Mammoth has treated them well. They have no wrongs to redress, no demands that are justified."

"How would you know?" she flared up again. "You've never lived with them. You've never eaten with them. You've never visited them in their homes. You never met them but the time Karsch threw them out. Masterton won't even acknowledge their demands much less discuss them. John, do you have any idea what economic slavery is?"

"No, I've never been invited into their homes. Have you?"

It made her stop and reflect. "Yes, I have. I declined, now to my sorrow. It seems my sense of community is no better than yours should be."

She had hit home. True, he hadn't come from a life of poverty, but his parents were descended from hard-working, blue-collar folk. His success had, so far, been largely due to his own efforts, no one else's.

"Mary, there was a riot. Violence begun by violent men, not the poor blue-collars you support. A man got killed, for God's sake!"

"Two men," she corrected.

"Kiril was an accident."

"An accident you could have seen coming from a long way off."

"Me? How?"

"He warned you," she insisted. "Michael told you. It was documented many times, in files that don't exist anymore.'

Michael. Fleming stiffened. He ignored the accusation about the files and went to the heart of the matter, his heart anyway.

"Is that it? Is it Michael Jensen that you're really thinking about?"

"No."

"Of course it is. Ever since the funeral you've been cool towards me. Ever since you saw him at the cemetery with his guard down."

He was right, of course. She realized it too. Since that day she hadn't been able to get him out of her mind; the thought of Michael shredding the wreath and flinging it back at Masterton, then standing so defiantly before the grave. He was like a dog over the fallen body of his master. She hadn't ever seen such fierce resolve in a man before. She had never imagined Michael could show such devotion and such emotion. But there he was, ready to die with his Kiril. She just couldn't get that moment out of her mind. Fleming put his arms around her waist and she shrank away.

"John, don't. People can see us."

"But you're shivering."

"Not from cold. I'm angry." But she began to relax in his continuing embrace.

"Then let's not talk of this anymore. I don't want it to come between us."

She turned and looked into his soft, gray eyes. They were warm but weak, lacking Michael's fire. But hadn't Michael rejected her? She sighed.

"I'd better go back to my work, John."

"Tonight? Can we see each other?" He asked it with a strong measure of encouragement.

"Tonight." But it was without warmth.

It was a troubled Fleming that listened to the end of Libby's speech and his anxiety increased even more when everyone followed her jubilantly into the Ore House. He saw no good coming from this, just more clashes with the miners and Karsch and he without the power to prevent it. He whispered a mild profanity and returned to his office and his pathetically small numbers.

Chapter 22

"**You** are Michael Jensenice," Flynn stated matter-of-factly, her emerald eyes looking deeply into his. That she knew his name caught him off-guard, still he made an effort to hide his surprise.

"Jensen. We dropped the 'ice' when we found so much here in Minnesota.

"No, Michael. They stole it from you at Ellis Island," she answered. "You should take it back again and remember with pride the ancestors that bore it. But I was told pride has never been one of your shortcomings, has it, Mikey."

She possessed a lot of nerve for a woman, he thought. "Don't call me that," he said. "My friends call me that." They had quickly arrived at a standoff, stared at each other and then his curiosity got the better of him. "So, who are you? Who told you this about me?"

"Michael is your proper name, isn't it? I'll respect that." That settled him down somewhat. "My name is Elizabeth Gurley Flynn. Libby, if you like. My adversaries call me the Screaming Bitch and, in time, you'll know why. I hope you come to prefer Libby. My predecessors, Heywood and Scarlett, told me what was going on before I came here. Kiril's death was in the paper, of course, and you were also mentioned. You were there when it happened. It must have been terrible beyond words." He didn't respond so she went on. "I also spoke at length with Tresca in Duluth and the Chinese Gentleman, Mr. Wong, who is a fountain of information and discreet to a fault, of course. He's obviously fond of you. I asked him if you were in the crowd and, when he pointed you out, I have to admit I liked what I saw. In fact, I think I like it even better up close." She made Michael blush.

"However, don't flatter yourself too much. I'm looking for leaders, not lovers."

At the sound of that word, Michael's natural instincts took over. "Why settle for just the one when you can have both?"

Libby smiled and took a drink then deliberately traced her finger around the rim of the glass. She looked at him invitingly, but her next statement was all business. "Will you help me? Will you help our cause?"

Michael leaned back in his chair. "Cause? Is that what it is now? Sounds very patriotic. You don't seem to need too much help, ma'am. Snap your fingers and a hundred miners come running. If you keep making speeches like that and follow them up with free beer, they'll stick around too, at least long enough to see the promises broken."

She nodded. "Today, yes, but I cannot afford the beer for long." She gestured at the crowd around them. "And when the novelty of a skirt on a soapbox wears off, they'll drift away. They will come to think the movement has abandoned them and so they will eventually abandon it."

"Hasn't it already? Tell me you aren't up here just to sweep up the pieces like a good cleaning woman." He said this while looking into his glass, then took a lingering drink. She wanted to knock it out of his mouth. She knew he was acting poorly and was determined to rise above it.

"Indulge me, Michael, while this 'cleaning woman' gives you a little history lesson. Are you familiar with the Irish potato famine? Eighteen forty-five it was and my forebears were in the worst of it. They were shanty Irish, not lace curtain. They were poor tenant farmers to a British laird who they never met. When the blight came and the potatoes rotted in the ground, they starved. A million good Irish men, women and children died and a million more were forced to leave their homes and Ireland forever. And do you know, Michael, what our good laird did?"

Michael stared silently into her fiery eyes.

"When we couldn't pay the rent we were evicted. He burned our cottage and ran cattle over the land; cattle that were fattened and shipped to England for the fat British bellies. My great-grandparents and I don't know how many of their children and cousins died from starvation and disease.

"My grandfather was sent to America and lived in the New York slums where he fought with the Italians over crumbs. He survived. He did well, bless him. He became a cobbler and then a shoe maker in Boston. He became a manufacturer. His daughter, my mother went on to Boston College, married well and I grew up with lace curtains but I've never forgotten my roots."

"But the famine," said Michael, "was no one's fault, was it?"

She gave him a condescending smile. "God made the blight. England made the famine. Think of this for a minute. In the middle of the worst of it, forty ships a day went to England loaded with mutton, beef, corn, wheat; all of it taken from the dying. Our cemeteries were filled with the graves of infants. No, Michael, be not mistaken, it was genocide all right. The more that died, the bigger the consolidation of the farms and the more bully beef for the lairds.

"A politician, his name was Nassau Senior, was quoted as saying that the famine would not kill more than one million people and that would scarcely be enough to do any good.

"I grew up hearing all the stories, all the injustices and I promised my dead ancestors that I would fight for justice and fairness as long as I lived. I've organized more workers out east than there are in this whole district; steelworkers, butchers, weavers. I've slugged it out with shipping kings and steel barons alike. I know what I can do. But I also know what you can do. My words. Your voice. Yes, Michael, I do need someone in pants for much of the work."

"What do you expect to accomplish with words, Miss Libby, that your Scarlett and Heywood could not?"

"Everything we hope to gain. Everything! Respect, living wages, safe working conditions. All of it."

"I tried words, too," Michael said. "They didn't listen to them and my brother was blown to pieces. Before that happened I didn't care much about your Workers of the World and I still don't. But the Masterton's will pay. And not with words, either. I'm going to use a better way and one I am more familiar with."

"No, please. You must not act on your own. If you act out of revenge, anything you do will be seen as an act of the I.W.W. Revenge gives rise to reprisals. They are only waiting for us to do enough violence to justify martial law. That will mean militia and a forced return to work justified on national interests and with no improvements in conditions. The war interests, Michael, will trump everything. So please, don't make my work more difficult than it is."

She was very pretty and quite convincing, this east coast Irish lady with the fast and educated way of talking. It was almost enough to convince him. Almost, but the roar of the blast and the sight of Kiril disappearing forever in a shower of rock was burned indelibly into his brain. It kept playing over and over again. It screamed at him. Revenge? It had become such a noble word to him.

Michael finished his beer and stood up. She didn't try to stop him. She waited patiently for his answer, already knowing what it would be. Still, he tried to compromise.

"Maybe I can help you, Miss Flynn. Libby. But I've got my own plans, too and nobody is going to change them." She watched him from the saloon and smiled at the prospect of having him yet. He was young and volatile, a bear cub just coming into manhood. And vain on top of that. She had known immediately that flattering his ego was the key to enlisting his support.

She finished the last of her beer and started to get up to go after him. If reason wasn't enough, she had other weapons at her disposal. Two miners came up to her and began to ask a question. She put her hand on their shoulders to stop them, thought better of it and invited them to sit down. Michael could wait for a while. Oh yes, she'd have him eventually, even if it would mean having to take all of him.

chapter 23

The Mammoth mine kept producing ore in spite of Kiril's death and the almost total shutdown of the Range, driven on by the strength of Masterton's stubborn determination and the rigidity with which Karsch carried out his orders.

Michael's crew had walked out and wasn't replaced. The remaining night crew was merged with the meager numbers of day-timers. Administrative people and foremen changed shoes and shirts and were sent to blast and dig ore. There were still a very small number of the poorest Zenith and Aurora residents reporting each day in spite of the threats and abuse. The Minneapolis, St. Paul and Chicago newspapers were having a field day playing the mine owners up as loyal Americans standing up to the avarice of the European immigrants. It played well. Wasn't it, after all, Europeans who were killing American doughboys in the trenches of France? The miners were seen as both greedy and treasonous at the same time.

One night Zenith trembled from an explosion. Sadie woke and ran screaming into Michael's bedroom and found him already standing at the window. He scooped her into his arms and stroked her hair until the shaking stopped.

"What was that noise, she said?"

He didn't tell her because he didn't want her to know. He was a little bit drunk that night, as he had been for the last week. He said nothing but stroked her hair and stared down the street where the home of a strikebreaker had just been blown into kindling.

Chapter 24

The weather turned hot and humid and as oppressive as the days were, the night brought little solace. By nine that evening, it hadn't cooled off more than two degrees since the sun set.

The oscillating fan hanging from the tin ceiling did little more than churn up the sodden air that hung in the nearly empty council chambers in the Hibbing town hall. The hall had been commandeered for an impromptu news conference. The parties sat in the chairs normally occupied by the council members. They faced a single, unarmed reporter whose reputation normally carried little weight beyond the North Country.

Masterton was stripped to his rolled up shirtsleeves. Large sweat stains radiated from under his arms. A tired and haggard Tom Booker of the big Oliver Mining Company ran a wet kerchief over his face. Matthew Deering, the independent mine owner and a man of little pretense, sat stripped to his undershirt sipping on his glass of bourbon and wielding it to underscore each of his verbal points. The diminutive reporter was Alexander Comfrey, the senior reporter for the Duluth Herald. As powerful as these men were, Comfrey knew they sold no merchandise and placed no ads in his paper. He owed them nothing beyond journalistic honesty and, if pressed, he would have insisted he owed that only to his readers.

Comfrey was born and reared on The Range and knew these owners as well as he knew his favorite waitress at the Harbor Cafe in Duluth.

"The strike is big news, gentlemen," he said, "big news, but I'm afraid it's getting somewhat shopworn. The people are losing interest. It has lost its shock value, has grown stale and the world still turns. Have you followed the news from Europe? It appears democracy is poised to triumph in Europe and our allies have found sufficient steel after all." Comfrey was parrying Deering's cigar with one of his own and waved a glass of whiskey in his other hand. "Our readers have a right to know the truth. The truth beyond the angry rhetoric, behind the bigotry and behind all the posturing rightousness." He got a mildly mischievous grin on his face. "Say, I just had a thought. What if my paper actually began printing it? Not just the lies and innuendoes. Not just the 'who stabbed who', but the truth. What say you fellas? Do you want to give me the truth? The truth untainted by international politics? The truth as it pertains to employees and employers. Work conditions, pay and poverty. Where do you see it all heading? What say us all?"

Booker laughed, unwilling to be baited into an argument with the press. "You can go to hell, Comfrey, you and your populist press. You wouldn't print the truth if it crawled up your pants and bit you on your private parts.

"Ouch," said Comfrey. "I sense your feelings may be rather truthful at that."

Masterton grunted for attention. "What is the truth, Alexander? Tell us. Whose point of view is best represented by the truth?"

Comfrey unfolded the latest edition of the Herald. "Let me quote from my own yellow rag, boys. Tom, your own Oliver vice-president, Pentecost Mitchell, claims the miners have never presented any demands to you and yet, every edition of the paper lists those demands. Every child on the street can recite these demands. Is it true that you have never heard these demands?"

"That's the god honest truth," Booker growled. "These so-called demands have never been presented by a representative committee of the miners. And by 'committee' I don't include those goddamn Wobblies. We'll never recognize those assholes."

"Tom, do you keep your doors locked during office hours?"

"Shit, man," Booker spat. "I'm as accessible as the next man. Under the right conditions."

Comfrey's pen was poised, his trap baited. "So under what specific conditions will you hear the miner's demands formally?"

Booker shifted uncomfortably in his chair but Deering cut off any answer that might be forthcoming. "Let them first quit the strike and return to work. Let them give us a gesture of good faith. They do that, then we talk."

Comfrey pursed his lips. "It would seen to reduce their bargaining position substantially, but still, that is the consensus of the mine owners?" There was a moment of restlessness before they assented. "And if they desire not to honor that 'request'?

"Then they can stay out until hell freezes over," Masterton bellowed.

"But even up here, that won't be for another six months." Comfrey made a few notes then referred back to the newspaper. "Mitchell made another comment here. When asked if the strike had caused any reduction in the production of ore, he replied, 'No, sir!' That's it. Right here on page one. 'No Sir!' with a big exclamation point. I assure you, gentlemen, exclamation points are expensive. We don't throw them around carelessly." Comfrey held up his hand, paused, and cleared his throat. "Boys, there are, by most valued accounts, sixteen thousand strikers on the range and maybe fifteen hundred wholly inexperienced, former North Dakota sod-busting strike breakers working. And Mr. Mitchell says there is no drop in ore shipped? Gentlemen? The truth? Are you all guilty of over-hiring and management malfeasance or has your tonnage actually dropped just a little bit?"

Booker chuckled and nodded, yielding to, and then ignoring Comfrey's logic. "You figure it out Alexander and then put yourself in our places. What would you say? Tell the world the bastards have us by the balls? Even if they did, and I'm not suggesting that, we'd never be able to admit it."

"Sounds a little like you're a bit ensnarled in a web of your own weaving." Then Comfrey dismissed the matter with a wave of his hand and went on. "That's the business of accountants, isn't it? But here, quoting from the paper: Eyewitnesses say the picket lines have been taken over by women."

"Is that so?" Deering smiled.

"Yes. The ladies claim they'd rather 'man' the picket lines than stay home and bandage their men."

Masterton poured himself a tumbler-full from Deering's bottle and offered Comfrey some. He accepted. Masterton took a long pull and leaned across the table. "If it sounds rough to you, well, rough is a two-way street, Mr. Comfrey. When they play rough, so do we."

Comfrey ran down a list in his notebook. "The hospitals seem to be filling up with beatings, pistol whippings, intimidation, unlawful arrests. Strange, but I don't see any of your special mine deputies on the police blotters, hospital admittances or morgue records. Apparently they are living wonderfully healthy life styles."

"We are the law!" Deering shouted. Booker made a gesture of apology to Comfrey but Deering wasn't finished. "You left out dynamiting, Mr. Reporter. What about everything that's being blown to Kingdom Come around here? Tracks, locomotives, wagons, shops. Houses, for god's sakes. So you can just take your sarcasm and, and, well just shove it."

"Sometimes our security gets a little excited," Masterton allowed. "Their lives are at risk, after all."

Comfrey decided to go off in another direction. "Apparently," he said, "to the point where the governor is about to step in." That brought their heads up.

"Where did you hear that?"

"Have any of you ever met John Keyes? No? He's an excellent man and a wonderful attorney. He could do wonders in one of your organizations but, at the moment, he's representing some of the jailed Wobblies. I understand he's in St. Paul tonight delivering a letter from the miners to the governor himself."

"What's in it?" Masterton demanded.

"Anticipating that just such a question might be given to me, he gave me a copy." Comfrey pulled an envelope out of his coat and unfolded it. "With your indulgence, I'll be happy to read it to you."

Chapter 25

John Keyes walked into the walnut-paneled office and looked around to take in the full-sized portraits of some of Minnesota's former famous governors.

The man sitting at the huge desk devoid of papers brought him back to the present. "Mr. Keyes, I presume. My own gubernatorial portrait is being hung at a reception next month."

Keyes came back to the moment and strode quickly to the desk. "Governor Burnquist, I beg your pardon. This is a beautiful office, sir."

Burnquist cleared his throat. "Umhmm. Your business, Mr. Keyes, involves the Iron Range?"

"Yes sir. This will just take a minute, governor. Five at the most, if I may have your permission?"

Governor J.A. Burnquist nodded soberly, stately. Mr. Keyes nodded similarly and began to read:

"*To: The honorable J.A. Burnquist, Governor of the State of Minnesota, St. Paul. Governor, in a recent order you instructed the sheriff of St. Louis County to disarm miners, peaceful citizens. We submit here with gross violation of personal liberty of the miners and ask you to remove all mine guards from within city limits of mining towns or to likewise disarm them. Otherwise our miners will be instructed to defend themselves by constitutional rights.*

"*In Gilbert on June 15, a Friday night, seven mine guards forcibly entered the home of strikers with drawn guns. They threatened strikers with bodily harm if they did not return to work. They snatched a baby from the arms of its mother and brutalized it. We are ready to submit facts to your representatives.*

"*Another striking miner, George Andreychine was imprisoned twenty-four hours in Itasca County without a charge being filed against him. Inquiry was futile. Are we in Russia? We only seek justice, not partisanship. Signed: Carlo Tresca, Joe Gilday, Sam Scarlett, M. Shustrick.*"

Keyes held up another letter. "I have several more, Governor, all requesting your intervention."

Burnquist held up his hand. "Fine, fine Mr. Keyes. That's very interesting. I'll certainly look forward to finishing the others later. Right now, I'd rather talk."

John Keyes was young, idealistic and still trusted, to some extent, the political system. He held his tongue and watched Burnquist push himself wearily out of his chair and limp over to a sideboard.

"Gout," he offered by way of explanation. "Get's so damned bad I can hardly walk. Too much shellfish according to my doctor. But I'd rather give up prime rib than go without lobster. Know what I mean? Coffee?" he offered. "Or Bourbon. I hear they drink their bourbon straight up on the Iron Range."

"Yes sir, those that drink it at all. The water has so many minerals in it, it turns the bourbon black. I'll take coffee, please, if you have it."

"As will I. Mr. Keyes, I can't help but wonder, where are the men who wrote that first letter? Why didn't they come in person?"

Keyes took a sip of his coffee. "They're in jail, sir. Two on murder charges, two on destruction of property."

"Hmmm," Burnquist nodded.

"However, where they are should have no bearing on the validity of their statements, governor. We have entered a plea of 'Not guilty' and will pursue it until they are completely exonerated."

"Umhmm. Of course."

Burnquist took the other documents from Keyes and sat down at his desk. He glanced over them without much interest. Personally, he disliked everything about the Iron Range. Northern Minnesota held little interest for him. His constituency base was south. His personal roots had been established at Carlton College in Northfield many years prior. He was a professor by vocation, an intellectual, and had no stomach for life's vulgarities, and specifically the current mine situation. He had never held pragmatists in much regard.

The governor smiled at the memories he had of northern Minnesota. He had made only one stop north in his entire gubernatorial campaign: Two days at a rally and dinner in Duluth and three more days in Bemidji, ostensibly for a fishing trip to demonstrate his bond with the state's outdoorsmen. In reality, he had sat in a drafty cabin the whole time swatting mosquitoes over endless games of cribbage while watching wave after wave of rainsqualls sweep across the wild waters of Cass Lake. Just thinking back on it drew forth a rueful chuckle.

"Sir?"

Burnquist looked up at Keyes, mildly surprised to see that he was still there. "I beg your pardon. I was momentarily taken hostage by some tortured memories."

"Governor, I was just asking if you could at least visit the northern towns and talk to the owners and representatives of the miners. Some common ground has to be established. Maybe you could clear the way for a settlement; get some meaningful talks started."

"Representatives? I thought the miners were being led by I.W.W. factions."

Keyes appeared puzzled. "They are. The International Workers of the World are the miners chosen representatives."

"But the I.W.W. isn't a recognized labor organization. Not in this state at least."

Keyes jaw tightened slightly. "They are recognized by the miners, sir. Shouldn't the miners have the freedom to choose who speaks for them? There are many legal opinions that suggest organizations representing labor need not nor should not be registered or controlled by any government body."

"Hmmm." Burnquist leaned back, his portly body disappearing into the padded leather chair and looked hard at the young attorney. Why did a man like Keyes ever choose to represent such rabble? Was his life still being guided by simple ideals? Youthful ideals, rightly founded but wrongly directed. Well, see how far that will carry him in life.

Burnquist took in Keyes clean-shaven youthful face, his poorly tailored suit and his slightly scuffed brown shoes. Personally, he would have chosen black wingtips but realized Keyes might not have but one pair of dress shoes. He was that way once, just before and after tenure protected him against the consequences of uttering liberal invectives in a conservative college. Times change, but even to suggest taking the position of the miners! They aren't even American citizens, most of them. They don't vote so how much attention can they warrant? The governor would rather put his attention elsewhere.

Burnquist's conscience quivered as his required course of action became clear. What sense would it make to go against his real constituents? The mine owners were the only true citizens in this deal and their generous campaign contributions proved it. He stood up and held out his hand.

"Mr. Keyes, it's been a very enlightening meeting but now it's late. I need to think about this for a few days.

"But sir, if…"

"Makes no matter, son. Tomorrow I'm entraining for San Francisco for the Governor's Conference and then I'm taking a few days in Yellowstone with the Roosevelts. Can't be helped. We'll talk again as soon as I get back." Burnquist had timed his goodbye to coincide with his arrival at this office door. He opened it. Keyes made a last desperate attempt.

"Governor, please, all we ask is…"

"When I get back, Mr. Keyes. Have a pleasant journey back to Hibbing. Goodnight now."

Burnquist shooed him out, closed the door, then turned and addressed the little man in the corner. He had been sitting in the shadows and, because Burnquist had ignored him during the course of their meeting, Keyes had assumed he was the Governor's secretary.

"You heard?"

"Yes sir." The response was timid.

"Their letters have a certain Jeffersonian ring to them. Rights and values; strong textures of populism."

"Yes sir." And very agreeable. "Very Jeffersonian."

But he knew the message the owners had sent him had a stronger ring of suppressed anger and power. Burnquist went over to the sideboard, dumped ice in a glass and splashed bourbon over it. He held the glass up searching for discoloration and sipped it tentatively, his tongue searching for the taste of minerals. There was none. He took a big swallow and turned back to his nephew and secretary, Gust Burnquist.

"Gust, while I'm gone, I want you to discreetly visit the iron range cities; Hibbing, Eveleth, Virginia, Mammoth. That should be enough. Look around. See what's what. Give me a full report when I get back. I need this to sound supportive of the generally inherent rights of the miners but not in relevance to the specific issues they want addressed. It wouldn't hurt if the owners came across as at least a little patriotic. The war effort, you know? Oh, and sympathetic. Let's have the owners demonstrate a bit of concern for the plight of their workers. Try to point out a healthy number of improvements in their life styles that the owners have unilaterally promulgated. I'm sure there must be a number of them. Let's see if we can help find a way out of this mess before the legislators return from the summer recess "

Lundquist came out of the shadows. He was short and round of body and face. It was ten-thirty at night but his face bore no trace of stubble. The man with the round, boyish face full of freckles was frowning.

"No. Next time, Gust," the governor consoled him. "The next conference I'll take you along. Maybe even the big one in Washington. That's a promise. Do this for me now, please?"

Gust, head hung in resignation, went out the door. His little hand on the knob looked like a man gripping a small melon. There wasn't much energy in his answer. "Yes, sir." There would be no Teddy Roosevelt in his future.

In parting the governor added, "And remember, Gust, no publicity. Keep your presence incognito. Be my spy, my Mata Hari."

"Yes, sir."

chapter 26

Comfrey was winding things up in Hibbing. He had gotten what he wanted from the owners and he'd write it as he had heard it knowing full well, as Keating and the others did, that his editors would tear the guts out of it simply because, as the governor ignored the miners because they didn't vote, the newspapers ignored them because they didn't read.

"One last question, gentlemen, and then let's all try to get some sleep in this ungodly heat."

His prey smiled wearily. It was after midnight and the four men had been circling each other like wolves for over four hours. Deering had already cursed the decision to hold the interview several times over but Booker held to the view that, if the proper news got out, the public would realize the wisdom of the mine companies, the miners would capitulate and the situation would resolve itself. Masterton was going along with it secure in the conviction that, no matter what was said, he could always deny saying it and go his own way.

"Shoot," Booker agreed.

Comfrey grinned. "Déjà vu, Mr. Booker. Tom Booker frowned. "You said, shoot! I'm going to say close but no shooting. You gentlemen have mentioned several times how damaging the vandalism is in your pits. I've heard of shoot-on-sight orders being given to deputies. Am I hearing correctly? I mean is this happening? Is this really necessary? Trade a life for a steamhose?"

Like a schoolboy on a Friday afternoon, Masterton raised a weary hand. "I'll field that one, Tom. Mr. Comfrey, I only own one mine, admittedly one of the larger ones but still just a single site to protect against your gentle martyrs. Here's what protecting it entails. Mammoth, the pit, is over half a mile long and just about fourteen hundred feet wide at the belly. That's more than fifty acres down on the mining floor. We have five pump houses, six miles of track, forty ore cars, two belly loaders and two steam dippers, not to mention a dozen other buildings: tool sheds, explosive bunkers, offices... all in the pit. On the surface we cover another fifty acres with the processing mill, shops, offices, more tracks, equipment yards, ore stockpiles. Then there's the company housing. I'd guess another thirty or forty buildings. You are talking about a small town here. I'm trying to protect it all with thirty men. The sheriff offered to take over my security with two. Booker here, with all his holdings; how many Tom? Yeah, a dozen mines. How many deputies did you put on?"

Keating's head dropped. "Three hundred ten."

A low whistle came from Comfrey.

"Can they do the job?" Masterton persisted.

"No. Every night. Every goddamn night something gets torched or broken."

"So why don't you settle and avoid all the trouble?" asked Comfrey. "Wouldn't it save you dollars in the long run? Would a greater share of the wealth be so out of character for you?"

Deering ignored the suggestion. "The miners have been warned. If they come onto our property during the shutdown, there's no question what they're after. If we see 'em, we shoot 'em for aggravated trespass and intention of doing grievous harm."

Comfrey looked at each man in turn. "How many? How many have died?"

"Only those that deserve it."

"Deserve it? Is there really that much sabotage happening that men deserve to die for it?"

Masterton rubbed his eyes, glad that school was almost out. "Even as we speak, Alex. Even as we speak."

Chapter 27

The profile of the Mammoth mine was more serpentine than round. Its banks undulated in and out of ore pockets like the pseudopods of a giant amoeba. There were over four miles of rim at the top. The sides were pocked with hundreds of gullies carved by erosion. There were plenty of places to drop in and climb out without being seen or heard. The two men had already dropped into the pit and, crawling cautiously between the many piles of equipment and ore, had already done their work and were picking their way back to the top, hidden in one of these gullies deep in one of the unpatrolled recesses.

Cresting the hole, they crawled through the heavy grass and brush until they came to the dark shadow of a pile of overburden. They waited. Dressed in black, their faces covered with coal dust, they were invisible to all but each other. A minute later, the slow match they had left behind reached the kerosene and touched it off. Far down in the mine they saw the pinpoint of light build as the back of a pump house burst into flame. A figure came running out the door. A cry for help and more men could be heard, shadowy forms rushing to the fire.

From the top they looked like ants, scurrying about trying to control the fire, torches in hand trying to find the arsonists. On the rim, Michael Jensen and George Andrychine shook hands in the dark and began to trace a cautious, circuitous route through the woods and swamps back to Zenith.

Chapter 28

When Michael wasn't at home sleeping or skulking about in the dark, he could invariably be found at the Ore House Bar. He was willing to drink with anyone who offered a pitcher or glass but shared his private thoughts with no one because he would never again have a confidant like Kiril. His soul echoed with loneliness.

Libby might have filled that void except for her narrow focus always directed to her job, and her travels, which swept her up and down the Iron Range cities. She spent a lot of time giving speeches and rallying the pickets to "another day, just give me another day". When she was in town, she would spend most of her time gathering the faithful together and sharing what was happening elsewhere.

Mary had become a distant memory. Michael had given up on her as both love mate and soul mate. He saw her rarely and then only from a distance. Occasionally she would stop, giving him the opportunity to approach her if he wished but he always changed direction to avoid her.

There was something of a spark between Michael and the embattled Wobblie queen. When they did get together, their conversations often became heated arguments over their radically different approaches to the situation, his vengeful destruction versus her peaceful, persistent agitation. And the more heated the talk became the more they became aware of the heat in each other. Finally one night, it was just she and Michael and a round-faced, fleshy stranger drinking after the closing hour.

"Mind if I join you two?"

Libby stared at the man until his confidence became so shaken that he began to tremble noticeably and actually backed away from them. He sucked in his lower lip for a moment and, when he expelled it, the words spilled out.

"I mean there's no one else and I still have this." He was holding up a nearly full pitcher in two hands. He waved it feebly about the empty room. Libby looked at Michael who gave a little shrug.

"Why not?" Michael pulled out a chair and Lundquist slid into it and gratefully put down the pitcher and rubbed his wrists.

"These things are heavy, aren't they?"

Michael picked it up. "If you want someone to help lighten it you came to the right table. Mind?"

"No. No, go right ahead. That's why I brought it. For company. I'm really not much of a drinker."

Libby smiled at the funny man. "Stick around here long enough and that will change. What's your name?"

Lundquist exhaled a sigh of relief. "I should introduce myself, should I not? My name is Maurice. Maurice Windfield."

Michael screwed up his face. "Maurice?"

"My friends call me Maury." Windfield said quickly. "You can call me Maury." He wrinkled his nose and waited to see if they decided to become his friends.

Michael was noncommittal. "So what do you do, Mo?"

"Do? Oh, do! Well, as to my occupation, I'm a writer; a novelist, actually. Yes, a novelist and I was drawn here by the spectacle of this strike. It has a lot of appeal for a writer. The monster owners against the hard-pressed underdogs. Man struggling against his pitiless masters. Power versus passion. All that raw, seething emotion." They stared at him. "Yes, there's much here to interest a writer," he finished lamely.

Michael raised his brows. "And you are going to write a book about us?"

"Almost certainly." Lundquist felt he had gotten over the first hurdle. "I want to write it from just that perspective. From the miners I mean... their perspective."

"For us, it's all about dignity," Libby said. "We're asking only for respect and dignity, and the livelihood that goes with it."

"I think much on that aspect of livelihood, or the right to one," Lundquist offered.

Libby threw down much of her beer. "It's a lie in any case."

Lundquist sat back abruptly. "What do you mean, madam?"

She narrowed her eyes and looked at him hard. "You sir, are no novelist. Maybe you are a greeting card salesman, but certainly no writer. No, you haven't got the moxie for real journalism. You don't look like you've ever been out of the greenhouse in your life. In fact, you've been in town for three days and we're the first ones you've even talked to. Surprised? Mammoth is a small town. Secrets are never as secretive as we wish. Besides, writers aren't bashful, Maurice, Maury, or whoever you are. They are 'in your face' assertive. So who in the hell are you?"

Lundquist looked around conspiratorially. "I'd rather not divulge that except to tell you that I'm here to gather information."

"For the governor," Libby said.

Lundquist's eyes widened. "My God, how did you know?"

Libby burst out laughing. He had been so easy.

"Well, son of a bitch," Michael swore. "What are you really up to, then? Is he going to help us or them?" Lundquist's upper lip was beaded with sweat. He took three deep breaths.

"In a way, both. I was sent here to observe and report back. Maybe try to resolve the dispute."

"Dispute?" spat Michael. "That's the first time I heard it called that. And as far as you being able to resolve anything, I sorely disagree."

Libby, taking a more placating approach, reached out and took his hands in hers. "Honestly? An honest report?"

Maury blushed red but came back with enthusiasm. "Oh, yes. I want to see it all. Both sides. Governor Burnquist specifically sent me for that. I'm his personal secretary, you know. My full name is Gust Lundquist."

"Where is he, Gust?" asked Michael. "The governor."

"On holiday. He's in the Badlands with the Roosevelt family, no less."

"Asshole." Michael spat on the sawdust covered floor. "Everyone knows he's just a puppet for the owners."

Lundquist was insistent. "Well, even if he might be, I'm most certainly not." He also spat on the floor but his phlegm caught on his lower lip and he drew a handkerchief from his breast pocket.

Michael reached for the pitcher again. "You haven't struck me as much of anything yet." Lundquist's lip trembled and perspiration ran down the creases on the sides of his mouth. Libby put her hand on Michael's arm by way of cautioning him.

They watched each other for a minute. Michael softened when he spoke again. "What do you think of the things the miners are pulling, Gust? The sabotage, they call it?"

Lundquist sipped his beer. "I've heard of it, but I can't honestly say I have witnessed any."

Michael grinned. "Want to?"

"Michael," Libby warned. "Are you drunk?"

"Are you telling me that you are a saboteur?" Lundquist's hands started trembling again.

"Oh, god, no!" Michael said. My mother would never let me do those things." He grinned, "I just hold the lantern."

Lundquist's face slowly dissolved into a smile of his own. Then he laughed and, in doing so, let out a loud belch and a smaller noise from under the table and they all began laughing together. "I told you beer gives me gas," he said lamely. "Both kinds."

Michael was beginning to like the little guy and helped him drink his beer long after Libby had gone back to her room. She was asleep when he knocked even though she was half expecting him to come. Throwing on a robe, she opened the door. He stood across from her, his arms resting on the frame. Her first impulse was to look over his shoulder.

"Did you bring him with you?"

"Mo? No, I left him degassing out behind the Ore House."

Standing there, she thought he looked very young and vulnerable. He was waiting for an invitation. Still, she made him ask.

"Can I come in?"

She wanted to make him beg so she could establish control over his will. "I'm married, you know."

"I didn't know. You aren't wearing a ring."

She looked at her hand. "It's an on and off thing. At the moment it's off."

He asked again. "I still want to come in." There was a long pause. "I need to."

"Why?" she said, as much to herself as to him. Then again, she thought, why not? She saw the pleading, lonely look in his eyes. The time for pretense was over. She stepped aside and shut the door after him.

Chapter 29

Mary looked up when Karsch walked in. "He's not in," she said. Karsch ignored her and went straight into Fleming's office. She heard him rummage around and a minute later he reappeared.

"He's not here," he said.

"That's what I told you."

"Where the hell is he then?" Karsch was rocking unsteadily on his heels. Mary stared at him. God, she thought, is he already drunk so early in the morning? Or is that still from last night?

"At his home, I expect. He hasn't come in yet so I don't know."

Karsch grunted and began mumbling. He was talking to her yet ignoring her at the same time. His eyes were roaming about the office.

"What are you looking for?" she asked.

He went back into Fleming's office and began rifling through the papers on the desk. His voice came back to her. "The damned payroll. It's payday and the troops are restless."

Mary stood up and went over to a bank of filing drawers. "I have the checks here in the cabinet."

From inside Fleming's office, "I wonder who's warm fanny he's cozied up to that he can't shake out of bed like the rest of us. Not yours, obviously."

Her fingers tightened on the drawer pull. She yanked it open and reached for the checks. In a moment he was behind her, hands on her waist. She froze.

"I've been wondering, Miss Savich, who's been cozying up to your fanny these days? I mean now that your Mr. Jensen's been nesting with that Wobblie bitch. But don't worry, I'm on to his tricks and in due time he'll be mine." His hands began to creep up her torso. They traced her ribcage and touched the bottom of her breasts.

"You bastard," she screamed and turned to hit him, but he caught her arm and laughed. His breath was foul in her face.

"Easy, girl. Where do you get off with that? You ain't such a lady, yourself." He bent her wrist back and slid his other hand over her breast. "Just a little good morning squeeze. A little kiss."

"Karsch!"

He wheeled at the sound of Fleming's voice. John was in the doorway, his face flushed and angry. "What in the hell are you doing?"

Karsch hadn't the decency to act embarrassed. "Morning, Fleming. Me and Mary here were just getting more acquainted 'till you come in."

"Get in here," Fleming said in outrage and disappeared into his office, unable to look at Mary. Karsch reached behind her and took the envelope of checks from the drawer, putting his face close to hers.

"Next time we'll have to pick a place more private, won't we?"

She shuddered and tried to strike him again but he stepped back and disappeared into Fleming's office. The door slammed behind him and she heard voices as they started shouting at each other. There was the sound of bodies shuffling and something slammed against the wall. A moment later the door opened and Karsch came out. He stopped and waved the checks at Mary.

"Next time," he reminded her. "A little more privacy."

"You bastard," she breathed and hurried into Fleming's office. He was on the floor, slumped against the wall, dabbing blood from his mouth.

He managed a wan smile. "Not my best attempt at protecting a lady's honor."

"John." She knelt beside him, but her thoughts were already beyond the room. They were intent on Karsch's threats. What could she do to avoid him in the future, if anything? John Fleming, her 'savior' had just demonstrated his impotence in the face of Karsch's brutality and in the back of her mind was the knowledge that barely an hour earlier she had heard Michael leave that Flynn woman's room.

Chapter 30

Going down into the dark mine had become a game to Michael. It was a dangerous game. Three nights a week, usually with George Andrychine, he went out to do some destructive mischief on the Mammoth property. On his off days he drank at the Ore House until his pain was properly anesthetized and then he would go home and sleep for twelve hours.

In the bar he had lost his cockiness; like a soldier who, after too many months at the front no longer looked forward to the end but only took each day of survival as a victory in itself. But he was not yet like the soldier who deserted out of weariness over the killing. He knew that each time he went down increased the probability that he would be caught and it took a heavy toll on his sanity. He began to wonder if he wanted to be caught. He fantasized about his capture by the guards and the pleasure they would take beating him. His maudlin behavior came to taint everyone who hung around him so very few men did. Only the young and restless came to see him as the symbol of leadership that Libby had hoped for. He was both a cause as well as a reflection of the dark unrest that settled on Mammoth.

The big frame house was now empty except for Katla, Sadie and Michael. Their boarders had given up hope of a settlement and joined the pilgrimage back to the Pennsylvania coalfields. That gave Katla more time for her garden. It was filling in, lush and verdant, one of a quilt work of plots connecting all the back yards and giving a veneer of prosperity to an otherwise depressed location.

Sadie was on summer recess and, now that Michael was officially a striker, and more than that, a leader of sorts, she had no want of friends to play with. On most days, Michael wasn't one of them. On this particular day, he woke up in the kind of mood that no child would want of a playmate. Katla and Sadie sat on the back porch shelling peas when he swung open the screen door. He stood there in his underwear watching them, his face unshaven, his hair slick and oily. Finally Katla acknowledged his presence. Her face was creased with the weariness of a mother who had grown tired of her child's manners and behavior.

"Close the door, Michael. You let in all the flies that your body odor attracts."

He stepped obediently onto the porch, the screen door slamming shut behind him. When he reached into the bowl for some of the green pearls, she slapped his hand.

"There now! Just look at your filthy hands!" He pulled back but it wasn't enough to appease her. "And your face. I wouldn't let one of my children into dinner like that."

"Ma, I am one of your children."

"But you don't look like one. So you can just go hungry until you wash. All my children have the faces of angels."

Sadie giggled and Michael tried to appease Katla by reaching down and tickling Sadie until she laughed all the harder. The tension eased and he made the next gesture.

"I'm going to take a bath right now, Mama. Right now." He didn't move but Katla took him back anyway.

"That's good. You are a handsome man when you want to be." She did a few more pods before adding, "You had a visitor last night. When you were out." She didn't suggest where he might have gone.

"Who?"

"That girl from the mines."

"Elizabeth Flynn?"

"No. The nice one. Miss Savich."

"What did she want?"

"Nothing. Just that you had invited her and she came to see you. I think to see where we live. I had her come inside." To see 'how' we live was more to the point he thought.

"And nothing more?"

Katla straightened up in her chair and brushed a spray of hair from her eyes and handed Sadie an empty bowl. "Here, darling, go see if we missed any peas in the garden." She waited until Sadie was gone and then went on. "We had some coffee and talked about the strike. I told her what a terrible thing it was, setting families against each other the way it has. I said it was a sin against God's people. She agreed it had gone too long and hoped the government would step in to end it. She agreed the miners have suffered too much."

"Aw, crap, Ma. She said that? She's one of them, Mama, that everyone's striking because of."

Katla looked at him hard. "No, she acted like one of us, Michael. I think she is one of us. She had our face and our hair and our eyes."

Michael stood up and went to the door. He looked out over the back yard, his eyes coming to rest on the big rock alongside the garden. "She's one of them, Mama. She doesn't want to be like us anymore. She thinks she's better than us." He turned and was halfway through the door when Katla's words reached him.

"Michael, she said for you to be careful."

He turned back and smiled at her. "I'm always careful, Mama."

Katla was more emphatic. "She said to be careful of a man. The one that bosses the mine police."

"Karsch?"

"Karsch. Yes. She said, 'Be very careful of Karsch' and, for goodness sake, shut that screen door quietly now."

chapter 31

Michael stood up from the table at the ore house and drained the last of his beer. "Come on, George. It's time we got on home don't you think?" It was getting close to quitting time.

"But we still have beer left," said Lundquist, gesturing at the last two inches left in their pitcher. Libby gave Michael a somewhat questioning, somewhat accusatory look. He returned it with a shrug of his shoulders.

"I promised Sadie we'd go pick blueberries tomorrow and it's late."

"I guess it is, Michael. Sleep well, if you can," she replied.

When Michael and Andrychine left the almost deserted Ore House home was not where they headed. Instead, they slipped into the shadows and went out to the main highway, walked east for two miles, then cut over to the Mesabi tracks. They moved cautiously as they carefully traced the railroad right-of-way back to the sorting mill. When its bulky outline began to loom in the distance, they slipped down into a cedar grove and followed a nearly invisible game trail that cut northwest towards the eastern lip of the mine. When they got there, Michael went into the bushes, retrieved a coil of rope they had hidden the night before and tied it off on a healthy sapling. Lowering it down, he slipped over the edge. George quickly followed.

The pit was always eerie, ghostly inhospitable at night; a broad, rocky landscape contained by the high, foreboding walls. The terrain was broken up by ore piles and layered with the working terraces. There were piles of equipment, storage sheds, pump houses and ore cars in abundance, and, with Karsch's guards prowling around, it was especially hostile.

He crouched behind a stack of rail ties and waited. This, he wondered, must be what real war was like; men hunting each other, each in their own turn prey and predator, striking out from places of dark concealment. He thought he would be a good soldier if it ever came to that, one of the survivors because the rush of adrenaline he felt was not from fear but excitement. He was still too young to know that fear was a healthy human emotion whose purpose was to protect and ensure survival, but only if listened to.

An hour went by, then another. They marked the positions of the guards by the flares of matches held to cigarettes, the sounds of shoes scraping on the gravel, the grunts of men relieving each other from their shifts and relieving themselves in other ways that brought a gentle poke from George in Michael's ribs.

When they were finally satisfied that it was safe to move, they crept forward until they were within fifty feet of the big steam dipper. The black silhouette of the shovel cast a prehistoric pall over everything else, like a tyrannosaurus dominating its domain. But this dinosaur was not so fearsome that it did not need protection. Two men, armed with rifles and a jar of dill pickles, had climbed onto the machine's tracks. They were looking in the general direction of the two intruders yet they saw nothing.

The wait had begun. They lay on the wet gravel and watched the guards eat their pickles and tease a pint of whiskey. They had collected a small pile of pebbles and began throwing them at a tin can.

"If they are holding there what it looks like from here," whispered George, "I do not want anything to do with them."

"Bullets only hurt if they hit you, Andy."

"They look like they will be there all night, Mikie."

"Isn't that why they call them guards?"

Another half-hour passed. Three more hours and it would be coming on dawn. Michael was ready to pull out and call it a wasted night when Karsch, drawn by the sound of the stones hitting the can, came around the corner. He grabbed a leg and threw one of the men to the ground. The other jumped down and came to a semblance of attention.

"What the fuck are you lazy asses doing? You've got thirty men scared shitless because of your goddamn rock throwing. I should paint a bulls-eye on your backs and run you off in the dark. You!" He pointed to the one still cowering on the ground. "Get over to pump house four. Tell them they can sleep now because you just volunteered to pull their shift."

He turned to the second man who had decided he wasn't going to be killed but still thought maybe he'd be better off that way. "And you stay off your lazy ass and start marching around this pile of rust, you hear? All I wanna hear from this end of the yard is the sound of your boots turning gravel into sand. You ever pull this crap again, you'll be lying under this shovel instead of sitting here farting on it."

The guard grabbed his carbine and hurried off. Karsch went over and picked up the can. He crushed it in his hands and threw it away. It landed four feet from Michael and skittered up against his leg, bounced back and came to rest just out of the shadow line of the ore pile. They froze. Karsch stared at their hiding place for a full minute as if he had sensed something. In fact, something inside his brain had registered error when the can had rolled back to him instead of bouncing on. There is something back there, it whispered to him. There is something soft enough that it made no noise when the can hit it. There is something out of place here because there should be nothing in that shadow. No, it's nothing. The can simply struck on its lip and kicked backward. It's nothing. He'd be damned if he was going to go over there and step in a pile of crap or a pool of piss in the dark. Karsch waited until the guard reappeared on his first circuit.

"Stay awake," Karsch reiterated and walked off.

Michael lowered the pack off his back and pulled out the two bottles of petrol. He pulled the corks and stuffed the necks with rags and inverted the bottles. The gas flowed out and saturated the bags. He handed one to Andrychine. "Here, Andy, don't let it drip on your hands."

They let the guard complete another circuit and then Michael whispered, "Now!" The match flared. He touched it to the rags and they caught. He stayed bent over the bottle until certain it was burning well, and they stood and threw. The bottles traced a bright arch through the sky and crashed into the wooden cab of the steel monster. It was immediately engulfed in flames. Michael stared in fascination at the spectacle.

"Come on, Mikey!" Andrychine was already ten yards away and running hard still, Michael beat him to their rope by fifty feet. Angry voices and rapid footsteps came close behind.

Michael went up the rope like a monkey. He reached the crest and threw himself down at the edge. George had started up when Michael was well along and he was halfway up by then.

"Come on, George. Go, man!" He was a bigger man with more muscle but much of it was in his legs and hips. He was laboring hard, his boots fighting for traction on the rocks. The voices were very near now.

"George, for god's sake!" He was almost at the top.

"There he is!" The lanterns shone on the cliff wall. Shots rang out. George stretched out a hand and Michael grabbed it and hauled him over the edge. More shots and bullets spattered around them. A second more and he was safe.

They lay in the grass catching their breath and letting the fear release its grip over them. The success of their foray had made them feel brave and courageous and a little foolish because it made Michael sit up. He started to throw rocks down on the guards.

The deputies were busy playing their torchlights off the rim and sending up random shots. They were still yelling and Michael could pick out Karsch's voice.

"Come on you sons a bitches! If you had any balls, you'd show yourselves."

But they weren't that brave and, instead, he threw more rocks. The rope danced and tightened. They had found it. Someone was climbing up. Pulling out his knife, Michael waited a few seconds before cutting the rope. There was the sound of someone falling followed by a scream, then a curse. More shots ricocheted harmlessly off the cliff.

"Karsch," Michael yelled back. "If you have to see someone's balls to recognize them, you shouldn't be working in an iron mine. Take that rope and piss up it, you ugly bastard!" The he slipped back deeper into the shadows.

"Come on, George. Let's go get drunk." George slowly rolled over and groaned.

"Michael, I think I am shot."

"What? You aren't serious. God, where?"

"I am very serious. They shot me. The dirty bastards shot me."

"God, no!" Michael began searching him. "George, don't worry. Where is it? Where?"

"I don't know. It doesn't hurt so much but I can feel it in me."

George coughed. He put his hand to his mouth and caught some of the oozing blood. "He moaned. "This shouldn't be. Mike, I think they shot me in a lung. I'm having blood in my mouth."

Now Michael was really scared, a new and different fear that gripped him like a vice. He grabbed George by the boots and roughly pulled him back into the tree line. It was still dark and only dogs could hope to find them now and it would take an hour to get dogs out there. But in an hour the sun would rise and they wouldn't need dogs. Michael tried to think it through. When they came to search for them it would be on the path they had taken down the railroad grade. Michael looked off to his right. It was the longer way home all the way around the pit, at least five miles and George might not make it. The very thought terrified him.

"You are going to be okay, George. You will be all right. We'll go to the doctor. He'll make it right" He eased Andrychine onto his side and ran his hand down his back. It felt wet. Michael pulled up George's shirt and braved a match. The whole of the back was bloody. Michael pulled off his bandanna and wiped it. Andrychine stiffened and gave out a little cry. He found a little hole in the ribcage where the bullet had gone in. Dark blood was still oozing out but it came slowly because it was clotting now, but it looked bad. He was familiar with bullet holes in the deer he shot and none ever survived to run away. Michael knew he had two poor choices: Leave the man here or take him out on the tracks. It wasn't really a choice at all.

"It isn't very good, George. We have to leave here now. I'll carry you."

George managed a poor laugh. "It will not work, Michael. A mule cannot carry a cow. I am too big for you."

"And you want to die here, instead?"

The prospect had already entered his mind but Michael saying it made it more real. "No. I do not want to die anywhere but for sure not here, Michael. Go get my sister," he murmured. "She will know what to do."

Michael ignored him. "George, we're getting out of here right now. They'll be coming after us soon. I can carry you. It's just you and me now. " He picked the man up and eased him onto his shoulders. He staggered for a moment and then started off. It was nearly impossible, picking his way along the narrow trail in the dark. He fell twice before they came out of the woods and got up on the level grade but they were still alone. He had beaten Karsch to the rabbit hole and avoided the noose. All the while he kept talking, trying to keep George calm. George made responses for a while then grew quiet.

Michael went as fast as his load permitted along the tracks, cutting off the east end of the tailing piles and along the path around the lake. His back screamed in agony by the time they reached the little footbridge where he had picnicked with Mary. He stopped to rest and gently lowered Andrychine onto the handrail. The man was unconscious but still breathing. He checked the wound. The bleeding had stopped. Michael wondered if there was any left to spill. Much of what had come out of George's mouth was crusted over his face. Michael's hair and clothing were matted with it and he could smell its sweet, gamey odor. Except for the dried blood, George had no color at all in his face.

To the east, the sky was turning grey with the approaching dawn. In ten minutes, the shadows would become objects and someone would see them.

"We're almost home, partner," he breathed, picking up his helpless burden.

He didn't go home. It was too far, too late in the day. Instead, Michael crept through the alley alongside the laundry and, crossing quickly to the front of the building, pushed open the door. He heaved himself up the stairs with the last of his strength, his footsteps falling dull and heavy. At the landing he turned right and pounded the door urgently, waited ten seconds, and hit it again. Mr. Wong opened it. He was dressed in a heavily embroidered silk robe.

"Who is it?" Wong squinted for a moment. "Michael? Who is that with you?"

Michael pushed past him. "Mr. Wong," he groaned. "Help me. I need help."

Wong had already made that determination. "Come over here," he said, scurrying over to the sleeping alcove. "Put him on the bed."

"He's all bloody."

"All the more reason. Do not mind the blood. I own a laundry you know." Michael lowered George onto the down mattress and tried to straighten up. His knees buckled and he collapsed. From the floor he looked at Wong with desperate eyes.

"He's been shot, Mr. Wong. He needs a doctor." Wong was already bent over Andrychine, his head on the man's chest.

Michael tried to stand. "I'll go," said the new voice. He turned to see Mary standing in the open doorway. Wong straightened up. The sadness on his face told them. "There is no need, Mary. The doctor will not be necessary."

Michael turned back to Wong, incredulous. "He's dead, young Michael. His soul has fled his body."

Slowly, almost grateful that the ordeal had ended, Michael sank back onto his knees. He felt a rending in his heart and the courage that had sustained him also fled. He reached out and put his hands over Andrychine's. His head fell on the bed and he wept. "Oh, God. Oh, God in heaven, why?" He squeezed George's hand hard enough to break the bones, trying to make the dead man scream with pain, acknowledge life again, but the only pain felt was his own.

Wong put his hand on Michael's shoulder and squeezed in another way, trying to tell him it was over. He could let go now and mourn. Mary came over and stood next to him. Not knowing what else to do, she went to the sink and came back with a basin of water and began cleaning Andrychine's face.

A door opened and footsteps came down the hall. Libby stood in Wong's doorway for a moment before coming in. She quickly shut the door and stood in the middle of the room as if that was close enough to see but far enough to stay apart from it.

"He's dead," she said matter-of-factly. At the sound of her voice, Michael released his grip.

"How did it happen?" she asked, then answered her own question. "They shot him, didn't they?"

Michael looked at her and nodded dumbly.

"In the mine?" She came across the room. "You went down in the mine you stupid fools. I told you this would happen. How many times did I tell you? You ignored me and now this man is dead. Are you finally satisfied? You just created another martyr."

"Shut up!" Michael pushed himself off the floor. "Shut up! What do you know about it? You and your Wobblies brought on the strike. You started all this. You shut the mines down and brought on all the killing. You want to help? Get the hell out of here. Call a cop if you want. Just leave us alone." He covered his face and another groan escaped. "It didn't have to happen. They didn't have to shoot him for chrissake. All he wanted was a decent job and a house on a dry street. Was that too much?" He threw his head back. "He had children. A family for crissake." Michael fell silent except for the sobs that came from him."

Libby's voice still held no pity. "Who killed him, Michael? Karsch? The guards? Or was it a hero like you?" Or was it agitators like me, she thought but she chose not to share his guilt. She went to the door. "God have mercy on him. And on you, Michael Jensen." She walked out.

Wong mixed a glass of sweet-tasting liquid and made Michael drink it. He ran a bath while he went downstairs and came back with a clean change of clothes. When Michael came out of the bathroom he looked exhausted but the tension was gone from his face. Mary was still there. She had cleaned Andrychine and covered him with a sheet. His profile under the cloth gave a macabre aura to the room. It was filled with the smell of jasmine incense burning in front of a smiling Buddha. Mary wondered what he had to smile about.

Michael's eyes began to grow heavy. He paced for a while and then, like a dog circling a bedding place, collapsed into a chair. "I'm going to kill Karsch," he said. The words came out slowly.

Mary stared at him. "You're crazy to even think that. He isn't a man, Michael. He's a monster. He'll kill you."

"He can die and he has to."

"You saw what he did to Ruffcorn. He killed him with his bare hands. You have to let it go, Michael. He'll kill you, too. You know that."

"It isn't over until Karsch is dead." And she knew he was right.

Michael looked at the body. "We have to tell his family."

"We can't," Mary said. "We can't be associated with this."

He shook his head. "She has to know." But the Mr. Wong followed Mary's reasoning.

"Young Michael, if the family receives the news from us, it will lead the authorities back to you. Your own life will also be in jeopardy."

"But we can't just bury him."

"No," Mary agreed. "We can't do anything we should rightfully do. We have to do what is best for you now, not for him." Her words stung because she had layered them with her own anger. But she was right. They had to abandon George Andrychine.

"Do we just dump him somewhere? We can't do that."

Mr. Wong sighed and nodded. "It is the only way I'm afraid. You must take him back to the mine and have someone discover him there. They may think he acted alone."

In the end his protests gave way to their logic. Mary and Mr. Wong left for their work insisting that Michael stay in the room until the next evening. Libby came back once more and looked at George again and gave grudging approval to the plan but she refused to offer any comfort beyond that. In her eyes, her young hero had lost his luster. When he looked at her she saw only a pleading, helpless boy who had been caught in his mischief and was being made to pay a heavy price for it.

In the afternoon, the Mr. Wong brought him food that went untouched and when the sun was well down, Michael carried George out. Mary went with him. It was harder now; he could barely lift him. The adrenaline rush to save his life had been replaced by the onerous task of carrying the stiff, cold corpse through the darkened streets and out to the park. They laid George at the edge of the lake along the path and, with him, Michael left the last of his innocence.

He was too numb even to appreciate or thank Mary for the help she had given, too hurt to realize the love that fostered it, but when they came back to her apartment, he let her hold him like a child and cried in her arms.

The next day, two boys, while fishing, found the body and ran to their parents who went to the police. After an autopsy, Andrychine was placed in a coffin and delivered to his home.

Father Basil refused to bury Andrychine in the Catholic cemetery because he had died while committing a crime.

"I am sincerely disturbed by this, Mrs. Andrychine, but Canon Law is very explicit. It can't be done."

George's widow was stunned but not silent, not even to a member of the clergy. "I do not understand, Father. George can't be buried? Where shall he go? How can you refuse to bury a dead man?"

"He can be buried, of course, but just not in St. Marin's cemetery."

"But I do not understand. Why?"

Basil was a traditionalist and strictly adhering to the rigid church law made it that much easier, but not much. He was also human. He knew he could have remained silent and performed the service. No one in Rome would ever find out. But there was the possibility that his bishop might and bishops could be peculiar. He might even order the body exhumed and moved elsewhere. That would create a nasty scandal. Basil knew he would finish his pastoral ministry in Mammoth in four years, but his retirement would be in Duluth where such a blemish on his record would be the talk of the Chancery. It wasn't the proper way to wind up fifty years of priesthood. He knew he couldn't make her understand how the implications might affect his own future so he fell back on the law.

"Mrs. Andrychine, the church cemetery is sacred ground and… how can I put this… your husband's presence would desecrate that ground."

"Desecrate? What does that mean?"

"He died in the state of sin not grace. Mortal sin."

"She was livid. "George? He never sinned. Not once! He was a saint to me and the children. He was a friend to everyone. You ask anyone!"

"But your husband was destroying valuable private property in the act of crime when he died and that is a serious sin."

"Is it a sin to defend yourself against the devil?"

"Please, Mrs. Andrychine."

She was on her knees, begging him. "He gave. He gave twenty-five cents. Every Sunday he put that money in your collection plate even if it meant going without. You ask the ushers if he didn't."

"I'm sorry."

"You cannot do this! God cannot allow it."

"I speak for God." Nobody, knew Basil, no matter how generous, could buy for himself a place in God's kingdom.

In the end Fr. Basil stood like a rock on theological principle so George's friends carried the body out to the old settler's burial ground and laid him in a rocky grave. Michael was among the mourners as was Mary. He talked to no one nor did anyone speak with him, but he was seen by all who knew him as the one who had abandoned his friend to die. Only George's wife, prostrate with grief, passed close to him and when he reached out to touch her, she gave him a look of such hatred that he shrank back in alarm.

The town was silent and sullen. It was waiting for the next tragedy that was sure to follow, as everyone knew they always came in threes.

chapter 32

Karsch was timing it carefully, waiting until the Ore House was crowded with men. Libby Flynn was on a table rallying the dwindling believers with her usual rhetoric and promising, as usual, a triumphant and imminent end to their sufferings.

"Men! Never lose heart! Hear me now. Never let your spirits give up the light of resolve that guides you. You are the pioneers of a bold new movement, a movement that will melt the shackles of bondage that threaten to crush the dignity of all other noble workers throughout the world. Your commitment to the cause is already legendary. In cities throughout this country our citizens are reading of your exploits."

She produced a sheaf of clippings. "In New York, Pittsburg, Omaha and San Francisco they are reading about you and eagerly awaiting each new day's developments. From one end of the Iron Range to the other, the miners have joined arms in solidarity, solidarity that will endure hunger and cold and the inhuman indifference the owners have heaped upon you. They have refused to hear our demands but, rest assured, they know them well. The very heavens echo with our cries for a living wage and working conditions that will entertain life. Your children now grow up illiterate. That will change! Your babies die in infancy from needless diseases. That will change! Your friends are sacrificed to the dangers of poor management. That will change! And your wives are sentenced to keeping families together under the burden of widowhood and that must cease immediately. The next great victory will be ours and that must begin today! Even at this moment the final obstacles to our victorious struggle are being eliminated." She paused for the expected applause but her words were only met with a disturbing sullenness.

Katla jumped at the heavy pounding at the front door. "Good heavens, Sadie, run to answer that before they knock it down."

Ignoring the little girl, Karsch and three county deputies burst in and rushed into the parlor. Katla looked up from her sewing. She had never met Karsch, but she recognized the ugly man immediately and shivered in revulsion. She tried to say something about their poor manners but when she opened her mouth, the words died in her throat.

"Where is he?" Karsch demanded.

Sadie had crawled into Katla's lap. "Mama?"

"Sush, honey. It's all right." She stroked Sadie's hair, drawing from her the miraculous strength a child possesses. "What are you men doing here?"

One of the deputies spoke up. "We have a warrant for your son, ma'am. You have to tell us where he is. It's the law."

"I do not understand you. What is a warrant?"

"It says we have to arrest him, ma'am. The charge is murder."

Katla's hands flew to her face. She drew several deep breaths and then quietly sighed. Michael's misadventures had finally borne the bitter fruit she knew would come. Now he was being sought by the law and something in her said that neither God's justice nor a mother's pleading could protect him. Still, she uttered the words any mother would have. "He's not home."

Karsch had already pushed past her and headed for Michael's room upstairs, taking them two at a time.

Chapter 33

Michael opened his swollen eyes and slowly focused on the gray stonewalls and steel bars of the Itasca County jail in Grand Rapids. He lifted his head off the thin mattress. A bolt of pain tore through his head and he fell back letting out a small involuntary groan. He tenderly probed his scalp. It was a solid tapestry of bruises and cuts; swollen like a melon, stitched up like an old sock and wrapped in bloody bandages. His hand dropped to his stomach and stayed there until he fell into a fitful sleep.

His first awakening the previous night had been no less startling. He had heard the pounding on the door and the short angry words of Karsch. He jumped out of bed, prepared to go downstairs and confront him. An inner voice told him to run but he finally gave in to indecision and stayed in the safety of his bedroom. He heard the footsteps mount the stairs and hid behind the door. When they came in the room he attacked them, hitting the first man alongside his head. Then Karsch gave an order and they swarmed over him beating him unconscious with their night sticks. They carried him out the front door past the stricken Katla and the screaming Sadie and dumped him into the paddy wagon brought along for the purpose of confining a violent murderer.

"Jensen. Michael Jensen! Wake up. You've a visitor." The voice drifted in and out of his head and held him suspended between consciousness and sleep. He vaguely heard the scraping of the key in the lock and the metallic sliding back of the door.

"Are you sure he's okay?"

"Oh yeah, he'll live. The doctor came in and stitched him up last night. A couple bumps on the head is all."

"How did he get these 'bumps' as you call them?"

The jailer admitted John Keyes, slid the door shut and bolted it. "You'll have to take that up with the sheriff. Then he added indifferently. "Sometimes they come in peaceably, sometimes they don't."

Keyes insisted on a more satisfactory answer, but the jailer didn't care. "You have five minutes."

Keyes was unwavering. "As his legal representative, I have as much time as necessary to prepare his defense. If you have any problems with that, you can take that up with the sheriff."

The jailer shrugged. "Suit yourself. I go to lunch down the street in five minutes and then you have to wait an hour until I get back." Keyes nodded and then he was alone with Michael. He moved to the side of the cot.

He studied the beaten face. Both eyes were swollen almost shut; his lips were blue and swollen as were his ears. A black line of ragged stitches crossed Michael's forehead while a pink bandage covered more injuries on his scalp. Keyes guessed that he had been brought in close to death.

The lawyer pulled a three-legged stool over and sat down. "Michael. Michael, can you hear me?" He shook him gently. "Michael, please wake up."

Eyelids fluttered. The cracked lips parted and the garbled words escaped. "Who's... there?"

Christ, thought Keyes. Have they blinded him, too? Then Michael's eyelids parted and he looked at Keyes. "Who... Who are you?"

Keyes permitted himself a faint smile. "So, you are alive then. I generally have poor luck defending corpses. They've so little to say in their own defense."

Michael silently stared at him. Keyes cleared his throat and started again. "My name is John Keyes, Michael." While he talked, he dipped a cloth in a basin of water and patted it on Michael's wounds. "I'm an attorney. I was retained to defend you."

"Retained?"

"Yes. Retained. Hired? Occupied?"

Michael stiffened and John was pleased to see the spunkiness. "I know what that means. What are you defending me for?"

"Against, corrected Keyes. "They didn't tell you? No, you don't know, do you?"

"They didn't give me much time to ask."

Keyes stood up and walked over to the barred door as if his next statement would require more space between them. "Murder, Michael. They've charged you with the murder of George Andrychine."

When it finally registered, Mike moaned and turned his head to the wall. Incredible as it seemed, he knew that whatever the owners desired, they would find a way to effect. "I didn't kill George. George was my friend." Then he added in a whisper. "I left him but I didn't kill him."

Keyes sat down again. "I know that. You don't have to tell me. They know it too, but there's a law on the books, Michael. It says anyone involved in the commission of a crime during which a person is killed is just as guilty of the man's death as if he killed him himself."

"What crime did I commit?"

"Someone set fire to one of their steam shovels. Burned off the cab. Did a pretty good job of it I was told. That would be a felony. It qualifies."

"How do they know it was me that did it?"

"Let's just assume for the moment it was you, Michael. Who knew you were down there that night?"

Michael studied the lawyer carefully. He didn't know the man. He didn't know that he could trust him. All he knew about him was what Keyes had told him and now he was being asked to confess to a crime.

"Who hired you?"

"The Industrial Workers of the World."

"I asked who?"

Keyes flinched. "Specifically? Elizabeth Gurley Flynn."

Michael relaxed just a little. "Why?" He remembered how angry she had been at Wong's apartment.

"I honestly don't know why. Because you're a miner in trouble, I imagine. She didn't say. Just give him your best effort, she said."

"She was against the trouble I was causing. Said it hurt the rightness of the 'cause'. Dirtied her noble enterprise. Wanted me to stop." Michael screwed up his face. It hurt to talk so much. Then he remembered Karsch. "I couldn't stop."

Keyes rinsed and freshened the rag and touched it to Michael's face. He winced and pulled away.

"Don't. It doesn't help."

Keyes dropped the rag, folded his arms and waited. They stared at each other for a while, Keyes patiently, Michael defiantly. Finally the patience ran out and Keyes stood up to leave.

"Wait. Please."

Keyes sat down. "I have to know everything," he said and Michael told him.

"Yeah, I was there. George and I were there together. We torched the shovel all right and got out of the pit but they shot George at the rim. In the back. I carried him out. To the Chinaman's place."

"Chinaman's?"

"Mr. Wong. He owns the laundry on Main Street. He can't be involved."

"Why not?"

"Because he's a friend. I trusted him," Mike shrugged.

"When did George die?"

"I don't know. Sometime after the bridge. The little bridge over Skunk creek. I carried him around by the lake. I guess he died before we got to Mr. Wong's."

"Who saw you?"

"When?"

"At anytime that night. Who knew you were out there?"

Michael thought back to that night. "We were at the Ore House until it closed. But we didn't talk about anything."

"At all?"

"Well, yes. No. Not about going down that night."

"Are you sure?" Keyes pushed the point.

"I'm sure, dammit! What? Do you think we sit around and brag about this stuff?"

"I don't know. Do you?"

Michael softened. "No. We don't."

Keyes marched on. "What about later? At the mine?"

"It was dark and we blackened our faces."

"Did you talk? Might the guards have recognized your voices?"

Again Michael thought it through. "They were too far away. Two, three hundred feet." Then he remembered. "I yelled something to Karsch but... I don't know. Maybe he knew it was me. He's got it in for me anyway."

"Don't worry about that now. Placing a voice in the dark is guesswork and won't carry much weight in court. Go on. Who else?"

Michael retraced his path. "We went around the lake. It was still dark and I didn't see anyone."

"Could someone maybe standing in the shadows have seen you?"

"Sure, but we were quiet and I didn't see anyone myself. I don't know."

"You had a two-hundred pound man on your back, stumbling around in the dark and you were absolutely quiet?"

"George wasn't very chatty and I was too tired to sing."

"Accepted, Michael. The … uh, Mr. Wong was home?"

"He has an apartment above the laundry. We went there because it was the closest place."

"Was he alone?"

Michael forced a laugh. "You don't know him, do you?" Then another memory came to him. "He's got two boarders that came over from next door."

"Who?"

Libby Flynn and Mary Savich.

Keyes noted Michel's familiarity with Flynn's name. He also remembered Savich as working for John Fleming.

"What did they say or do?"

"Libby stayed just a minute. She was mad, said so, and left. Didn't want to get involved. Then she came back the next day for a few minutes. That's all."

"She didn't want to get involved," Keyes mused. "Still she sent me to you. Do you have a personal relationship with her?"

"What does that matter?"

"It's all relevant. Believe me. So, do you?"

Michael shut his eyes. "We did. Not anymore."

John forged ahead. "Miss Savich. She works in the mine office, doesn't she?"

Michael nodded. "Did you have a relationship with her also?"

Again Michael's guard went up. "Why are you asking this?"

Keyes shook his head at the stubbornness. "Mr. Jensen, all one has to do in Mammoth is to make a few inquiries. You ask the time of day and someone will be only too happy to build the proverbial watch for you. There are very few secrets in the privy and none in the bedroom as my father used to say."

Michael picked up the rag and wiped his mouth. "My father was like that." He dropped it back in the basin. "Well, if you know that much, then you know it wasn't much of a deal, Mary and me."

"I heard that also. I also heard that, as your interest waned, hers increased. John Fleming also carries a bit of a torch for her, I understand?"

"Other way around."

"So. Anyway, there seems to be quite a few torches burning out there and maybe someone got burned to the point they wanted to get even. I was just thinking that, anyway."

They were quiet for a time until Michael said, "I was pretty tired. Mr. Wong gave me a sleeping powder of some sort and I took a bath. I had his blood all over me. Mary stayed to clean up George and helped me carry him back the next night. I was pretty tired. I don't remember much."

"Back?"

"To the park where they found him. She said if I turned George in or told his wife, the police would have me."

"She was right. So now the whole town persecutes you for abandoning a dying comrade."

"Yes. I would if I was in their place."

Keyes pulled a sheet of paper out of his briefcase. He studied it quickly and went on. "Michael, the primary evidence in this case is circumstantial at best and it hinges on one piece of material property."

"What are you talking about? You lost me."

"They found a red kerchief, monogrammed with your name, on the body. It was stuffed in the wound, under his shirt. They claim it places you together at least sometime between Andrychine's shooting and his demise. In short, it puts you right in the middle of it all."

"I think I remember he borrowed it to blow his nose at the Ore House."

"So it was your handkerchief?"

"Someone made a copy of mine and put it there to make me look guilty. There's a lot of guys in town that don't like me so much."

"Better."

Michael slowly sat up. His head was swimming. They had to have taken the kerchief out of the wound to examine it and for sure to clean it. Mary was there all the time, a lot of the time when he was asleep. She had helped with the cleaning; done most of it herself. She had even helped carry the body back to the bridge. She had the opportunity and, as Keyes implied, a probable motive. It came together quickly and he voiced it in three words.

"That goddamn bitch!"

chapter 34

A grand jury was seated and met in the case of Michael Jensenice versus The State of Minnesota on August 1, four days after his arrest. It was held in Grand Rapids, the county seat, and because of that there weren't a lot of spectators, at least from Mammoth. Between the cost of travelling and the general animosity towards Michael, the locals stayed home and the public benches were peopled with the regulars that normally attended those public entertainments.

The prosecutor moved the deliberations along quickly. Karsch took the stand early to swear that he heard a voice that he positively could identify as Michael's. Yes, he would swear to it. The stiff, bloody kerchief was waved before the jury and duly entered. That's when Sadie started crying. Katla was a silent, ghostly presence during the entire ordeal, having been conditioned by her ancestry to expect and accept a life full of tragedies

Fleming and Savich were present, one as a company representative and one for personal reasons. Libby Flynn sat in the back, jammed next to the lugubrious little Lundquist in the one row that was filled to capacity. Of that internecine group as Lundquist referred to it, only Flynn went to the stand. She denounced the entire proceedings as a witch-hunt and a shameful waste of the taxpayer's money. She held up Michael as a symbol of the devastation being wrought on the miners and portrayed him as a puppet dangling helplessly over a fire of self-interest. In effect, she offered nothing of substance on Michael's behalf. It made good copy for the newspapers but had little effect on the grand jury. It took less than thirty minutes for the jurors to order Michael bound over for trial in the murder of George Andrychine.

"I have never in my life seen such a boldly pompous display of power mongering." Elizabeth Flynn was churning like a freighter though the tempestuous waters of the Itasca County legal system.

"Murder? Not just trespass? Not just misdemeanor damage to private property? Murder? Who in the name of God shot who? I ask you. Who? Do they own everything up here including the judges? The damned mining companies?"

"It was just a hearing, Miss Flynn. The trial, I assure you, will be quite a different affair." Lundquist was carving on a slab of roast beef. His words came out full of hope and promise but his plate gave him away. They had learned by now that when he was in a bad mood, he ate heartily and tonight his platter was full.

Keyes was the third member of the group that gathered for dinner at the restaurant in the Grand Rapids Hotel. He thrust his fork in a challenge to Lundquist. "I agree with you in principle, Mr. Lundquist. However, the case will eventually be tried on merit, not factional influences. On merit, I believe the evidence is wholly circumstantial and possibly heavily fabricated. I also believe Mr. Karsch would not hesitate to lie in order to implicate Michael even if it wasn't his voice he heard. It was his voice, of course, but you still can't convict a man on a lucky guess." Why, he wondered, should it be that those cornerstones of our value system should be so mutually exclusive?

"Well," Lundquist whimpered, "all I know is that Mr. Jensen merits the best effort you can make."

"Even at that," continued Keyes, "there's still the mystery witness to deal with."

"I beg your pardon?"

"Yes, Mr. Lundquist, there is a player yet to be announced; someone who knows what happened, maybe saw what happened, and perhaps, even went to the police with the information." He turned his attention to Libby. "Someone who somehow managed to plant Michael's red bandana, or a startling replica on Andrychine's body sometime after his death and before his discovery."

"The scoundrel! Who is he?"

Keyes laughed at Lundquist's outburst. "I don't know. There are only suspicions at the present. Perhaps Mary Savich. Or Mr. Wong. Or even Libby here. They all had access to the body. Or it could have been any number of people who knew about Michael's trademark kerchief and stumbled on Andrychine's body?"

Libby nodded and smiled vaguely. "It seems you still have much to investigate in the matter."

Lundquist's mouth was full of food but still he blurted, "I don't know about Savich or Wong, but you can rule out Libby here. The woman has devoted her life to the cause of mankind. She has no motive whatever." He put a comforting hand on Libby's forearm. She stared at it before bursting out with laughter at his unpretentiously forward manner.

"Exactly," reiterated Keyes, digging into his mashed potatoes. "No motive whatsoever that we are aware of."

Chapter 35

"**Over** here, dolly." The grating voice oozed out of the shadows between the two vacant houses. She knew it immediately as Karsch's. A shiver ran up her spine and she cautiously closed the distance between them to half. She wanted to stay out of the alley and in the open.

"What do you want?" Mary answered.

"I said come here, Miss Savich. I have a proposition for you and your Jensen friend."

"I would rather stay out here, thank you." She said it bravely but she was already shaking with freight.

He moved out of the darkness and was on her so fast she tripped in her attempt to step away from him. She drew her shawl tighter about her. He picked her up and pulled her into the alley. Mary shut her eyes and was about to scream but didn't. There was too much at stake.

His broken teeth flashed. "Damn it girl, now I got you all excited again, didn't I?" He was drunk again. He was always drunk now. "I don't mean to, at least not so soon. You know I have that effect on women."

She brought her hands up and curled them into trembling little fists. God, how she abhorred this man. If she had any alternatives, any at all, other than outright abandonment, she would never have come.

She had already gone to Fleming on Michael's behalf but Fleming, again, only distinguished himself by his frustrating predictability.

"Mary, it's out of my hands. We can't stand in the way of justice at this point."

"Justice? You call it justice? You mean injustice, don't you?" She said. "There is no evidence against him. None. He would never shoot a friend of his. What kind of stupid logic is that? Go arrest the man who fired the fatal shot. Go and have your Karsch arrested."

He gave her a damnable patient smile. "You understand the law as well as I, Mary. If he was even there and committing a crime, he is guilty. The little red bandana weighs heavily as evidence, Mary."

"You can buy them at the store by the dozens."

"Monogrammed?"

"You can buy needle and thread there also. Isn't this obvious to you? It was taken from Wong's and planted there to…!" She had said it without thinking and trapped herself.

"So you were there? That night?" he guessed correctly.

"Yes," she nodded. "I saw the body. At t Mr. Wong's. I helped him but the kerchief wasn't with the body at the park." She was sure of this because she had removed it herself when she cleaned the wound at the Chinaman's. She knew it had been put there later.

"You could testify to that, Mary." John suggested but he immediately rejected the idea. "No, that would only prove that he was there after all. It would implicate you and your, ah, friend also. No good. No good at all."

About as no good as your help, she thought. "No, telling the truth would serve no purpose now," she agreed sullenly.

"Mary, I'm sorry. I really am. There's nothing to do now but try to conceal the truth of the matter as much as possible to keep you out of it and let the jury decide his fate."

"So you can do nothing? You are unwilling to do anything?"

"No, there is nothing I can do. It's out of our hands now. It's in the courts." He looked away. "And I have more important matters to deal with right now, matters I still have some small measure of control over."

She despised him for saying it as well as for his unwillingness to take a hand in the matter. But, after brooding over it, she realized how powerless he really was and her anger simmered to a kind of pity that such a remarkably capable man should have been so easily cuckolded by men less intelligent and competent than he. That was why she was willing to arrange a meeting with the one man who might control the situation, knowing how difficult it would be to control him.

How cold she felt, how desperately alone. She had no power now but prayer.

"Free him," she begged.

Karsch feigned surprise. "Free him? Your miner? How can I?"

She had had enough of his abuse. "You can do it! You said you heard his voice. You were mistaken. Recant your testimony."

"I don't think so."

"Rethink it. Please. Michael is not a murderer and you know that."

"Why should I?"

"The kerchief won't stand up by itself. People lose them all the time. They borrow them. They…"

"Stuff them in bullet holes."

Mary stiffened and played her final card. "I'll swear he wasn't with Andrychine that night. I'll…" she hesitated. To even voice this cheapened her. "I'll swear in court that he was with me that night."

Karsch exploded in laughter so cruel that she finally broke out in tears. They washed over her like a wave, a final blow to her courage.

"Savich," he said. "I can find twenty men willing to swear that they saw Jensen carry Andrychine away from the mine. I can produce ten men that will swear they saw him drop the body in Lake Park. I can produce five men that will swear they had spent the night with you although the price for that will be admittedly higher. I can guarantee that your lover will hang and, if not hang, then waste his life in a prison cell."

Her knees gave way and she slumped to the ground sobbing. The suddenness of it caused Karsch to look around. The streets were empty. He picked her up like a grownup grasps a child about the shoulders. He pushed her up against a wall until the sobbing dropped to a low whimper. Then he pressed his mouth close to her ear.

"Or," his breath heavy with sour whiskey, "I can get a hearing problem if it will help your boyfriend."

His words sunk in slowly and she answered just as slowly.

"You would do that? Why?"

He exhaled slowly and paused between each word. "I will make you a trade." His lust was dripping from every word. "I want to bed you, woman. It's that simple."

Coming from any other man, it would have seemed ridiculous, but hearing Karsch say it almost stopped her heart and having to deal with it nearly killed her.

"I know you hate me, Savich. You hate my guts, what I do, every-thing about me. They all hate me, even my deputies. I can live with that. I hate them too and I get by because there are men that pay me well to do it. Don't act smug. You're no different. Understand me? They hate you too because you refuse to be like them. You won't share their filthy misery. See? You're just like me, Mary Savich. You take the best of what life gives you and then steal a little bit more than you deserve because you're as greedy as the rest of us."

He was talking fast, trying to wear her down before she screamed in panic and tried to rip his face off which he knew she wanted to. He was still holding her face against the wall. "But, listen now. When I strike a bargain, I keep my word. Ask anyone. And I can keep a confidence."

Mistaking her silence for no, he went on. "You ain't no virgin, Mary. You and I both know it. You're a bitch and I'm a bastard. You got looks and I'm as ugly as sin but in a dark room there ain't no difference between me and pretty boy Fleming. One night, one time. For his life. And another thing, you make him promise to stay away from the pit. Stay home and let things go their own way. If I see him anywhere close to the mine again, I'll kill him for sure. Wherever I lay eyes on him, he's dead." He let her digest this for a moment but not too long.

"Deal? Or maybe death. Or don't you care enough?"

She was trying to think. Her mind was racing, trying to find another alternative. To save the life of the man who had rejected her? She had used Michael for her own misadventures but they were more mischievous than devious. The thought of Karsch laying on her, pressing his smelly body against hers, putting his gross saliva in her mouth and forcing himself into her? She shook her head, praying that when she looked up he'd be gone. Karsch thought she was saying no and shook her hard. His hand slid around until it found and squeezed her breast. The vomiting would come later. She couldn't look at him and could barely force out the word. But it did come.

"Yes."

Chapter 36

"That's what I said, Masterton. I'm changing my story."

"That's what the hell I thought you said." Masterton's face was rigid with anger. "What I want to know is why? Why are you letting this man go? If we convict and ship him out of here it'll put God's own fear into any other man who thinks of harming Mammoth again."

"I decided I can't positively swear it was Jensen up on the rim."

"You could last week! You could three days ago!" Masterton had run out of patience. "Is your mind so full of shit it can't hold that single thought until we… the jury finds him guilty?"

Karsch took the insult without flinching. "There was a lot of voices that night, a lot of gunshots. It echoes bad down there. I can't rightful come down on a man who may be innocent now can I?"

"Aw, crap. When did the truth ever stop you?"

Fleming had been watching them spar. This had been their campaign from the start, Karsch's and Masterton's, and his own opinion had never made any impact. Now it was nice to see Karsch on the grill and nicer still to see Masterton so distraught. He wasn't expecting it when Masterton suddenly turned on him.

"Fleming! Did you have anything to do with this?" Karsch turned to the window, to his private thoughts. Fleming was tempted to avoid his wrath with a simple no. Whatever made Karsch change his testimony, he seem determined and content to stick by it. He could let it go at that. Still, for Jensen's sake, he felt compelled to say more. Jensen had stuck with the Mammoth long after the others had walked out. He had a proven loyalty up to a point. And then there was the thing between he and Mary Savich. Whatever she was looking for, he wished her the best. She was on her own now. So, amazingly, he backed up Karsch, a man he openly hated. But then, everyone hated Karsch.

"No sir, I don't know what changed his thinking but I think we can turn it to the mine's advantage."

"What in the hell are you talking about, Fleming?"

Fleming tried to sound as logical as possible. "Well sir, there is still enough evidence that Jensen will likely be convicted. Much of it circumstantial to be sure; no smoking gun so to speak, but still enough. If this happens it will be based on the State's evidence not our testimony. The kerchief, no alibi, blood on his clothing, a history of depression, anger, etc. The mine won't be personally associated in the prosecution; the town can't hold any rancor toward us. They'll see you as a man of fairness and integrity," he lied, "and Mammoth as a victim of Jensen's destructive tendencies. And if he isn't convicted, it will still put such a scare into everyone that only a fool would dare try such a thing again."

Masterton ran his fingers through his hair. He didn't know what all testimony had been lined up against this Michael Jensen, but he had heard the rumors of a surprise witness that could tie him solidly to the crime. Yes, it had certain logic all right. There were as many Mammoth residents who sided against the strikers as with them. Logically it seemed that no more harm could be added to that already done.

"Oh, yes. Only a fool, indeed, John. Mammoth seems to be nothing but fools. I don't know." His disloyal employees outnumbered him. "I've got a palooka known for his guts who's turned gutless on me, and a gutless manager who's suddenly found the guts to stick up for him. And what if he does get off?"

Karsch growled, "Oh, he'll try to get back at us. Revenge is a powerful motive and I've already fixed that. I'll still get him for you, Masterton. In my way, I will. That I will swear to."

Masterton shook his head, "I don't want to hear any more about this, but let me know how it turns out."

Chapter 37

The trial began at eight in the morning in the courtroom of Judge Harvard L. Molde. By three that afternoon, the jury had gone into deliberation and an hour later returned their verdict.

True to his promise, Karsch had taken the stand and slowly but emphatically backed away from his earlier version of that night. After five minutes of badgering, the frustrated prosecutor grew weary, threw up his hands. "Your honor, I don't know who or what was able to change the witnesses testimony but he can no longer be heard on behalf of the prosecution. I'm dismissing him as a hostile witness. I have no further questions. Your witness, now, I believe, Mr. Keyes."

Keyes smiled and simply said, "Thank you, Mr. Karsch. I have no questions."

The bandana had been the most damaging piece of evidence offered but it never had too much impact. The judge excused Sadie, as a minor, from testifying as to its origin so it was never explicitly identified as belonging to Michael. The implication was duly made but the defense attorney countered by arguing that anyone could embroider a kerchief with any name and there were any number of young women who might have the temerity to make such an item for Michael without having the courage to actually give it to him. That drew a relaxing round of laughter from the gallery but not as loud as when twenty friends of the Jensen's suddenly pulled out red embroidered handkerchiefs and tied them around their necks.

Keyes garnered more points when he noted that there were also any number of angry men who might have planted one on the expired body and that drew a murmur of agreement.

Keyes scored again right after lunch when the prosecutor asked if Michael might be willing to take the stand to clarify the ownership of that particular red bandana. Keyes gallantly suggested that only a man of great insensitivity would risk losing the favors of many women for the sake of recognizing the sewing capabilities of one. Michael stood by his constitutional rights and remained mute.

The prosecution paraded a number of disgruntled miners and mine employees who testified to overhearing Jensen talk of forays into the mine and substantiated his close relationship with Andrychine. Kiril's death and the vendetta motive were developed quickly and convincingly. Even John Fleming spoke of the animosity between Karsch and Jensen, which might have led him to his despicable actions. Everyone the state called spoke of seeing a red bandanna around his neck that he would proudly attribute to his little sister. As the day wore on any impartial observer could sense the ebb and flow of the jury's inclinations.

The prosecutor was already sorting through the notes of his closing argument when John Keyes announced his final witness, the surprise witness that everyone expected to testify for the other side.

"Your honor, I call Mary Savich to the stand."

The prosecutor jumped to his feet. "I object, your honor. I have not been given previous notification of this witness and the opportunity to prepare for her testimony."

Judge Molde took out his pocket watch and noted the time. It was coming on to dinner and his wife, an exceptional cook was making chicken and dumplings for dinner. "Overruled. You may call your witness, Mr. Keyes."

The bailiff swore her in. "State your name, please."

"Mary Savich."

Keyes approached her. "Thank you, Miss Savich. Would you please tell the court what your position is with Mammoth Mines?"

"I work in the office as a personal secretary to John Fleming."

"And your relationship with Michael Jensen."

"We're… friends. Just friends."

"Just friends?"

"Yes." Her head was down, her fingers nervously teasing the lacy edge of her hanky. Whatever had possessed her to do this? In front of her sat an ashen-faced Michael. Was she about to betray him? She had already done it once, was she here now to drive the final nail? No, that made no sense. She was Keyes' witness, not the State's.

Keyes asked the question. "Could you shed some light as to Michael Jensen's whereabouts on the night of George Andrychine"s death?"

She looked at Michael. His eyes were filled with questions, hers with tears and love.

"Miss Savich?"

She gave a start. "I can. Michael was with me that night."

"You were together then?" Keyes rephrased the question.

"Yes."

"For how long?"

"From the time Michael left the Ore House until he left to go home the following morning."

The courthouse burst into a rumble of voices and Molde's gavel crashed down on the stand. "Order! I caution you to keep order in my court."

"And exactly where were you and Michael? Surely not in the Mammoth mine pit burning steam shovels?"

She spoke in a barely audible whisper, her words quickly lost in the gasps of the gallery. "No. We were in my room. All night."

That simple sentence got Judge Molde home in plenty of time for his dumplings that evening and netted him the entire next day off for some bass fishing.

chapter 38

"**Why** did she do it? Why did she destroy her reputation by saying that?" Jensen asked Keyes over a quiet celebratory dinner.

Keyes shrugged. "If you don't know the answer to that, then I can't help you. I'm an attorney not a psychologist."

Lundquist was wolfing down his supper and spoke through gopher puffy cheeks. "Guilt? Maybe she realized this thing had gotten out of hand and she couldn't live with the guilt."

Michael didn't buy that. "Then why did she turn me in to begin with?"

"Did she turn you in? If you believe that, why don't you ask her?" Suggested Keyes.

"I would advise you not to go near that woman," Libby cautioned.

Michael flashed his first smile in a long while. "Jealous are you?"

Libby put her hand over his. "We can talk about that later." They did, in between their lovemaking that began anew with his freedom and redemption and, although it was good, the very intensity of it told Michael that is was more of a farewell than a new start.

A quiet truce bound up by Karsch's recantation and Michael's close brush with a hangman's rope held for a week and, with it, the strike violence went elsewhere.

"Any news, Mr. Wong?"

"Yes, young Michael. In Cohasset, an engineer for the Armco mine was awakened in the middle of the night by noises coming from his garage. When he ran out there he found his car on blocks, the tires gone. He followed their trail in the grass to an open field and found the tires. When he returned to his house, the garage blew up."

"Well, at least he *had* owned a car."

"Seven Chisholm woman were arrested for throwing rocks at a car full of mining company executives."

"The Chisholm men never could throw worth a damn."

"By August 22, over three thousand miners have left the district, many of them Wobblie sympathizers who have run out of patience."

"Who wouldn't run out of patience? They got tired of just sitting on their butts watching scabs take their jobs and steal their paychecks."

"Martin Teljer. Did he ever arrest you, Michael?" asked Mr. Wong. "The Hibbing chief of the Oliver police was stabbed four times when a riot broke out at the Seiler pit. Many men were arrested, many injured."

"At least they didn't make their women fight for them."

The papers are full of talk opposing the miners, Michael. They have very few friends."

"Sure. All the newspapers have sided with the owner bastards. The priests and lawyers, too. They all want to sleep with the wolves. They think the miners are all German immigrants conspiring with the Kaiser. All except Mr. Keyes, anyway."

"Ah, a good man, John Keyes. But the others, they just want it to end I think. That is all. It is good that you are out of it."

"I'm done because the judge told me to be done."

"He gave you good counsel."

"It's wrong, if you ask me."

"So are many things people are doing in the name of justice."

"Judas Christopher! Now you're talking like my mother."

Perhaps if I had listened to my mother, I would still be in San Francisco sweeping gutters, thought Wong. They were alone, yet Michael moved even closer to confide something to him.

"Mr. Wong, I didn't thank you. You could have gotten in big trouble, too."

"Oh, yes," Wong nodded eagerly. "There is much prejudice against people from other countries. Especially the orient. I am very grateful to be an American even if others don't think me so." He winked at Michael. "I think we dodged a bullet in several ways."

"Barely." Michael smiled back at him and then became serious again. "There would have been no trouble if that woman hadn't gotten me arrested." The thought of her deceit made him grimace with anger.

Wong clucked his tongue and in a gesture strange for him, he grabbed Michael's arm and shook him gently. "Be wary, Michael. Youth may be the cause of much stupidity but it is not a justification for it."

"What?" Michael pulled away but Wong pursued him.

"Michael, forgive my honest approach, but you are often a mule in your thinking. You have made judgments based on the weakest of facts and ignore the obvious good things Miss Savich has done as being suspect and motivated by her own interest."

"What in the hell are you talking about, Mr. Wong?"

"Who, Mr. Jensenice. Who. Like the wise old owl. Miss Savich, your comely heroine who lied for you. You wonder why? I begin to wonder myself if you have no clue as to the mysteries of love. I do know that love can never beget betrayal."

Michael stared at him in stupefaction.

"Michael, I confess, when you knew why you did what you did and everyone disapproved, you were more the man than now when you do not know why you act even though everyone nods their heads and say, 'Michael. Now that's a good boy'" Then Wong dismissed him. "You must excuse me now, Mr. Michael. I have a pot roast in the oven and must baste it." A second later all that was left of Mr. Wong was the soft padding of his sandals on the stairs.

Chapter 40

Libby was one of those who thought Michael a good boy and, in recognition of his good deportment, she continued to take him as her lover as she was available. He accepted her on those terms because they were all she offered and the best he had available but the suppleness of their lovemaking had begun to grow dry and routine. It was over but, like any metamorphic process, the change was so slow that, at times, it seemed there was no change at all. Then one day Michael realized he hadn't seen her for a week and that was how it eventually ended.

Libby's cause was not only going poorly but was about to come to an end. Tresca, Heywood and the others, originally charged with murder, pleaded guilty to a lesser charge of instigating a riot and were clapped in Duluth jails for ninety days. In a bizarre show of lack of support, the national I.W.W. headquarters refused to send replacements because they decided to keep the incarcerated men on the payroll. Libby visited them and asked for their temporary resignations but, being family men, they didn't want to give up the income. This left her virtually alone and required so much travel up and down the Range that she had come to see Michael less and less often and, when she did, her disposition was so fitful and ill-tempered that the lovemaking became little more than rutting.

On one occasion, the last time the two were to be physically involved, Michael left her room in a huff. He passed Mary on the landing. Their eyes met for a moment and then parted. Mary clutched at her handbag while Michael hastily finished buttoning his shirt and then she rushed past him down the stairs. But they had been close enough for him to feel her warmth and for her to tingle at the scent he still exuded from his lovemaking. He told himself later he would have spoken, given time, but in his confusion and embarrassment he couldn't.

He spent most of the next day memorizing a couplet from Hamlet, the better to be prepared for their next meeting and oblivious to the events which were about to shatter the fragile truce.

The following week, the I.W.W. removed Flynn from her responsibilities because of her generally poor management of the strike and her specifically poor performance in the defense of her cohorts in their trial. She hurriedly packed her bags, said goodbye to no one, and left town on the morning Greyhound bus.

Chapter 41

On August 30, Michael was taking his breakfast with Katla and Sadie. The house seemed cavernous with just the three of them. The table talk was quiet and sporadic, filled with trivial observations and courtesies. Several replacement miners had inquired about renting rooms but Katla turned them away rather than provoke her son further. She was basically satisfied. They lived frugally, only occasionally dipping into one of her cash reserves to keep the store accounts current. In addition to her splendid garden, her little hen house held fifty young pullets that were coming up to roasting size. Michael, when not lost in his moping, was spending precious time with Sadie and that brought him a goodly amount of favor with his mother.

"I told them you were only doing it because they made you, Mikie," Sadie volunteered through bites of jelly bread.

"Who? Do what?" he asked.

She took a big swallow of milk and caught her breath. "I told Theresa and Margaret that you stayed home and helped in the garden instead of fighting with the miners because otherwise the judge would lock you up again."

Michael nodded abstractly. "Un-huh"

"I told them you weren't afraid. I made them take back what they said about you being afraid."

Michael watched her intently and he wasn't smiling. Sadie thought he was going to beat up her friends so she began to defend them. "Mikie, don't be mad at them. I think they just heard that stuff from their papas."

Michael sighed and pushed back his chair.

"You haven't finished," Katla said.

"I've had enough, mama. It was good."

"Where are you going?" Her brow creased with concern.

"Out back, to work in the garden, like a good boy." The screen door slammed behind him. Sadie jumped up.

"And you, my little troublemaker?" Katla asked.

"I'm going out with Mikie."

"No." Katla steered her away from the door. "Leave your brother alone for awhile. He has to think."

"Can I go play with Theresa?"

"All right, Sadie, but no more talk about your brother. Do you understand?"

"Yes, mama."

"And don't get your dress dirty. I just washed it."

Katla watched through the window as Michael grabbed the hoe and chopped in a disinterested manner at some encroaching purslane. He worked his way to the end of a cabbage row and stopped in front of the granite boulder. She saw him stare at the hoe as if it had just dropped out of the sky. He let it fall and sat on the rock, tracing his fingers over the name Kiril had carved.

Chapter 42

Fleming picked up the envelope that Mary had placed in front of him. What's this?"

She had already started out of the office. "I thought I'd save you the trouble of letting me go."

"What? Is this a resignation?"

She nodded.

He read it, then carefully put it back in the envelope and handed it back to her. "I can't accept this." She began to protest. "I don't want it, Mary. It isn't necessary."

"Oh, yes it is, John. For me it is necessary. A woman is only allowed one reputation per town."

He wanted to tell her it didn't matter, that he still wanted her and would protect her, but he couldn't because he knew it was over between them. Instead he tried to meet her halfway.

"Listen, Mary. What happened between you and Jensen doesn't have to ruin your life. If…"

She put her hand over his mouth and, when she spoke, a glimmer of her former self came out.

"John, don't be such a fool. There was nothing between Michael and me. It didn't happen."

His mouth opened slowly.

"I lied," she said.

"But why?"

She shook her head at his thick headedness. "If you could only understand something so simple as that, maybe things would have been different between us. Maybe I would still think I was in love with you." It was the way he looked at her then. "No, not again. Not anymore," she said with finality.

"But if you did this for Jensen, he must know how you feel."

"Michael is still a child.." She shook her head. "Nothing had worked out the way it should have. I have to get out of here. I'm leaving Mammoth on Saturday. That should give you time to find a replacement."

He didn't know what more to say. His silence was taken for assent but Mary wasn't quite finished.

"I'd like to make one more request, please."

He look up and quickly agreed. "Yes?"

"Make arrangements to meet Mr. Karsch somewhere other than here."

Fleming's eyes darkened. They reminded Mary of a small dog she once had that defended its chewed-up bones so courageously.

"Has he bothered you again? Has he touched you?"

Then she grew tired of the martyrdom.

"Oh, you fool. You pampered, high-born, over-civilized fool! Haven't you seen through it yet?"

His voice rose reflexively. "What are you talking about?"

"Why do you think he changed his testimony? Why do you think he's been so openly abusive since the trial?" She wanted to cry now. "Why do you think I'm so joyless at the freedom of a man you presume to be my love?"

Fleming's face was a big question mark.

"Do you want to know who my latest lover was? Do you want to know who I most recently and painfully took to my bed? Do you?"

"No."

"Can't you guess, John?"

"Mary, for god's sake."

"Yes! I bought Michael's freedom by bedding your man Karsch! Masterton's trained ape. Do you want to know what it was like? Good? Better than you? Aren't you wondering even a little bit?" Drained of all her rancor, she slumped into a chair.

He came around his desk.

"God, Mary. Not him!" He tried to pull her into his arms but she brought up her hands and waved him off.

"No! Don't touch me! Ever!" She still wasn't crying. Her agony had gone beyond tears. Fleming stood helplessly while her pain poured out of her. Finally she gathered her shattered dignity like an old woman gleaning straw in a barren field and stood up.

"I… am still a lady, after all." She walked into the front office. Fleming followed her timidly. He would have still tried to comfort her but the outer door opened and Anson Peterson, his transfer agent, burst in.

"Mr. Fleming. Thank god you are here." The man was nearly as agitated as Mary had been. His face was flushed and he was greatly winded.

"Peterson, what is it?"

"You have to come quick, sir. There's been a shooting."

"Where?"

"Zenith," gasped Peterson. "The mine police just shot a little girl."

Chapter 43

Four Mammoth mine deputies had gone into Zenith, in direct violation of Sheriff Meinie's orders, to confiscate a rifle. Alphonse Trebal, a militant, had an old Spencer carbine and, being broke and desperate, was making noises about using it against the deputies. When the threats got to Karsch, he had sent out his cops.

They got there ready for a confrontation and were surprised when Alphonse met them at the door and invited them onto the porch. They refused the cup of barley coffee he offered, but demanded the right to search the house. When Alphonse stood on his legal rights to keep them out, they shouldered past him into the little four-room frame building. His wife and two young sons were cowering in the corner of the tiny parlor and presented such a tragic picture that they stayed away from them. Had they been less polite and more careful in their search, they would have been alerted by the family's very cohesiveness. They would have become alarmed by the hatred in the woman's eyes and, perhaps, discovered the rifle hidden under her skirt. They were done in by their own compassion.

They left the house, passed through the crowd of curious neighbors and were about a hundred fifty feet down the rutted street when she came running out on the front porch screaming, "You bastard killers," and began firing in their direction. The police captain whirled around and, seeing the crazed woman and her wild shooting, shouted to his men, "Men, don't shoot! For God's sake, don't shoot that woman." Then a poorly aimed bullet struck a deputy, passing through the flesh between his thumb and forefinger. The man fell to the ground, largely in fright, but Alphonse thought his woman had killed someone and that cast the final dice against them.

He rushed out the front door and grabbed the rifle from his wife, waved it at the police and yelled, "Yah, you got yours, now get the hell out of here!" Whether he actually aimed the weapon at them or only held it out to show he was in control of it became inconsequential. He, being just a man, and a striking miner at that, the deputies opened fire with their pistols and Alphonse began to fire back in self-defense. The crowd, caught in their crossfire, scattered, falling over each other in panic.

It was long range for the .38 caliber pistols and their six-inch barrels but with four men giving it all they had, the bullets eventually found the mark. Alphonse took bullets in his neck, chest and both legs. It was one of the leg wounds that toppled him off the porch. He got back on his feet and, for a moment, stood with the onlookers, ready to trade shots, but the police had cut the distance by half and one well-placed bullet struck him just below the left eye and he fell dead.

Eight feet away lay Sadie Jensen, a dark-red stain slowly spreading over the front of her newly laundered dress.

Two blocks away, Michael had heard the gunfire and ran out through his back yard. Gripped by a sense of dread he vaulted several fences and broke through another. He passed the mine police who were running from the scene and got to Sadie first.

"Sadie! God no, Sadie! Sadie!" He put an arm under her and a hand over the spreading red stain. She was unconscious. He picked her up, held her tight, and ran off to the hospital.

By the time Fleming arrived, the people of Zenith were in a seething uproar.

"You did this, Fleming. You and your goons. Our men haven't quit protesting so now you're killing them. And children, too!" They wanted to do him likewise but Karsch came up and protected him. John was stricken with a rage of his own. He wanted to scream back at them that the deputies weren't his men but he knew they were.

Mary had seen Michael running with Sadie through Mammoth and was already waiting in the treatment room. Michael had squatted down in a corner, his head in his hands and mumbling unintelligibly to himself. She watched him, a man adrift again, caught in another situation beyond his control. He wanted to scream at someone, to assign guilt and mete out a violent punishment but when he finally looked up and saw her he just sighed heavily and shook his head. Eventually he stood up.

"I've got to tell Mama. Maybe she already knows and I have to be there. But I can't leave Sadie."

"I'll stay until you get back," she said. Michael didn't object. Then she went up to him until she was so close he could see deep into her eyes. They were filled with tears. She tried to speak but there was so much to say she couldn't say anything. They stood like that for a time and then he edged past her. In doing so he found his hand in hers. He held it for a moment in a way that said everything he felt in his heart, then he hurried home.

Chapter 44

It was getting into the evening with a sun setting behind tall thunderheads from the northwest. Michael, amazed at the speed of his mother, hurried back to the doctor with Katla to find Sadie still alive but in severe distress. The bullet had passed through her between her heart and lung, miraculously missing both but causing heavy hemorrhaging and she lost a lot of blood, so much so that Doctor McKenzie was unable to render a prognosis until the next morning assuming Sadie survived the night.

He was too busy to offer more than that. He also had the deputy to patch up and Alphonse's body to examine. The authorities would want to know which wound had caused his death. That he was shot to death was not in question. That took only a few minutes of arbitrary examination but, as a medical examiner, it was worth five dollars to him and he didn't want to cheat the County out of its money.

After dark, when rain began falling, Michael finally left Katla in Mary's care and went back to the house. He carefully, almost reverently washed Sadie's blood off his hands and changed into dark clothing. He forced down some food, threw on a rain slicker and went out on the back porch. He sat there and stared at the garden for four hours, watching the rain increase in intensity until the granite rock was only visible whenever a bolt of lightening crossed the sky. Finally he stood up and turned to the night.

"For you, Kiril," he whispered. "And Sadie. And Papa. What I am doing, I do for you."

Katla was also whispering on her knees beside Sadie's bed. "Papa," she prayed, "Go to Jesus. Go to Him right now on your knees and tell him to give us a miracle. We never bothered him before but this we must have. I don't want to live without my little Sadie girl. Go to Him!"

"Mama, don't you know? I have been with Him all day."

Michael went alone this time; first down to one of the mine shops off First Avenue, the street that separated Zenith from the mine facilities. With a crowbar he forced a window, crawled in and stole a length of rope. Dropping it out the window, he took a small drum of kerosene and balanced it on edge with a small cord hung from a rafter. The cord ran around a post and back out in front of the barrel and through a notch cut in a miner's candle. Michael lit the candle and watched to make sure it was burning well. In an hour it would burn through the cord, tipping the kerosene over the flame and set the warehouse ablaze. He wanted a big fire to make a nice diversion.

Masterton and Karsch were having it out with Sheriff Meinie in Fleming's office. Meinie was standing in the center of the room, legs spread and neck bowed forward like the bull he was. He had gotten the call and came down on his motorcycle immediately. Standing there in knee-high leather boots, dark-green jodhpurs, leather helmet and his brown leather John Browne belt with holstered revolver, he was a man to be reckoned with. His face was screwed up in a fierce scowl hung over by a walrus-sized handlebar moustache and he was bellowing.

"Listen here and listen good, Masterton. I don't give a good crap who the hell you are. I've had enough of your vigilante shit. It stops here and it stops tonight. If not, I'll throw the whole lot of you in my jail. Am I making myself clear?"

Masterton, torn between confrontation and appeasement, chose the latter. "Now, Joe, let's not blow this out of proportion. It was an accident, just a tragic accident."

"Accident? I'll give you proportion, mister. You kill a miner, you probably kill a little girl, that's a hellava proportion."

"Go easy, Joe. Truth is, we don't know who shot the girl. Could have been that Czeck." Then he cut off Meinie's next blast and, in doing so, abandoned his conciliatory tone. "This is an election year, Sheriff, and you aren't going to get elected by any immigrant miners. Remember who pays for all your pretty posters and ice cream socials."

Masterton had woefully underestimated the extent of Meinie's anger, anger and the fear that his jurisdiction might be taken over

by a regiment of National Guard soldiers and martial law. He got
the message when Meinie stepped up to him and grabbed him
by his lapels. Karsch made a move but a sharp look from Meinie
stopped him. He turned back to Masterton.

"Listen and listen well, Bart. I get paid to protect people. Rich
people, poor people, voters, drifters, they're all the same in my
book. I don't make political promises. I only uphold the law. And
that law applies to your damn 'cops', too. You understand me?" He
loosened his grip. Masterton had flushed scarlet and was sweating
heavily. Karsch cut in.

"We're the law here, Sheriff. You deputized us."

Meinie turned and shot a finger at him. "I never did like you,
mister. Especially I don't like trash like you calling yourselves police
officers. I made a mistake. That's all through now. You've just been
de-deputized." Karsch's eyes narrowed into slits. They reminded
Meinie of pig's eyes, the mean little razorbacks he had gown up
with on the farm. It occurred to him that Karsch could be mean
enough to come at him right in Fleming's office. I'll have to shoot
the bastard if he does, he thought. He'll kill me if I don't. But when
Meinie spoke again, it drew the attention away from a showdown
even though his eyes never left Karsch.

"What are you saying, Meinie," Masterton asked.

"I said just what you heard, Masterton. As of right now your
mine police are nothing more than security men. They take their
authority off your property, I'll run 'em in. They shoot unarmed
men, even if they catch them in your toilet, I'll charge them with
murder. I want all their weapons turned in and locked up." This
time he didn't have to ask if his message was understood. The slack
in Masterton's jaw told him it was.

"Good," Meinie said in self-confirmation. "Good." He nodded
twice, looking them over once more for good measure. He threw
on his slicker and left. Over the rain they heard his cycle roar to
life and he was gone.

Masterton looked around the room, cursing the Sheriff under
his breath. Fleming was there, too. He had been satisfied to sit at
his desk quietly the whole time. His only desire had been to convey
to Meinie somehow that he wasn't really one of them. He stood
now. Masterton turned on him.

"A couple of worthless traitors you are. Hell of a lot of help you were, Fleming."

John Fleming cleared his throat as if he were about to deliver a speech. It was a short one. "What do you want me to say? The girl drew first?"

Karsch smiled at Fleming's audacity. Masterton was tempted to hit him but he had enough of fighting for the time being. Fleming was almost disappointed. During Meinie's tirade he had been writing his resignation but now he needed a little more goading to get up the nerve to deliver it. He was about to say something that might provide it when the phone rang. Fleming picked it up, listened and hung up.

"Karsch, that was the watch house. You might want to take a look outside."

Karsch went to the window and peered out. Rain was still pelting the glass.

"Down by the stores," Fleming said. "Warehouse #3 is burning."

"Stupid fool," Karsch muttered, his nose pressed comically against the glass. "Trying to torch buildings in the rain."

"Do you blame them?" Fleming said. "They had a rough day. If the Jensen girl dies, we'll be fighting a war tomorrow."

"What'd you say?" Karsch whirled around.

"I said if…"

"You said Jensen girl. Michael Jensen the driller?"

"His sister, Sadie. Why?" But Karsch had already turned back to the window. The flames were licking through the roof of the warehouse, fighting against the downpour. He watched the shadowy forms of his men running back and forth in its light.

"So, Jensen," he whispered. "You broke your promise, haven't you? It took bedding your girl and shooting your sister to draw you out, huh? Now I can keep my promise." Throwing on a raincoat he went outside, grabbed a torch and headed for the pit.

Chapter 45

Michael threw his coil of rope over the rim and started down. He ran short of line ten feet from the bottom, but that didn't stop him. He pushed off the wall, and dropped in. He looked back towards the top, invisible now, and knew he'd need to find another way out.

He ran across the bottom unconcerned about discovery. The rain made him nearly invisible and the wind soundless. Once he heard a challenge from an unseen and nervous guard but he slipped by and the miserable sentry shook it off as a storm noise. When the low, squat shape of the dynamite shack loomed ahead, he slowed, moving more cautiously. It was deserted. Michael guessed those who weren't fighting the fire were sheltering somewhere out of the rain.

He came around to the side of the building, crept to the corner and took a quick look around. A lone safety lamp swayed from a crooked pole ten feet in front of the door. It gave off just enough light to define its presence but not enough to cast shadows.

He went to the door and ripped off the lock with his crowbar. Putting his shoulder to the heavy oak door, he pushed it open and slipped inside. It was cool inside by nature of its design; two log buildings laid up one inside the other. The inner one was two feet smaller in every dimension. The open space between them was packed with rammed earth. In contrast, the roof was flimsy; spruce pole rafters covered with several layers of corrugated roofing that rattled like snare drums in the wind. It had been designed so, in the event of an accident, most of the blast would be directed straight up. Whichever way the blast went, Michael knew there was enough dynamite stored there for a big one; ten thousand pounds at least. He threw the light switch. Nothing. The storm had taken out the power line from the generators. No matter. He knew the layout well. There was a small vestibule just inside the door with smaller doors leading off to the five powder chambers.

He groped his way into the center one, went in and worked quickly. If anyone came around, they'd see the broken lock for sure and come in to investigate. Michael found an open box and took out a cylinder of nitro. With a small, pointed stick he poked a hole in one end. Taking a blasting cap, he pushed the fuse into it, crimped it with his teeth and slid the cap into the end of the dynamite. He put the stick back in the box and uncoiled the fuse. It would burn at four seconds to the inch. He cut it at three feet and pulled out a match, struck it and touched it to the fuse. It caught immediately. Michael laid it on the wet, sawdust floor and slipped out.

He shut the door, slid a new lock onto the iron hasp and snapped it on. He jerked it once and hurried to the shadowy corner of the building.

"Got you! You son-of-a-bitch!" Karsch clamped his hand over Michael's throat and threw him against the wall, holding him there, faces inches apart, the hatred in Karsch's face reflecting off the horror in Jensen's.

"You're mine, Jensenice! I got you cold and I'm going to kill you, nice and legal, you scum." He pulled Michael's head away from the building and slammed it back, again and again. Michael was staggered, flashes of lightening burst through his head. A trickle of blood began running down the back of his neck. His vision blurred and he lost sight of Karsch. The man was there somewhere right in front of him but his arms were long, miles long. His hot, laboring breath beat into his face. Karsch was sexually aroused by the thrill of killing him. It reached across the seeming miles that separated them. Karsch meant to beat him to death and toss him around like a dog gripping a rabbit by the neck.

Michael was seconds from passing out and then Karsch stopped and threw him to the ground. It was too easy. Karsch wasn't getting enough satisfaction. "I got more fight from that bitch of yours," he smirked. Michael tried to back away, his fingers biting into the sodden ground. They found the crowbar and tightened around it. Karsch bent down and picked up a big chunk of ore and held it over his head.

"I didn't tell you, did I? I bedded your girl. She gave me her sex and I gave you your freedom. I knew you'd come back, come back to die at my hands just like swatting a deer fly."

He was standing directly over Michael, straddling his legs. Another lightning flash lit up Karsch's demonic face. It was an aiming point. But it was too high above him, to far across the miles between them. In desperation Michael swung the crowbar and the hooked end drove into Karsch's side. The point tore through the skin and crashed against the ribs, crushing one. Michael pulled down hard and the crowbar tore loose and came free trailing blood and muscle. Karsch screamed and staggered back against the dynamite shack. The boulder fell and missed Michael's head by inches.

"You bastard!" he screamed, ripping his shirt off beneath his arm. In the security light he inspected the damage. Particles of rib and cartilage stuck out of the ragged tear in his side. "Lord, you what you done! You tried to kill me, dammit!" But Michael wasn't looking nor did he have any faith in the fatality of his blow. He was clutching his throat, fighting to recover his breath and crawling away to increase the distance between them. Fifty feet away, he stood up.

"It won't kill you," he whispered in a raspy voice. "I wish I had a stake to drive through your heart." Then he was lost in the dark before Karsch could come at him again.

Karsch tore off the rest of his shirt and tied it around his chest and stumbled over to the shack. He fumbled at the lock. It looked all right. He gave it another jerk, harder, and the hasp came free. He swore, swung open the door and peered inside. The acrid smell of burning powder came to him. He slammed the door and got away seconds before it blew. The blast tore up through the roof, carrying wood and metal hundreds of feet into the sky. Night became day. The walls bulged, held for a heartbeat and blew out, driving before it logs, rocks and any equipment in its proximity. It shattered windows in Zenith and Aurora and destroyed every surrounding building in the pit. Everything was moving in fluid, destructive motion, from big machines down to pencils. The debris rained down like newspaper drifting down a windy street. And nearly as suddenly as it had come about, the echoes were lost in the wind and only the steady drumming of the rain intruded on an eerie silence. The only evidence that the shack had ever existed was a smoldering thirty-foot deep crater.

A hundred yards away, the initial blast threw Michael into a sump hole and saved his life. Broken pieces of destruction hurtled past him and smaller pieces rained down on him. He lay there at fortune's mercy and survived. When it stopped he crawled over to the edge and dragged himself out. A dozen fires were sputtering behind him. He wanted to stay there but he knew men would be coming soon. The whole town had to have heard the explosion.

He stood up and moved west toward the spider webbing of timbers just visible in the distance. In five stumbling minutes he reached the tracks laid on the dirt and gravel incline that led up to the long, curving wood trestle that carried the ore cars to the sorting mill. It was the trestle his father had helped to build and died on. He mounted it and began climbing. The grade grew steeper. Soon the banks were twenty feet high, and then forty and they abruptly ended and continued on over the latticework of wood poles and braces. Another bolt of lightning tore across the sky, lighting the slick, wet bed of cross ties. They were spaced four inches apart, wide enough to slip a foot through or, worse, slip off of and pitch over the edge.

Michael bent low and put one hand on each rail. A wave of dizziness came on and he held on. When it passed he went out on the trestle. The water streaming down into his face made it hard to see but it had stopped his bleeding. The lightning was steady enough now that the entire long trestle was strobbing in stark detail before him. It was five hundred feet long and, at its highest point, a hundred and fifty feet tall. It fed into a deep cut at the lip of the mine, then climbed another fifty feet to ground level.

The going was tortuously slow with Michael fighting to keep his balance in spite of the rain and the pounding in his head. He had walked the trestle erect before, in daylight and no wind. But tonight was different and he moved with the clutching caution of an old man.

Fifty feet. A hundred. Another flash of lightning stabbed the sky. It blinded him for an instant and he waited through the rumble of the thunder. He started out again, stumbled, then caught himself. Too fast, he thought. I'm going too fast. Slow down, there's no hurry. He shut his eyes, counted ten, opened them and extended his right hand. It found the steel rail and he held on. He slid forward on his left hand and picked up his right. He moved with glacial slowness.

Suddenly he was pinned! Something had grabbed his wrist. He screamed in terror and pulled back. Something incredibly powerful held and hurtled him forward bringing him down hard on his chest. His face struck a crosstie and the left side of his head went numb. Stunned, he rolled over on his back and held on as Karsch came on to the trestle.

The ungodly monster stood there, almost naked from the waist up in the pounding rain. The wound under his shirt bandage shone dark with blood. His short-cropped hair was gone, burned off by the blast. His pants hung in shreds and his chest and back were covered with deep lacerations. His left hand, broken when the shack blew, was thrust into his belt.

Michael wiped a hand across his face and stared in disbelief. He had survived? He had climbed the trestle with just one arm? It hit him with awesome surety. The thought hammered into his throbbing brain. This man could not be killed because he wasn't a man. He was a mythological beast and had come to kill him. I'm going to die, he thought. Maybe he deserved it. They both did. Maybe it was the divine retribution that Father Basil had preached about so stridently. Had God ordained that this Satan, this unkillable beast should be the hand of the Lord's justice? Had his world now turned to such absurdity?

Karsch reached down and grabbed Michael by his shirt. With one arm he pulled him off the trestle. He held him so close that Michael could see the yellow on his broken teeth, the torn lid that hung over his left eye. Karsch growled low and mean like a Doberman about to tear out his throat.

"You can't kill Karsch, Jensen. Nobody can. You tried. They all tried and they all lost. You spilled my guts and now I'll spill yours like your father's. Spilled guts is all you're gonna be."

"No! Please. Don't!" Michael's anger had been reduced to blind terror and he was begging for his life.

Karsch began to swing Michael over the edge. Michael hit him in the face but his wet fist slid harmlessly off Karsch's cheek. Karsch only grabbed him harder and began to taunt him.

"You are dead, little man. You hear me? You weak, gutless ass!" He spit blood and saliva in Michael's face. "Maybe we should die and go to hell together."

Michael's flailing feet found the gap between the ties and he hooked his boot under one and held on.

"She was a good woman. Did she tell you? Did your little whore tell you what a real man feels like?" He spat again and laughed but his words had brought about a change in his victim. Mary. At the moment of his death the truth of her love was made clear. She had saved him, not betrayed him. It was Libby. The thought cleared his head. He was suddenly not afraid for himself but for the others that this man would hurt. The paralysis of fear giving way to the strength of rage. When Karsch attacked him he had preyed on Michael's weakness. When it came to that, Karsch had no peer because his strength was greater than any others but, when he attacked people Michael loved, he was attacking something stronger than either of them because there was no strength like that which protected another.

His body tensed and Michael rolled up for another attack. "Noooo, dammit!" He swung again as Karsch dropped him and this time his fist found the hole in Karsch's side. Karsch screamed and cursed, doubling over in pain. The man had felt pain! Michael's back hit the rail. The edge of the ties bit into his spine and he hung there for an instant then slowly pulled himself back. With his free boot, he kicked out at the dark mass above him, catching Karsch in the groin. Karsch staggered and bent down. Michael kicked again, hitting him in the face. He kicked again and this time heard the jawbone snap. Karsch fell back and a gurgling sound came from him. Frantically he grabbed for a hand-hold, sat down and slipped over the edge. He held the rail for a moment then lost his grip on the slippery steel. He looked up and reached out a hand but none was offered. Michael gave him one last kick in the chest and he was gone. He dropped over the edge without a sound.

Jensen knelt on the trestle waiting for the knots in his stomach to ease and then he vomited. He sat there in the darkness for a long time letting the water stream over him, cleansing him. Eventually he crawled to the rim and oblivious to any guards that might be about, walked home and fell unconscious into his bed.

chapter 46

The sun was high over the eaves when Katla padded into his room. She raised the shades and lowered herself onto the edge of his bed and silently watched him for awhile then left and came back with a bowl of warm water and began sponging his beat up face. He winced and opened his eyes when she attacked a crusted scab on his temple.

"Ma, ow! Be careful. That's tender."

"So you woke up finally."

He took her wrist. "Mama, don't. Please. It hurts more when you do that."

"Nevertheless, all cuts must be cleaned," she answered going about her task. After more dabbing she said, "One day it will stop hurting and you will know you are dead. Such is life."

He gave her a weak smile that she returned with a frown.

"I won't ask where you went last night. I think I know. Some are saying it was the lightning that did it." She caught his eye. "Do you think it was the lightning?"

He nodded weakly. "It was a bad storm. Very likely the lightning."

"Michael, I have more than enough gray hairs without always finding my children on death's door. Look here, your cheek is all blue. I think you cracked it."

"Ow! Don't touch it. Please, Ma."

She sat back and patiently watched while he probed the tender spot. Yes, it definitely could be a cracked cheekbone. Well, he gave better than he got. And if Karsch really was part of Fr. Basil's plan to wreck retribution on him than he had cheated the devil. He heard Katia sigh and saw the worry in her eyes.

"I'm sorry, mama. No more. I swear." He sat up abruptly. "Sadie? Is... is she?"

"So now you take the time to think about your little sister." Her eyes moistened and her lips trembled a little. "You father spoke to Jesus and He made a miracle for me and gave her back to us."

Michael sank back onto the bed and took her hand again. He carried it to his cheek. It was wet with tears.

"I am really sorry, Mama," he repeated. "I didn't know what else to do." He paused. "I had to do something for them."

She looked at him as if she were taking the first good look in years. He was no longer her little child, nor was he even an innocent young adult any more. He looked older, mature and weary. He looked like Ernest had in his day.

"Like your father," she said. "Stubborn, but always faithful, too." Katla bent down and kissed his forehead and Michael wrapped his arms about her. He held her for a long time and then she left him to sleep some more.

He rose at noon and limped down to the bathroom. The cold shower felt good. It stung his cuts reminding him that he really was alive even if life that morning was so painful.

Katla wasn't in the house. Michael checked the garden and poultry house, tore a heel off a fresh loaf of bread and walked downtown. He found her at the little hospital. Sadie looked much as he; pale and drained, but sleeping soundly. How small and vulnerable she was, he thought, laying like a little toy on the big hospital bed. Michael reached past Katla and touched his sister. She moved slightly. Katla scolded him gently with her eyes.

"Sshh. She's sleeping. Finally."

"Finally?"

"She hurt too much last night even with the medicine. Such a little bundle, he couldn't give her too much. Mr. Wong came in and gave her something. That worked."

Michael nodded at Mr. Wong's solicitude. "How long have you been here, Mama?" Her look said forever. Michael pulled a chair beside the bed.

"Why don't you go home and sleep. I'll sit with her."

Katla's eyes flashed protectively. "I'm her Mama. I'll go home when she does."

Michael looked around the nearly empty ward. "Then lie down over there," he said gesturing to an empty bed. "I can wake you if she cries out."

"If she cries out I will hear her," Katla said but after a mild protest, she consented and in minutes she, too, was sleeping.

He took Sadie's hand and sat with her through the rest of the afternoon. He remembered the other times, the good, tender moments they had shared as well as the not so tender. He thought of one time she had talked him into taking her with him deer hunting. She was seven then and he had thought it inappropriate because she was a girl and too young. Sadie persisted all that evening so the next morning he woke her before dawn, piled on all the clothes she could carry and they went out into the big cedar swamp south of Mammoth. It was a mild day for November and that had irritated him because it took away his final argument against Sadie.

It was frustrating and often all he could do to be civil to her. She moved through the dark like a little heifer busting around in the alder brush and chattered incessantly. Even when he got her to speak in a whisper, it still wasn't quiet enough because, like all little children, Sadie knew that darkness would swallow quietly spoken words that would normally be heard so easily in the daylight.

Three times that day they saw deer. Just at daybreak something crashed in the gray mist in front of them and a big doe bolted out the far side and they caught only a glimpse of its proud flag going over a little rise.

"See," Michael scolded, blaming her. "You scared it away. It was a buck, too."

"I didn't see any horns," she corrected.

"Antlers, not horns, and you didn't see them because you had your scarf over your eyes. You wanted to come so be still now."

"Okay, Mikie." But she just couldn't.

Later he gave up his stand and they walked down a narrow logging road. Coming around a bend in the trail, they discovered another doe with a late-born fawn foraging on clover in the middle of the road. Surprisingly, this time Sadie froze in her tracks, more in surprise than because of good hunting instincts. The doe, alerted to their presence, stiffened, ready to bolt. She tested the air, but the little breeze was blowing away from her. She pawed the ground and tossed her head but she couldn't spook them. Sadie and Michael stood as still as marble statues, Michael because he understood such things and Sadie because she was just then experiencing the most thrilling moment she had ever known and something in her said, don't move, don't ever move again.

Eventually the deer, not possessing particularly good eyesight, went back to browsing. The little fawn chased his tail in two complete circles and lay down; fell down really. Another minute went by. Sadie was wondering if Michael would shoot the mother deer and was tempted to speak. Michael thought he might have shot her if Sadie wasn't along but it didn't bother him because he was as entertained by their display as she was.

Suddenly the woods exploded to their right. A huge buck crashed into view, snorted and whistled in alarm, wheeled and bolted away, rattling the brush with an incredibly large and many-tined rack. Sadie was jolted from her trance and jumped back against Michael who was trying to bring his rifle around. It disappeared in a second. He looked back down the road and the doe and fawn were gone, swallowed up in the undergrowth.

They ate their sandwiches by a small lake and later followed a well-worn game trail around it. By now the sun was going down and Michael decided it was time to start home. It had all worked out all right after all. He knew where to come back in the morning.

They had their third encounter as they came down into a small creek bottom. It was a buck, as big as the one they saw on the trail with fourteen points on his antlers. It was dead and Sadie saw it first.

"Mikie! Look!" Her voice filled with awe but the animal didn't spook like the other they had seen. "Is it sleeping?"

Michael knew. "No, Sadie, he's not sleeping." Someone had shot the old buck in the hindquarters. The bullet had gone through the left leg and genitals but the sturdy animal hadn't dropped. It had fled down to this protected copse and, when its blood had drained out, it stiffened and died.

In his heart Michael cursed the fool who had shot such a magnificent creature but didn't care, or know enough, to track it to the end. And he was angrier still that his little sister was there to see it. As much as he enjoyed hunting and shooting, Michael respected the rules, especially the unwritten ones. He put his arm around Sadie and tried to comfort her.

"The poor guy. He almost got away, didn't he? But at least the hunter didn't get him, did he?"

"He's pretty, Mikie. Can I pet him?"

She held his hand while she tentatively stroked its coat. The deer had been there for some time, laying half in and half out of the small creek. The body was stiff and a white mold had begun to form over its rump. The meat had long since gone bad. It needn't be a total waste, he thought, so he took a small hatchet from his belt and began chopping off the big rack. At his first strike, Sadie went wild.

"Mikie! No!" she screamed, grabbing his arm.

"Sadie. It's okay. The old guy's dead. It doesn't hurt him." He attacked the skull plate again and Sadie shrieked and ran up the bank and stood there sobbing. He finished with the antlers and went up to her but she ran off still crying and screaming at him. Michael dropped the antlers and caught up with her. She was cowering against a tree.

"Sadie, what is wrong with you? Tell me."

She punched him on the chest. "You took his horns, Mikie. They were his, not yours."

"But if we left them some porcupine would just come and chew on them anyway. Sadie, we'll take them home and hang them up where they'll be safe."

She tried to make him understand as she did and the deer would have. "But they were his best things. It was all he had left. You can't take his best things."

He felt like laughing but didn't. It wasn't until much later that he did begin to understand what she was talking about. If Sadie had been familiar with the words pride and dignity she would have used them.

The antlers had given that deer its self-esteem. He came to recognize that, even lying there in a creek bottom, shot through the balls, the animal still looked magnificent. It still had some dignity. It had eluded the man who had killed it and cheated him out of a trophy rack. But Michael ruined that when he stole his dignity and left it mutilated.

That winter Michael took the rack off the side of the chicken coop and wrapped the skull plate in velvet and polished and varnished the antlers and hung them in the parlor. He did it with a pronouncement that now the buck would always have a place of honor in the Jensen house.

Then one day when he was at work, Sadie took them upstairs and hung them in her room because she knew better than he how the deer had felt and the antlers eventually became something that bonded them even closer than before. That's when he came to understand. Recalling it now, he finally knew the enormity of her empathy.

"You do know these things, don't you, kid? You always did." He touched her cheek and her eyelids fluttered. "It's not about the money or the work. It's not about winning or losing something. It's not about clubs and speeches and agitators from the other side of the country telling us what we should do or believe. It's not even about pride. It's simply a matter of dignity. It's just being able to keep your head up so you don't notice your toes sticking through your shoes. And that's something you should not have to fight for. Ever."

The rich owners never could understand poverty so how could they sympathize with the poor. Karsch didn't. Michael smiled at his own stupidity. Mary did. That was all she ever wanted out of life, to come out a little better than she started. Pa, too. Just a house, a family and a garden. Not much but enough for him to have a little dignity. Not the entire world, just a backyard full of vegetables. Those were a man's best things.

He kissed her, went over and did the same to Katla and tiptoed out of the room. The afternoon sky was full of dancing cumulus clouds that traced scudding shadows over the ground. He drew in the warm summer air and realized how close he had come to losing everything. Kiril was gone but God had given Sadie back to them. Katla's love and Mary's, too, if he was willing to try hard enough.

He felt a strong desire to find her and salvage what he had tried to throw away. He wasn't sure what was left between them or if she cared enough to consider a future together. He did know now that he cared enough to forgive her for everything and hoped she could forgive him. His mother had forgiven him for Sadie and Kiril and all the others he had hurt. Maybe, he thought, by making peace wherever he could, he would find the love to forgive himself. It was something, anyway.

Chapter 47

An angry mob was gathered around the Mammoth office. There had always been a few pickets, even when the strike was at its low ebb but today was different. They had started gathering in the morning and the numbers had kept growing until now there were several hundred of all ages and sexes with a hardcore of dozens of angry men and women suddenly possessing a spirit that for a long time had been knocked out of them. Sadie's near tragedy and the previous night's explosion had given it back to them and gave them the strength to stand as one and speak as one.

Michael ran straight to Mary's apartment and pounded on her door. There was no answer. He crossed the hall and tried Mr. Wong's with the same results. Coming down he took the steps two at a time and nearly ran over Wong out on the sidewalk.

"Oh, it is you young Michael. I am elated. I was afraid you might have been hurt in the trouble last night. But I am sure you were spending the night with your sister." He finished with a knowing smile.

Michael's pulse was racing now. He put his hands on Wong's shoulders to get his full attention.

"Mr. Wong," he panted, "please. Have you seen Mary?"

Wong backed away. "Young Michael, you are in such a hurry. Has something happened other than that which I know?"

"No!" Michael suddenly became self-conscious, knowing that Mr. Wong knew what he was thinking. "It's nothing. I just want to talk with her."

Wong nodded sagely. "Oh, yes. Talk between young people is more valuable than anything. Talk with words but also with the eyes. By the way, one of your eyes looks terrible. Did you walk into a door?"

"Have you seen her?"

Wong smiled at the young man's transparency. "Yes I have. Someone else wanted her presence. A man from the mine came here a short time ago and took her back to the office. There was considerable urgency to his actions."

"Why?"

"They are very concerned about the miners today. The big explosion and fires last night have given the miners new heart. Perhaps they seek more of the same. Myself, I think there is little left to destroy. In my heart I fear they will continue on until they destroy each other."

"Dammit!" Michael jumped off the walk and ran down the street. Wong watched him race off and remembered the words his father had spoken to him many years ago. "So slowly the young men reach for truth, so quickly they rush to destruction."

Twenty guards armed with clubs, and both in defiance of Sheriff Meining and out of fear, pistols and even rifles, were lined up in front of the main gate. They had taken ore carts and formed a barricade. Ten more were standing on the office porch behind desks, files and anything they could carry out and use for shelter. The tension was etched deeply on their faces. There were still a lot of shotguns and deer rifles that the miners had kept hidden and were unaccounted for. Sheriff Meining was standing across the street with a score of nervous sheriff's deputies. He was giving them final instructions in the event of real trouble. Between them milled the angry miners and their families ready to explode into violence.

Children were running among the grownups, playing tag in the sea of legs and dresses. A few were clutching adult hands; others tugged at the hard objects they were clutching. Two boys had found sticks of their own and were playing pirates, cutting and slashing across the decks of their galleons. On the porch of the café four old men were playing Euchre, chewing on unlit cigars and feigning indifference to the action around them.

One family had spread out a quilt and was setting out a picnic lunch. There were dogs everywhere, barking and snarling, all caught up in the excitement. Little girls taunted, shrieked and danced away from them to hide behind their mothers. It could have been a church outing but for the hate-filled language that erupted continuously. It was a ringing counterpoint to the frenzied oratory of the gaudy speaker perched on the bed of a wagon. From half a block away Michael recognized Libby. She had come back!

She stopped in mid-sentence when she saw him coming down the street. "There! There now!" she shouted, pointing at him. "That is the kind of hero who acts on his convictions. There is a man the movement must follow."

It struck him how well and often she climbed onto bandwagons and then tried to get in front of the marchers so she could tell them which direction they were to go. She called for him to join her but he ignored her invitation and began shouldering his way through the crush of people that kept grabbing for his hands and pounding his back. He finally broke clear at the steps of the office.

"Not one step further." A tall, lean mine guard held a club across his body, barring the way. The mob, thinking that Michael was intent on rushing the office, surged behind him.

"We're with you, Jensen! Let's kill them all and burn the damned office."

Michael looked back in horror at the mob that was rapidly transforming itself into an out-of-control riot. "No!" he tried to shout above their shouting. "I am not here for any of this. I am not here to fight anyone." He turned to the guard. "I've got to see Mary Savich. Is she here?"

"It doesn't matter if she is. No one can come in." The guard's eyes were darting everywhere. He raised his voice even higher. "We're shut down."

A cheer erupted from the miners. Michael ignored them and stepped up on the porch.

"I don't care what you are. I don't care what you say. I'm taking her out of here." Cowered by the look of determination in Michael's eyes, guard began to step aside.

A second deputy, apparently less wise than the first, came over and struck Michael in the chest with his rifle butt. Michael fell backward off the porch. People tried to catch him but missed and he went sprawling into the street. A vicious cry rose and men charged the guards. Weapons appeared and the air was filled with flying rocks. Meining grabbed a megaphone.

"Stop! Everyone, stop what you're doing. Back off now! Finally he threw it down. "Oh, hell! Come on, men. Let's try to save the women and children, anyway."

Michael got to his feet and was immediately knocked down again. A woman with a brick in her hand hurried by him with a rustle of skirts and a guard appeared in her wake. It was one of the nasty ones he remembered from the pit.

"You started this, you little bastard." He pulled a pistol from his belt but was instantly clubbed down from behind before he got it aimed. His eyes rolled up and he fell in a heap next to Jensen. The pistol fell out of his hand. A miner saw it and tried to pick it up.

"No!" Michael screamed. He grabbed the revolver, shielding it from the others. Then a familiar voice cut through the din behind him.

"Jensen! Jensen!"

He spun around and froze, the blood draining from his face. Standing ten feet away, bent and bandaged among the churning mass of miners was the devil Karsch! But for his voice he was almost impossible to recognize and because of the crutch, a splinted leg and his left hand a solid mass of bloody bandaging, no one was tempted to touch him. His head was wrapped and he had a big bloodstain where the crow bar had done its work. His one uncovered eye shone like a black devil's jewel. That the man was slowly dying was obvious but he was taking an incredibly long time doing it. He still had some strength in his voice and he spoke like Satan himself.

"Look at me, Jensen. Look at your future and your fate."

"Karsch. You're dead."

"Not quite I ain't dead. But you are now."

A rifle rose in his good arm and he centered it on Michael's chest. Michael tried to get to his feet but his legs wouldn't respond.

"No, don't. There's no reason anymore."

The hammer came back and Karsch's finger tightened on the trigger and the thin, hard grin came on him. It happened so fast that it seemed to take forever. There was a scream. Who? Is that me, he thought? Then he felt himself falling. The rifle went off. From somewhere back in his head he heard another scream. Is that me? And he felt something fall against him. He heard Karsch screaming now with more obscenities towards him and saw him struggling to chamber another round. Then it speeded up too fast to follow. He tried to raise the pistol. His thumb fell off the hammer. Karsch swore again. He got it cocked and heard the roar of the gun. He felt nothing, no recoil, no impact. He was floating. More screaming. Is that me? It was so close he thought it came from another voice within him and then he took a blow over his eye and fell back and rolled on his side. He reached out and grasped something soft. What? A hand? He held onto it in desperation, afraid that if he let go he would fall into a bottomless abyss. He heard moaning. Is that me? Then he slipped into unconsciousness.

Chapter 48

There was a rattling of keys and the sound of a heavy door sliding back. It had a ring of familiarity. Leather soles fell on the hard stone floor. The sounds were distant but intrusive. They came closer and finally stopped. Soft, muted voices exchanged words. Someone shook him and the terror returned.

"Michael. Steady there. It's okay now. It's all okay."

He relaxed a little. There was a trickle of water over his forehead and the touch of a damp cloth on his face. When it touched the blue welt over his eye he cried out.

"Aah. Now we're reaching you. Again I have the honor of calling on you in your private cell such as it is."

Michael opened his eyes and they focused on the familiar face of the other man. "Keyes. I... what? What happened?"

"And where are you?"

Michael tried to take in his surroundings. "And where am I?"

John smiled down at him. "Well, who else would be coming to visit you with such regularity but in a jail?"

Michael's gaze drifted around the room, at the stone walls and the sparse furnishings that stank of urine and damp mustiness. He groaned.

"No. No. Not again." It began to come back to him. "Karsch! I killed the bastard, didn't I?"

Keyes chuckled. "Uh, Uh. Sorry. There will not be another murder charge to dodge. From what I understand, you couldn't kill him if you put a stick of dynamite up his ass. You are only here for your own safety this time." Keyes saw Jensen's confusion.

"Sheriff Meining locked up you and a dozen others just to help clean up the situation. There were more than a few guards who would have liked to have your scalp right then. More than one tried. Their take on the situation was that you brought it on when you rushed the office. Other than that, you are free to go right now. There won't be anyone charged for anything as I understand. Not good for my fee but wonderful for the little people."

Michael got up on his elbows. "God, my head is killing me." His voice was raspy.

"I should think so. You've been out for sometime. Sixteen hours?" Keyes took a dipper of water from a bucket and handed it to him. He drank it, then another.

"What happened? I mean after," he said testing the knot on his head.

Keyes returned the dipper and settled back in his chair. "Frankly, all holy hell happened. There was a full-scale riot, a lot of hitting, a few guns going off. It filled your local hospital and two or three others on the Range. I think the guards got the worst of it but then Meining's deputies were pretty selective on behalf of the miners. Lundquist got on the telegraph and raised such hell with his uncle, the governor called out the National Guard. Next day they went house to house and disarmed everyone, miners and cops, clubs and guns. The mine cops were disbanded on the spot and run out of town. The range is under martial law at the moment."

Michael stared at Keyes who made a gesture with his hands. "It's over, Michael. Finished."

"What about Karsh? He isn't here?"

"Jailed? God, no. Dead. There you are. No, not by your hand. Witnesses swore that you never got a shot off. Oh, don't misunderstand me. He's dead, all right. Took a bullet right through the heart. They said he still called you a few choice names while he was falling. I'm sure he thought it was you."

"Who shot him?"

"Care to guess? Well, it might surprise you to know that it was your good friend, John Fleming, that saved your life."

Michael shook his head in disbelief. "Fleming?"

"He grabbed a rifle from one of Karsch's own guards and ran up behind you. Apparently Karsch was so intent on you that he didn't even see him. Karsch got off the one shot just as Fleming did for him."

Michael stood up and slowly moved around trying to tie Keyes' words in with what he remembered. At the end there was still some missing pieces.

"Someone pushed me. I was trying to get the gun up and just as he fired I felt someone on me. I remember hearing a scream. I thought it was me."

Keyes came over and put his hands on Michael's shoulders. "You'd better sit down, son."

Michael shook his head. "No, tell me what happened."

Keyes cleared his throat. "First, there's something else you should know although I think you already suspect. Mary Savich never betrayed you. It was that Flynn woman. She wanted you off the streets, taken out of the action. She felt you were giving her movement a bad name. I don't believe she ever considered that it might result in a murder charge; maybe trespass or involuntary manslaughter. Suspended sentence or hung jury stuff." He paused. "I guess you might know what kind of deal Miss Savich made with Karsch to get him to change his testimony."

He remembered Karsch's words that night in the mine. It was all falling in place. He knew what Keyes was coming to.

"Who?"

Keyes' words came out in a barely audible whisper. "Karsch's bullet struck and killed Mary while she was saving your life for the second time."

Michael's knees buckled and he fell. "Michael, I'm so sorry."

chapter 49

Sadie was lying on a bed on the back porch. She was propped up on a nest of pillows, watching her Mikie work in the garden while swatting the occasional fly that dared land on her. Her brother was cutting cabbage for Katla's kraut tub. He worked methodically but without his usual youthful energy and, when Sadie called to him from time to time with a question, it was all he could do to raise his head and nod at her.

The back door opened with a squeak of the spring. Katla came out followed by a man Sadie didn't know.

"Do you need anything, honey?" said Katla. Sadie shook her head and watched the man. Katla pointed at Michael and spoke in the manner she reserved for strangers.

"There he is, in the garden."

Fleming smiled at her. "Thank you, Mrs. Jensen. I'll just go out and visit with him there if that's all right."

Katla nodded. "Yes. Would you like a glass of cool water?"

"No, thank you. I don't care for anything," he said.

"Or, I have some coffee from this morning. I could warm you a cup."

"No, really, thank you. I'm fine." He insisted. "Is this pretty little lady Sadie?"

"Yes, this is my little Sadie, Michael's sister. Sadie, this is Mr. Fleming, Michael's boss from the mine."

"My brother doesn't work for you anymore," muttered Sadie.

"That's what I came to talk to him about, Sadie. The Mammoth mine sure misses your brother."

"So you can pick on him again?"

"That's enough, Sadie. Hush now. I don't think Mr. Fleming came to talk to us. Mr. Fleming, you go right down to the garden and have your words with Michael. That way you can be private." She ended with a sharp look at Sadie.

"Thank you, Mrs. Jensen. I will do that."

Katla nodded again and went to sit with Sadie. They watched Fleming go down the steps and across the short space to the garden. He picked his way through a tangle of spreading tomato vines and quietly came up behind Michael. He stood there self-consciously, not knowing how to begin. He had spent the entire morning deciding to do this and still didn't know what he wanted to say. He only knew that he had to do something to put some kind of closure on everything. In the safety of his office he had thought that he might patch things up somehow but, as he stood there in the garden, he realized how shattered things really were.

Mary was right. He wouldn't want to live here. He was extremely uncomfortable just visiting even though these were the homes of the people who had built the mine that permitted him to live in comfort as well as put money aside each month.

He looked back at Katla and Sadie as if they might help him. Sadie waved back and then, as if she had read his mind, yelled at her big brother. "Mikie! Turn around."

Michael glanced back and saw Fleming's polished shoes. He rolled down from his stoop until he was resting on his haunches and squinted up at his visitor. Fleming moved around a couple of steps until he was out of the sun. When Michael recognized him, a small unhappy sound came from him and he slowly stood up.

They stared at each other. Fleming thought Jensen looked old, much older than the first time he had seen him carrying Mary across the muddy street. Now he had the tired lines that so many of his men who had left their youth down in his pit carried.

Michael was cradling a head of cabbage in his hands, balancing it back and forth like someone might test the heft of a rock he wanted to smash up against something, or someone.

"Back up."

Fleming was startled.

"You're standing on my squash vines. They're still growing."

"Oh! I'm sorry." Fleming quickly backed up a step and the distance between them became tolerable. Michael became conscious of his family on the porch. He gave them a small wave of his hand as if to say it was all right.

"What are you doing here? You've never come into Zenith before.'

Fleming tried to make a beginning. "No I haven't. I just came to... well, yes, there is something. I came to see how things are with you. With us. I mean you and Mammoth mines. I wanted to talk to you about coming back to work. I want you to come back"

Michael didn't answer immediately.

"How are you, Michael?" Fleming persisted.

"How am I? Do you really have to ask? I have no job and no money. I can't buy a beer with my friends of whom I have few. My best friend is dead and my sister nearly an invalid. But I'm doing well. I'm a farmer, Fleming, a very prosperous one. I have one fiftieth of a hectare under my hoe. I'm growing corn, tomatoes, and cabbage. Over there I've got a good... a good..." His voice trailed off. He took a deep breath and was about to begin again.

Fleming cut him off. "Stop it, Jensen. Please."

"I'm sorry. Stop what? Stop my farming. Stop breathing? Would you prefer I just stop living so you can pretend none of this ever happened; that none of us ever existed? Or died. That's how you feel, isn't it? That none of us exist? Well, dammit, I ask God every day for that same wish and He just won't make it better. I'm still here every day hating my life."

Fleming held a hand up against Michael's anger but he was not to be denied.

"You want me to kiss your ass for killing Karsch and saving my life? Is that it, because I couldn't you know. I tried my damndest but I couldn't. As for saving my life, stand in line. It's Mammoth's biggest pastime. Let's save Michael from himself even if it costs us our own lives. I'm a big supporter of that one.

"Or are you here to remind me that if I hadn't been there, she'd still be alive? Don't you think that doesn't tear at my heart every damned minute of every day?" He spun and hurled the cabbage against the hen house. Chickens scattered in panic from the flying pieces and then cautiously came back to peck at the cabbage.

"I would have killed you, too, if I had a chance. I had gotten to the point where I didn't need a reason any more. I must have been out of control, huh?" His voice cracked and died.

Another long silence ensued before Fleming brought it to an end. "I know. I probably would have deserved it and, God knows, more so than some that did die. We, the mine, brought a lot of pain to your house. I am truly sorry for that and even sorrier that I can't change what happened. I never was a very strong man. I'm an engineer. My weapons are the slide rule, compass and pen. I can't apologize for men like Karsch and Masterton and I can't fight them. I can only try to pick up the pieces and go forward. I hope you can accept that, Michael."

Micheal's tone was becoming one of resignation but hadn't yet arrived there. "Forward to what? More horseshit working conditions? More dynamite going off whenever it wants too? More good men dying? No thanks, Mr. Fleming. I'll iron shirts for Mr. Wong before that."

He may have been a poor fighter but John Fleming was a patient negotiator. As Michael's anger became more exhausted, Fleming grew slowly more convincing.

"You don't understand, do you? You won. The Minnesota Senate has named a select committee to look into the whole situation. They're already drawing up a list calling for better roads, schools and hospitals, safety programs and pensions. The owners are ready to talk. They're as tired of all this as anyone. They're beaten. Improvements in the lives of Mammoth are a foregone conclusion. It's only a question of good, honest men leading the town now." Fleming's third-person reference to the owners wasn't lost on Michael.

"What about Masterton?"

"His own hand-picked Board of Directors rose up against him. He's been censored and barred from active management for twenty-four months. By that time he'll have been bought out by the other shareholders. There's a provision in the agreement that provides for that."

"Where do you stand?"

Fleming shrugged. "I still have a job but no friends on either side. I might stay for a year, anyway. After that, I'll probably go east for awhile."

Michael showed the start of a smile. "If it gets too rough for you, I could use a little help here on the farm."

Fleming smiled back. "Thanks, but until then I want you to come back. I am very serious. I need you."

"For what? So the others will follow. I won't do that for you or anyone again."

He didn't understand. "They are back," Fleming answered. "Since yesterday, but they need a good leader. A pit foreman position is open. I'm offering it for both our sakes."

A quick look of surprise crossed Michael's face. He hadn't heard but then, he hadn't left the back yard for a week. He stared at the ground and sighed. He had been going over the last few months in his head all week but still hadn't resolved anything and, meanwhile, the rest of the world had forged ahead ready to forgive and forget. It was no different than the woods after a fire. New growth emerges before the ground has even cooled and life goes on, different but always the same. It wasn't going to be that easy for him.

"I'll think about it," he finally answered, already knowing he had little choice in the matter.

"Do that," Fleming encouraged him. "You're still the best driller I ever had. We've hired a lot of new men. Someone has to teach them to do it right."

"I'm the best damned driller you'll ever have," Michael muttered. He turned back to his work and Fleming turned to go. Halfway across the garden he stopped and, without looking back, said the other thing that was on his mind. It was the one thing he had resolved for sure.

"She loved you, Jensen. From that first moment in the street, it was really only you. Maybe she tried to deny it for a while but... maybe you were too much alike to know how much you..." He shook his head at his own stupidity. "At first she thought she wanted to use you to get to me but it turned out the other way around. All the time it was really you. I am truly sorry about Mary."

Michael dug his hands in the dark soil as if he would get up again but he didn't. He was rooted there. "You did Karsch in good," he said grudgingly. "I couldn't but you did. You did save my life. I had come to believe he was the devil himself." Finally it came. "Thank you."

Fleming nodded again. "Devil he was, not us. You are welcome." Then he left.

When Sadie hobbled down to see her brother, he turned away from her so she wouldn't see the tears in his handsome, dark Slovenian eyes.

chapter 50

Sadie looked down at Eric. He was sitting on the ground, leaning against the old boulder, his head cradled in his arms. Poor child, she thought. Your old gramma bored you silly with her ramblings. You did hear half of it anyway, didn't you? Well, fair enough, it's my story, after all. You've a lot of time yet to make your own.

The sun was putting a big, red cherry on the end of the day. It was time to go home. She gently stroked his hair.

"Well, Eric, that's enough talk from me. Your mother will be wondering what became of us."

She pushed her body off the rock, letting her spine gradually straighten from the long sitting. "Oooh. Grandma shouldn't sit so long like that. My rheumatism is kicking up a fuss."

Eric stirred and lifted his head. "All done, Gramma?"

Sadie smiled lovingly. "All done, honey." She pulled a tattered red kerchief from her pocket. "Say, those red berries over there are currants. Bet you didn't know that. If you help me pick some, I'll make current tarts for tonight."

"Sure, Gramma." He jumped up and dashing off, began stripping the fruit.

Sadie reached down one more time and felt the words on the rock. She closed her eyes.

"Well, Mama, life goes on, doesn't it?

"Yes, it does seem to, Sadie. "Yes, my little Sadie girl, it is ours for just a little while and then we give it over to someone else."

"How is papa?"

"Ernst? Not getting a day older. Sadie?"

"What, mama?"

"Mikie sends his love."

Tears were already coursing down her cheeks. "I know. I always know that."

Suddenly Eric stopped and turned. "Gramma Sadie?"

"What is it Eric?" she said getting up and going to him.

"Did he get yelled at?"

"Did who get yelled at?"

"Mikie. Did he get yelled at?"

"Yelled at? For what, dear?"

"For smashing the cabbage. Did your mommy yell at him?"

Sadie bent down and gathered him in a big hug. She was wiping her hot tears on his cool cheeks and crying openly. He would remember, enough anyway.

"No, Honey. He didn't get yelled at. No one ever yelled at your uncle Mikie ever again."

THE END